SILENT STRIDERS
&
BLACK FURIES

BY CARL BOWEN &
GHERBOD FLEMING

WORLD OF
DARKNESS
www.worldofdarkness.com

Gashwrack's eyes darted from Arastha to the tired wolf at her side. The wolf let Arastha stroke his fur, and he stretched his neck out every time Arastha's fingernails scratched him between his ears.

"I don't understand."

"Aren't I wicked to tease and confuse him so?" Arastha said to the wolf on her bed as she stroked his long right ear. "I need you to return to the caern from which you came to us, Gashwrack. Temporarily."

"Why?" Gashwrack asked. He never wanted to think of that place again, much less return there.

"To act as my field commander," Arastha said. "And as an escort to an honored warrior. And to help you bond with your new pack."

"What warrior? And what pack? I haven't taken—"

"I know," Arastha sliced through his protest. "But you will. Tonight before you leave. Shrike's Thorn will perform the rite."

"Who?"

The wolf beside Arastha raised his huge head and regarded Gashwrack with clinical indifference. As the two males stared at each other, the dire wolf's body stretched, melted and drew itself out until only a naked man lay by Arastha's side. Tightly curled black hairs dusted his chest and shoulders, except for the bald patch of the spiral glyph on his right shoulder and the crescent moon patch on his opposite shoulder. Intense silver-white eyes continued to peer at Gashwrack, and silky, black hair framed his face on both sides.

"It's almost time," the man said.

CONTENTS

SILENT STRIDERS

Acknowledgements

My thanks to Ethan Skemp, who did everything he could to help me with this book—which includes not chasing me out of his office with a broom when I kept coming in to ask him questions. Thanks also to Bill Bridges—although he won't know the true extent of why I'm thanking him until after he reads this story.

And thanks again to Stewart for the fistful of opportunities he's presented to me.

Chapter 1

Monuments to the honored dead stood before a lone figure upon the Hill of Lamentations, casting their long shadows in the last light of dusk. The figure stared at the monuments in silence, watching their shadows slide along the ground toward him like outstretched arms. The setting sun highlighted rough cairns and singular stones that stood in memory of heroes whose remains lay under the hard ground. The monuments were suited alternately to men and to wolves, as intricately sculpted or roughly hewn as befit the dignity and temperament of the heroes for which they stood.

What was more, each monument bore a touch of the spirits of those who had been left behind upon the heroes' passing. Where glyphs or carefully chiseled epitaphs recorded the heroes' greatest deeds, the telling was colored by whomever had created each monument. The remembrance of the honor, glory and wisdom of the fallen was wholly at the mercy of those who had been charged with passing it on.

The figure standing before these monuments considered himself charged thus, but the stories that these monuments told were not familiar to him. They spoke of heroes who had died long before his birth in a place far from the lands he thought of only hesitantly as home. None of his people were buried here among the hallowed heroes. Doubtless, many of his kind—the Silent Striders—had visited this place in its long history of bitter siege, internal strife and weary determination to persevere. Surely some had fought in its defense or brought timely news of dangers that it would face. Maybe some of his tribemates had shed their blood or even died here. However, no Silent Striders had been laid to rest in the Sept of the Anvil-Klaiven. This graveyard was a place of rest for only those who called the sept home, and no Silent Striders had ever done so. Although they were welcome at this sept and many others around the world, the werewolves of the Silent Striders tribe called no place home. The lone figure brooding at the boundary of the graveyard scowled at the monuments, feeling the weight of his entire tribe's ages-long isolation.

"I shouldn't have come here," Mephi Faster-Than-Death said aloud to no one in particular. His breath frosted in the cold of early night, and his fingers curled more tightly around the walking staff that had been his only reliable companion for more years than he cared to admit. The icy white string of spoken words drifted off over his shoulder in a steady wind that cut straight across the top of the hill. It carried the scent of smoke and scrubbed stone and even a faint trace of water somewhere far in the distance, but it carried no odor of man or beast. Mephi was alone with the dead.

Even after the words came out, though, he wasn't sure if he was referring to this graveyard or to the Sept of the Anvil-Klaiven itself. He had crossed an ocean via a moon bridge to bear witness to an event that had never actually occurred. Like many other visitors to the sept, he had come to see a legendary villain meet justice; but that villain had never arrived for the final hearing he'd been granted. Mephi had wasted time that would have been better spent back in the United States—where he was better known and better able to do his solemn work—just to witness this "historical" event. His few steady allies and even fewer friends must surely think that he had died since they'd seen him last. When he finally returned, he'd have to soothe hurt feelings and deflect accusations that he was shirking his local responsibilities. He'd done the same plenty of times before after long, unexplained absences, but those absences had come about for good reasons. This time, he was just a tourist who hadn't even found the thing he'd come so far to see.

On top of that uncomfortable realization, Mephi had to admit that he had little to show at all for his prolonged and unannounced sojourn here to this bitter and unforgiving Norwegian caern. He knew no one at this sept personally, and he was familiar with the reputations and legends of only a very few of them. Of course, he hadn't gone out of his way to try to get to know any of the werewolves at this sept either, despite his indulgence in their hospitality and their strong drink. The only werewolves he'd socialized with were visitors as well. In fact, he was more familiar with the lives and deeds of the hallowed dead of this sept than he was with any of the living warriors who called this place their home.

Digging the blunt end of his staff into the ground, Mephi considered that it might just be the fact that he'd spent too much time here doing nothing that had given rise to this lonely and morbid speculation. He could never really settle down to rest, even in places that were familiar to him, yet rest was really all he had done since coming here. He always had other responsibilities to take care of, other stories to learn and other dead souls to lay to rest. He had memories of other fallen warriors to preserve, be they heroes, cowards or traitors. The longer he stayed in one place, the longer he shirked those responsibilities that waited just down the road. It wasn't his nature to rest when there was work to be done. Nor was it his nature to let himself believe that he'd found even a temporary home.

Then again, maybe it was just the graveyard that had imposed this dour introspection on him. Most of the werewolves in the sept came here only when one of their shield-brothers had died. Although they honored their fallen and told the stories of those heroes' glorious deeds, they did not come to this place to remind themselves of them. Werewolves such as Mephi—a werewolf of the Galliard auspice—were charged with reminding the others. It was a Galliard's responsibility to make sure that these monuments and the tales they told didn't die with the fallen heroes.

Mephi considered it one of his many responsibilities to come to these places of the dead and learn what he could from them so that he could pass that knowledge on to all other werewolves who would listen. Although such places reminded other werewolves that they probably wouldn't live to see old age or victory against their ubiquitous foes, Mephi sought them out. These places reminded him that every life was worthy of some remembrance. As the hours stretched on and the sun set in front of him, Mephi had begun to believe that he was one of the only werewolves left on Gaia's green earth who still believed that.

"Hell, it's probably all wishful thinking, though," Mephi murmured with a self-deprecating smile. "Self-important, self-indulgent wishful thinking at that." With a twist of his wrist, he rotated his walking staff so that the hissing golden cobra head at the top was looking him in the eyes. He regarded the gleaming, handcrafted snake with the same sad smile and said, "But who knows? Maybe only the forgotten dead get any rest, yes?"

The scuffling sound of footsteps on the rocky incline leading up from the Aeld Baile drew Mephi out of his reverie, but he was not embarrassed by the sudden intrusion. He'd been caught talking to himself too many times for it to still bother him. When the footsteps drew no closer, Mephi decided to turn around.

"Excuse me," a man said in bland German. "Are you Mephi Faster-Than-Death?"

Mephi nodded and stood up a little straighter. He recognized the stocky, blond-bearded man from when he'd arrived at the caern, although he didn't know the man's name. All Mephi knew was that the fellow was one of the sept's Guardians under Brand Garmson. He wore a thick, wool-lined coat against the cold, sturdy work pants and heavy boots like those of a lumberjack or a construction worker.

Mephi himself wore only a thin, gray shirt, sun-faded jeans and a tattered tan duster jacket, the sleeves of which hid the heavy golden bands on his biceps but didn't quite cover the golden bracelets at his wrists. The cold didn't bother him, though, since he'd taken on his more bulky and hirsute Glabro form against the chill hours ago. He felt the chill on the tips of his ears, and the flat golden necklace he wore hung like a block of ice, but he felt it as if from some great distance within himself.

"Would you come with me, then?" the man asked, gesturing back toward the House of the Spearsreach. He showed none of the classic signs of being intimidated by Mephi's appearance. Doubtless, this man was used to tussling with or fighting alongside the locals, whose average muscle mass in their Homid forms almost doubled that of Mephi's tall and lean frame.

"Am I somewhere I'm not supposed to be?" Mephi asked without making any move to comply. The gruff cadence of a challenge rumbled in his voice, but it was just as much a factor of his current shape as his irritation at not realizing sooner that the man was coming.

"No," the man answered, bristling but minding his manners all the same.

"Then what do you want?"

The man clenched and relaxed his jaw before saying, "You're sent for. The Greifynya would speak to you. And the others."

"I see," Mephi said with only a shade more respect. Although he was being fetched, he was being fetched by Karin Jarlsdottir—the leader of the werewolves of this sept. "What 'others'?"

"Margrave Konietzko is among them," the man said, letting hero-worship glaze his eyes for an instant. Mephi understood the man's reaction, for he had heard of the Margrave even on the other side of the Atlantic. Although Konietzko was a Shadow Lord and an heir to the mistrust that werewolves of the other tribes often directed toward Shadow Lords, the Margrave's tactical genius and inspirational courage had led those who followed him to victory throughout Europe time and again.

"And one of those who are leaving tomorrow," the man added, as if in afterthought. "From the Roving Wind."

Mephi frowned. Word was going around the sept that the Roving Wind pack had volunteered to take on a mission that had some bearing on Margrave Konietzko's campaign against the forces of the Wyrm in Central Europe. Although Mephi didn't know the specifics, he'd heard the gossip like everyone else.

"I see," he said to the Guardian with a growl. "Margrave Konietzko and someone from the Roving Wind. What do I have in common with them that the Greifynya wants us all together?"

The local shook his head with a frown when Mephi finished talking, and he paused to reshape his thoughts.

"You misunderstand," he said. "The Greifynya and the

others have sent for you. They all wish to speak with you."

This time, it was Mephi who paused and frowned. "Why?"

"I didn't ask them to explain," the Guardian said.

"I see," Mephi sneered. "Well, aren't you a good boy? Why don't you show me where they are, then?"

The Guardian's blue eyes blazed like welding sparks, but he held his tongue. Apparently, he knew better than to push a touchy subject with a touchy werewolf. That, or he knew that he had a job to do, and he intended to do it. "This way," he said. He turned when Mephi nodded and began to walk back the way he'd come.

Mephi glanced at the cobra head atop his walking staff with a mixture of amusement, petty satisfaction, and a sliver of disappointment that the pissing contest hadn't come to blows. He hadn't been in a good fight—for which the stakes were his pride rather than his life—in months. No bar brawls, no shoving matches, no screaming rows with jealous women who wondered where he'd been since they last saw him. Nothing. The anger was building up in him and festering with nowhere to vent it. It always happened when he stayed in one place too long.

He shook his head and started walking. Once he found out what Karin Jarlsdottir and the Margrave wanted with him, he'd have to get moving again. He needed to get back to the States, where he could at least do some good.

Chapter 2

Gashwrack didn't slouch as he made his way along the dank hallway. To slouch would not be seemly, and it would invite attack even in such a place as this. The paramours of Arastha who lived in this Hive always lurked in corners and the mouths of empty tunnels that connected to the main hallway before Arastha's chamber. When word spread that someone had been summoned into the Lady's presence, the deluded, jealous fools staked out the main hallway to wait for the subject of the summons. If the summoned Dancer showed any sign of weakness, he was likely to be challenged and set upon regardless of whether he had actually provoked the challenger. The only justification that the survivor of the fight could then offer for what he had done was to say that the victim had been weak, and unworthy to disgrace Lady Arastha's presence.

Gashwrack knew from experience that projecting the impression of strength forestalled most such vain ambushes, but he was also well aware that simple posturing would get him only so far. If he didn't look out for an actual assault, it wouldn't matter how strong he looked.

The flickering light from the torches pressed the ceiling down on him and made his eyes dart into the shadows. However, even the shadows writhed and twisted in the torchlight, making Gashwrack think of diseased lovers sharing one last embrace. He saw no one nearby, but he kept on guard nonetheless. The undulating shadows could conceal unmoving forms. The echoing rhythm of his boot heels could cover the sound of someone breathing. His sense of smell was all but non-existent in this form, so only the foulest offal would even make his nose twitch. He might be alone in the subterranean hallway, or he might be surrounded.

Gashwrack's vigilance saw him safely most of the way to his destination, but trouble was waiting for him nonetheless. A shaggy mass of matted and blood-gnarled orange fur crouched just outside the bone-lattice door of Lady Arastha's chamber. The ugly hulk looked up at Gashwrack, and his pus-yellow eyes rolled in anticipation. The thick and ragged flaps of his ears perked up. Gashwrack could just make out the excited swish of the Crinos werewolf's tail on the floor. Gashwrack recognized the monster immediately.

"Splinterbone," Gashwrack growled, looking his adversary in its dancing yellow eyes. "Get out of my way."

"Arastha is busy," Splinterbone growled back, rising halfway to his full height. His hands shook when they came up off the floor, and his long, chipped claws chittered against the stone.

"I'm sent for," Gashwrack hissed through clenched teeth. Although he wore only his Homid shape, he glared into the Crinos werewolf's eyes without fear. With Splinterbone half-crouched, Gashwrack didn't have to look up and expose his neck to do so. "Arastha wants me."

"I'm standing guard," Splinterbone rumbled. His splotchy tongue licked his fangs. "Go away."

Gashwrack sneered, baring his teeth. "If you're the lady's only guard, she must want to die."

Splinterbone's eyelids peeled back in outrage and he stood to his full height. "I'm guarding!" he bellowed, thumping his chest with a hand that could crush a man's skull. He took a step forward and snarled down at Gashwrack. The beast's sulfurous breath blasted Gashwrack in the face, and oily saliva fell on the floor between them. Gashwrack pivoted his foot to keep his boot from being slobbered on. He counted it a victory that Splinterbone didn't simply slap him into the wall headfirst. Splinterbone was young, fanatical and tough, but he was too stupid to act first. Obviously, this "clever" ruse had used up his allotment of wits for the day.

"In that case," Gashwrack said as rage began to churn somewhere between his stomach and his heart, "go and announce me to Lady Arastha." He was careful to make himself look annoyed rather than furious. The human expression did not forewarn of an attack. It made Gashwrack look more like he was ready to submit to Splinterbone's ludicrous claim to authority.

Splinterbone's massive head twitched at Gashwrack's words, and his pupils dilated in hazy contemplation. "Announce…"

"Hurry up," Gashwrack snapped. The rage in his middle began to push outward, and he had to restrain himself from taking on the Glabro shape just to ease the pressure. "Go inside and tell Arastha I'm here!"

Splinterbone stepped backward toward Arastha's door with a dimly amused look in his wild eyes. The faint gleam in the murky orbs indicated that he thought he'd gotten away with something. "Announce you," he said. "Yes." His breath began to come out harder, and his next words were thick. "Wait."

"Stop stalling!" Gashwrack shouted in feigned frustration as the fury filled him at last. He clamped his hands into hard knots to keep his fingers from quivering. "Just go!"

Gashwrack was all but forgotten in the behemoth's mind already. He took another step back toward Arastha's door, then turned to open it with a faraway look in his eyes.

As soon as those eyes dismissed Gashwrack, Gashwrack let his fury burst its dam at last. Exploding into Crinos form, he leapt forward and drove his claws through the hair, skin and muscle of Splinterbone's back. Two vicious arcs flayed Splinterbone from tailbone to shoulder blade. In surprised agony, Splinterbone arched back onto the tips of his toes with a cub's terrified yelp.

Riding his initial wave of forward momentum, Gashwrack crashed into Splinterbone and pressed the attack. He raked the claws of his right foot down the back of Splinterbone's right leg, leaving a bloody rent from testicles to knee, and he wrapped his long arms around Splinterbone in an iron embrace. With his elbows pinning Splinterbone's arms, he crossed his wrists and drove his claws into the ropy muscles on either side of Splinterbone's throat. Splinterbone mewled, and a red froth dribbled out of the side of his mouth onto Gashwrack's wrist.

"How much do you love me, you tangled fool?" Gashwrack growled into Splinterbone's ear once the larger werewolf was immobilized. He nipped the tip of Splinterbone's flapping ear off to punctuate the question.

Splinterbone didn't answer.

"I asked a question," Gashwrack growled again, letting his tongue brush Splinterbone's cheek. "Do you love me more than Arastha? If you do, you live."

Splinterbone's head wiggled in what was either a feeble nod or an attempt to swallow more blood before it could run out of his mouth and down his face.

"Say it," Gashwrack said, flexing his fingertips as Splinterbone's skin tried to heal around them. "Say you love me."

"Love...you..." Splinterbone gurgled as best he could. His arms hung slack at his sides, and a frail, thin whine escaped his throat.

"More than Arastha," Gashwrack demanded, biting off a larger piece of Splinterbone's ear. He used his tongue to put the torn scrap of flesh into Splinterbone's mouth. Splinterbone didn't even try to bite him.

"More..." the brute gasped. "More...Arastha...."

"Good boy," Gashwrack snarled. He slackened the pressure on Splinterbone's neck, but he didn't let go. Instead, he leaned forward and nuzzled Splinterbone's head roughly in the direction of Lady Arastha's bone-lattice door. In the wide, diamond-shaped spaces between the slats, the two of them could see the silhouette of a tall nude woman. The woman's slim fingers poked through the lattice slats as she watched the two of them. Splinterbone whimpered and started trembling.

"Let him live, overzealous Gashwrack," the woman said. She might have asked for a kiss in the same tone of voice. "Stop hurting your new pet. Come in to me."

Gashwrack snorted in disdain, but he did as the Lady Arastha bid him. With a twist and a shove, he sent Splinterbone spinning to the floor. Splinterbone landed on his face, then scrambled to his hands and knees. He put a hand to his bleeding neck and tried to push himself upright despite the agony in his back. He spit, and a wad of phlegm and blood hit the stone floor with a smack.

"Go make yourself well, Gashwrack's pet," Arastha crooned. "You'll have need to attend him when he leaves me. Hurry along."

Without another word, Splinterbone gathered himself up into a three-point crouch and shambled away with his tail limp behind him. He spared only an instant to glare back at Gashwrack before disappearing down the first available tunnel.

When the fool was gone, Gashwrack's rage began to cool. As it did, his body melted and folded back in on itself until he looked human once again. Only the flesh and hair that clung tenaciously to his fingernails connected him to the monster that he had just been and the work he had just done.

"Magnificent," Arastha cooed from behind the door. "That was beautifully done."

Gashwrack was sure that she'd have said the same to Splinterbone had things worked out differently. Lady Arastha encouraged this perverse courtship among the Hive's strongest males. "Young degenerates always fall for that," he said back. "Let me in."

"Am I so eager?" Arastha teased. "What if Splinterbone had been my favorite?"

"He wasn't," Gashwrack rumbled, stepping toward Arastha. He put his hand on the door so that his fingers came through the lattice next to hers. He restrained himself from trying to open the door without her invitation or rip it down regardless of what she wanted. Although his blood was up after the fight, his excitement hadn't stolen his mind entirely. He didn't even touch Arastha's fingers. "If he was your favorite, you would have sent for him."

"True," Arastha said, stepping backward into the shadows of her chamber toward her bed. She ran her fingers along the nearest wall over a mural mosaic of bone and glass that depicted the Defiler Wyrm; Mahsstrac, the Urge of Power; and G'louogh, Arastha's patron totem spirit. The sound of Arastha's fingernails sliding across the exquisite work of art followed her into the dark.

"Come inside then, eager Gashwrack," she said as she disappeared. "And shut the door behind you."

Chapter 3

Mephi followed the silent Guardian to a squat wooden lodge hidden in the shadow of the House of the Spearsreach, where he was ordered to go inside. The others, he was told, were waiting inside for him, and they could not begin with their business until he joined them. Without a word to the Guardian, he nodded and went inside.

Inside, the lodge was even smaller than it had appeared from outside. A single room comprised its interior, with a stone fireplace at the far right side and a low wooden table dominating the floor. A stout war hammer that looked older than the combined ages of everyone present hung on the wall facing the fireplace. The wall opposite the door was decked out with animal skins and a few impressive hunting trophies. Although the room had only two small windows, the light from the fireplace and that from a hanging lamp illuminated the space well enough.

What brought the walls in closer, however, were the other werewolves already in the room at various positions around the low, circular table. The table was strewn with maps and what appeared to be hand-written documents, and the people in the room were all looking down at them rather than at the door that had let the cold in. A hardy local woman with a thick golden braid stood directly across the room from him, and she was the first to look up. Her blue eyes were striking despite the grim thousand-yard stare that leached warmth from them. The hard lines and sharp angles of her face might have been carved in oak or granite. Mephi recognized her right away as Karin Jarlsdottir, the Greifynya who had summoned him. She was much more attractive at this range than even she had seemed from the distance at which he'd seen her around the caern.

As Mephi cleared his throat, melted down into his Homid form and leaned his walking staff next to the door, the other werewolves in the room glanced up to regard him. The first to do so was a lean female who sat on her haunches in Lupus form next to Jarlsdottir. The wolf's fur was char-black, with russet undertones that the firelight behind her set off to good effect. Her shoulders and haunches were trim and strong as if she'd spent a lot of time running. She looked up, sniffed once, then turned back to the maps nearest her on the short table.

The only other man in the room crouched on the opposite side of the table from the wolf, and he stood with the careless ease of a man less than half his age. The way he moved displayed the perfect synchronicity between human and lupine grace that it took some werewolves a lifetime to achieve. This was no wolf tottering on two human legs, nor was it merely a man who could also run on all fours. He was a hunter's spirit clothed in changing flesh. His muscular body coiled like a spring, and an iron-gray mane hung to his shoulders, just brushing the fur-trimmed black cloak that hung on his back. The appraising stare Mephi got from the man shone with an unflinching expectation of command. A heavy broadsword hung from his wide leather belt, and he placed a casual hand near the hilt without even seeming to think about it. The Margrave Konietzko was even more impressive at arm's length than he had been when Mephi had first seen him across the Aeld Baile. Mephi felt suddenly self-conscious in his beat-up golden bands and travel-worn clothes.

Swallowing a surge of awe, Mephi turned to the blond woman across the table from him. He nodded and said in Nynorsk, "Greifynya, you sent for me."

"Welcome, Silent Strider, to the Sept of the Anvil-Klaiven," Karin Jarlsdottir said in English. "I apologize for not meeting you personally when you arrived. You've been treated well?"

"As if I'd come home," Mephi replied. Although he said basically the same whenever he was welcomed to a caern, the repetition made the words no more true. He looked at Konietzko and said, "Margrave Konietzko. I've heard of you even in America, sir."

The middle-aged Margrave nodded, but the canny, appraising look never left his eyes.

Finally, Mephi turned to the wolf at Jarlsdottir's side and nodded once again. "Ma'am," he said with nothing more to go on.

"This is Rain-Hunter," Jarlsdottir explained. "A Red Talon of the Roving Wind pack. She's a guest here, as you are."

Mephi nodded to Rain-Hunter again, wondering why the Greifynya hadn't mentioned the wolf's home sept as well. Maybe the Roving Wind pack didn't have one. While such a thing was a little unusual, it was not entirely unheard of. Mephi himself called no protectorate home.

"I thank you for coming to us so quickly, Mephi Faster-Than-Death," Jarlsdottir continued. "We'd like your help in a very important and timely matter. One concerning the plans that were made in our fellowship hall."

"What about them?" Mephi asked. He'd been leaning against the back wall when the Margrave and the Jarlsdottir and Antonine Teardrop had proposed a series of excursions south into Central Europe, but he couldn't imagine what it might have to do with him. Or rather, he didn't see how it might immediately apply to him. Maybe these three wanted another Galliard's opinion on how to interpret the Stargazer's bizarre Riddle of Threes. Mephi would have obliged without reservation if he could have offered any insight, but he had no idea what the old man had been going on about.

"You're aware of the Wyrm and Weaver's growing influence on this part of the world," Margrave Konietzko said in thickly accented English. "You have been informed, even in America?"

"I'm aware of it, sir."

"And you understood what the Stargazer said when he spoke his riddle?" the Margrave continued.

"As well as I could," Mephi said carefully. "He was talking about the dangers growing in Europe's heart and a threat to our Garou nation's past. He wasn't very specific."

He uncovered a path to follow, Rain-Hunter said in the lupine language of growl and posture that all werewolves understood. He warned of its dangers.

"I don't follow your path," Mephi said. Gauging the look that Rain-Hunter turned on him, he amended that statement to, "That is, I don't see what you mean."

"Regardless of the exact meaning of what Antonine Teardrop said," Karin Jarlsdottir said, "Margrave Konietzko and the other war leaders in this part of the world have come to believe that steps must be taken to gauge how much of a threat the Wyrm's legions actually pose us here. Therefore, two select groups of Garou have been chosen to answer this call to action if they can."

"Right," Mephi said. "I know about all that. Mari Cabrah and your Warder's pack are going into Serbia overland for recon." He looked at Rain-Hunter and said, "Your Roving Wind's going on a different quest. I caught that in passing, too. But did you say it'll just be two packs?"

"Yes," Jarlsdottir said with a patient look. "The first pack is coming together to take on a quest into Serbia. The American Black Fury will go with them."

"And the others?" Mephi asked. "The Roving Wind?"

"The others are going into Hungary tomorrow night at moonrise," Margrave Konietzko answered. "They're going to the fallen caern of memory hidden within Hortobägy National Park."

"You're here because we hope you'll go with them," Jarlsdottir said, a beat after the Margrave finished talking.

Mephi blinked in surprise and stood up straight. That'd come out of left field.

"The glory and honor of this quest would be well worth the difficulty," Karin Jarlsdottir said when Mephi didn't reply. "We know how dangerous this will be."

"I'm not worried about that," Mephi said. The last thing he wanted to do was leave this Get and the other two werewolves with the impression that he was stalling because he was scared. "I just don't understand this. I don't know anything about this fallen caern. I've never been to Hungary. I've never even been to this caern before. What made you think of me for this?"

Your skill is known to us, Rain-Hunter said.

"That's very kind," Mephi said, as curiosity and pride rose

inside him. "Do you know Storm-Eye? Is that who told you about me?"

When he'd arrived, Mephi had been surprised to find his sometime comrade among the other visitors to this sept. He hadn't been expecting to see Storm-Eye so far from her home protectorate. As fiercely territorial as Storm-Eye (and most of her Red Talon tribemates) could be, getting her to leave her home and come so far took a matter of singular importance.

No, Rain-Hunter told him. Not her.

"You were asked for by name," Jarlsdottir said.

Mephi was tempted to look at the Margrave, but he knew that the Shadow Lord hadn't been the one who'd suggested he be involved in this. The older man had never seen—and likely never heard of—him, and Mephi wasn't vain enough to think that the reputation he'd garnered in the States had preceded him. Even considering Rain-Hunter's assertion that his skill was known here, Mephi had a tough time figuring out how his renown had gotten all the way to Eastern Europe if not from one of the Americans who'd come to this concolation.

We asked, Rain-Hunter said when confusion clouded Mephi's face. My pack.

Mephi didn't ask the wolf why outright, but his expression asked the question for him.

My alpha asked, Rain-Hunter said. She who always finds the light, even in her sleep.

Mephi's eyes registered his surprise, and uneasiness blossomed in his stomach. "Melinda Light-Finder, you mean? She's in charge of Roving Wind? I didn't know she was here."

"Yes," Karin Jarlsdottir said. Her eyes took on a suspicious aspect when she saw Mephi's expression. "The Roving Wind volunteered to take on the quest, and they are asking you to join. Light-Finder would have asked you herself, but the Margrave thought it best to speak to you first since we hadn't heard of you."

"This is true," the Margrave added. "Since you would be traveling through my protectorate into strategically important territory under my supervision, I insisted I meet you. You are not known here."

Except by she who always finds the light, even in her sleep, Rain-Hunter said. And those she tells about you.

"You see," Konietzko said as if no one had spoken after him, "this mission is important, regardless of what that Stargazer said. I must be sure that the soldiers who agree to take it on are worthy and able to do so."

"You can be sure of me," Mephi said without thinking. "And of Melinda Light-Finder's judgment. She and I worked together plenty of times in the States. If she's volunteered for this, I'll be right there with her. Gladly."

"Spirit," Jarlsdottir mused with a light smile. "You don't even know what she wants you for."

"I don't have to," Mephi said. "If I knew she'd volunteered before she knew I was here, I'd have offered to go with her." Just don't ask me why, he thought. Not if you like having a pretty face.

"Well enough," the Margrave said. "Then pay close attention to what I'm about to tell you. You can talk over the specifics with the Roving Wind tomorrow before you leave, but this mission's foremost goal is simple." His face was graven in iron as he took a knee beside the table. Jarlsdottir matched the movement. Rain-Hunter had remained seated throughout.

When Mephi crouched, the Margrave touched a topographical map of Hungary and the countries surrounding it. He traced the line of the Danube River to where it crossed the Tisza River in Yugoslavia, then traced the Tisza upstream through Hungary toward that country's border with Romania in the east.

"This is the Tisza River," the old man said. He pointed to another line that crossed into Romania and said, "This is the Viseu River. In March of 2000, a burst dam at a mine here—" he pointed to a spot on the Viseu near where it met the Tisza "—spilled heavy-metal sediment into the river. This spill followed an incident in January, in which a similar accident on the Somes River dumped cyanide into the river that was carried almost all the way to the Danube in Yugoslavia."

"I've heard about this," Mephi murmured. "On CNN...the Internet..."

"Yes," the Margrave said with thin-eyed disdain. "What you did not see there is what serious effect this disaster has had. The creatures that lived in the river were poisoned and killed. The animals that ate those creatures were poisoned. The corrupt chain of predator and prey has spread this poison wider than the river's banks and even wider than the flood plains that flank it."

He traced two thick fingers along the middle stretch of the Tisza River that ran through Hungary. "In the Umbra, all of this territory has died and become a Hellhole. Each tributary is another vein carrying the poison on this plane and the spirit plane as well. The Wyrm's soldiers are growing strong here. Stronger than the forces we had in place at the time."

"Terrible," Mephi murmured.

"Understated," the Margrave said. He tapped a section of the map that lay next to the Tisza but not terribly far. "This is the location of the Hortobägy National Park. It is only 520 square kilometers, but it is one of the few wild places in this part of the country that the humans have thought to protect. Five years ago, the Roving Wind discovered a weak, natural caern of memory hidden deep within this park. Warriors from the Sept of the Night Sky and a lesser sept in Romania have only recently cleared away the Weaver's trappings there and awakened the caern's spirit. The Roving Wind undertook a quest to find a pathstone for the caern as well. The place is called Owl's Rest."

"It was," Jarlsdottir added. The muscles in her jaw were tight, and hatred boiled in her clear, blue eyes.

"What happened?" Mephi asked.

Overrun, Rain-Hunter growled. Her tail dropped flat against the ground where she sat. Too many, too fast.

"Yes," the Margrave said. "The soldiers of the Wyrm overtook the caern when the devastation of the Tisza River disaster was at its peak. The caern is small, and only a few souls had yet arrived to defend it. Some cowards fled. Others had left already to ally with my forces in other theaters of conflict before their position was secure. The defenders who were left were caught off guard by the disaster, and the caern fell."

"It was a small caern?" Mephi asked when the Margrave

paused. Rain-Hunter indicated that he was correct.

"Very small," the Margrave said. "But strategically important. You see, its pathstone was connected to other more powerful caerns in the region. There were also plans to use it as a staging area against the Wyrm's forces in Serbia. Had it fallen in that conflict, our soldiers there could have fallen back to the Sept of the Night Sky and continued the fight. Besides all that, although it is not powerful, it is still a holy place of Gaia."

"Then the Roving Wind and I are to try to take it back?" Mephi asked with a reasonable show of conviction.

"More spirit," Jarlsdottir said. This time, however, her words dripped with a caustic gallows humor that seemed to leave a bad taste in her mouth. The weary expression that came along with it made the Get of Fenris look at least ten years older than she was. She was too young to be Greifynya, Mephi knew from listening to the gossip around the sept. Being reminded by example of what would happen to her home if ever she was weak was not kind to her.

"A pack of strays will not take back what has been taken from my war-forged soldiers who stood their ground to the last," the Margrave sneered. "No, such a thing is beyond you and the Roving Wind alone. And this is not the time. Instead, you have a different and more immediate responsibility. Do you know what a pathstone is?"

"I know," Mephi answered, trying to keep indignation out of his voice. He wondered if the Margrave talked this way to everybody, or just everybody who wasn't a "war-forged" Shadow Lord.

"Good," the Margrave replied. "The pathstone at Owl's Rest is the object of your mission. You and the Roving Wind are to go there, get it and bring it back here before the Wyrm's soldiers make it their own. That stone is linked to the pathstones of the surrounding caerns. If our enemies take it, our caerns in this region will be vulnerable to attack."

"I beg your pardon, Margrave," Mephi interrupted. "But if the caern has fallen, doesn't the enemy already have the pathstone?"

"Wyrm legions would have attacked the exposed positions

already if that were so," Jarlsdottir said, "and the Margrave would be home defending his territory."

"Yes," the Margrave said with only a quick glance at the Get of Fenris. "The Warder and Gatekeeper of Owl's Rest were under orders to hide the stone if the caern could not be secured before it came under concentrated assault. We have not been attacked since the caern's defenders fell, so we must assume they were successful in that."

"I see," Mephi said. "So then we're to find this stone and bring it back here as quickly as we can."

"Without bringing the Wyrm's legions here with you," Karin Jarlsdottir said. A moment later, a savage smile broke across her face, and she added, "Well, not without letting us know you're coming first."

Mephi smiled with her, remembering what had happened to the group of Wyrm-spawn who had come to this place since he'd arrived. Set's teeth, that had been a massacre.

"You'll bring the pathstone to me at the Sept of the Night Sky," Konietzko said, showing no sign of catching Jarlsdottir's black mirth. "That is your primary objective. We also want you to perform basic reconnaissance. Look for how well entrenched the enemy is, and bring that information back to us. If you can eliminate targets of opportunity, do so. If you find any deserters or survivors, deal with them. Lead what survivors are healthy enough to return back to the Sept of the Night Sky. Kill any deserters that you find. Even if they haven't rolled over for the Wyrm."

"I understand," Mephi said.

"But even if you fail in those secondary goals," the Margrave said, "return the pathstone."

And remember the Stargazer's words, Rain-Hunter said. We must try to understand for his words.

"Yes," the Margrave admitted with a lingering shadow of disdain. "That, too."

Afterward, the Margrave was silent for a long while, during which only the crackle and pop of the logs in the fireplace made any noise inside the lodge. Everyone looked at Mephi, but he had nothing to say. He'd already given them their answer as soon as Melinda's name had come up. He was in.

"Are you still eager to follow the Roving Wind, Silent Strider?" the Margrave asked. "If you have pressing matters to attend to at home…"

"I haven't changed my mind," Mephi said. "When do we leave?"

"Tomorrow at moonrise," Konietzko said. "Be ready."

"I will," Mephi said.

"Good."

The Margrave inclined his head in a nearly imperceptible nod, looking one last time into Mephi's eyes, then he left the small lodge with only a mumbled parting word. His exit let in a rush of cold air that stirred the embers in the fireplace, and Mephi and Karin Jarlsdottir put their hands on the table to keep the maps from stirring or blowing onto the floor. The chilly rush subsided when the door closed again, but it did little to improve the temperature. Even the scent of the burning logs seemed dim under the scent of hard, hoary earth from outside.

"Do you have everything you need?" Karin Jarlsdottir asked Rain-Hunter.

Enough, Rain-Hunter replied. My pack will make ready. We go when the moon rises.

"Very well," Jarlsdottir said, standing up and retrieving the enormous rune-etched hammer that hung on the wall. As she balanced it on her shoulder, Mephi admired the bunch and flex of her muscles beneath the tight flannel shirt she wore. Her pants made no mystery of the shape of her powerful legs either. "Strider, I welcome you again, but I also say good-bye. I have to talk to my Warder and his pack one last time before the night gets any deeper."

"I understand, Greifynya," Mephi said. He rose, making it look like he was rising from a deep and gallant bow, and he pulled the door open for her. Jarlsdottir gave him a knowing and semi-amused look before taking the door from him and shutting it behind her with a thump. Mephi's walking staff clattered to the floor, and he bent to pick it up with a smirk. When he had it propped back up next to the doorjamb, he turned back to face Rain-Hunter.

She will not see you tonight, the wolf growled before Mephi could even say anything.

"What?"

I will not bring you to she who always finds the light, even in her sleep.

"Why not?" Mephi asked. "Surely she wants to—"

No, Rain-Hunter replied. You can find her tomorrow.

"Is that why you're here instead of her?" Mephi asked with growing frustration. "Even though she's in charge and you're not?" If he wasn't careful, this frustration was going to give way to anger.

We all found the memory caern together, Rain-Hunter answered. We found the caern's pathstone together. We all know enough.

"And why did Melinda want me along for this if she doesn't even want to see me?" Mephi pressed, ignoring the evasion for what it was worth.

Ask her, Rain-Hunter said with the lupine equivalent of a shrug. Tomorrow.

Mephi gave up at last. He knew better than to argue about a stubborn werewolf with a stubborn werewolf. He'd just have to wait until tomorrow. Perhaps by then he could think up some way to talk to Melinda Light-Finder about the last time he'd seen her, more than ten years ago.

Chapter 4

After following Arastha's undulating backside and her three swaying, frizzy braids into the deepest recesses of her private chamber in the Hive, Gashwrack was more than a little disappointed to find another male already waiting there for the two of them. The intruder lay on Arastha's bed in the shape of a dire wolf with his head on his forepaws. The tangled and fluid-blotched bedcovers lolled from the end of the bed in the same way that the dire wolf's tongue lolled from his mouth. The black and gray hair at his shoulders and neck pointed in all directions, and four deep furrows that crossed the glyph of the simple, tapered spiral on his right shoulder were just beginning to close up. The fire between Gashwrack's heart and stomach began to grow.

"Gashwrack," Arastha said, walking to his side and stroking his shoulder. "I want you to satisfy me. To make me very happy." Her other hand traced a long fingernail down his spine.

Gashwrack's eyes narrowed, and he glanced sideways at Arastha. She gave off coalfire warmth as she pressed against him, and she reeked of bed scent, but Gashwrack knew enough to realize that he was being manipulated. These blunt and clumsy words were enough to give Arastha away. He looked back at the wolf in Arastha's bed. The wolf met his eyes but seemed too tired and content to move.

"How?"

Arastha stepped behind Gashwrack, sliding her nails across the back of his neck then down his shoulder to the front of his chest. She stepped in front of him at the same time, cutting off his view of the male on her bed. She was shorter than he by half a hand, but her overlarge cave-sight eyes trapped him.

He could not even bring himself to glance down at her sweat-streaked and claw-welted breasts. The cunning gleam in her eyes betrayed her tired smile for the stage dressing that it was.

"No longer so eager, Gashwrack?" she purred, letting her thigh brush his.

Gashwrack took a long breath through his nose and looked down at Arastha's smooth, athletic body. He resisted the temptation to look at her bed again. He knew better than to take his eyes off her at this distance. "I can tell you've been satisfied already," he said. "I came to fill what needs you have left over."

"Yes, you have," Arastha said. She stepped back from him, and her predatory eyes narrowed. The cast they took on filled her false smile with more genuine life. "Tell me, then, Gashwrack. Are you happy here?"

"Yes."

Arastha backed away and sat on the edge of her bed beside the huge wolf. The wolf's tail flapped once. His silver-white eyes turned to regard her. "Were you terribly sad at your old home?"

"Yes."

"Don't lie," Arastha purred. "You were happy there. Determined. Respected."

"I was misguided," Gashwrack admitted with a downward glance. "Naïve."

"Proud," Arastha went on. "You had a good home."

"I have a better one now," Gashwrack said.

Arastha focused on him once again. "But you had a good home. And a position of honor."

"I don't want to talk about this," Gashwrack snapped, which earned him an amused twinkle in Arastha's eyes. Amused but not conciliatory. "Ma'am."

"I do, pet," Arastha said. As she spoke, she combed the fur of the wolf beside her with her fingernails. "I'm very interested in your former home. I think I might send you back there."

Gashwrack's jaw clenched, and his toes curled in his boots.

"Don't be afraid, loyal Gashwrack," Arastha said. "That place is ours now. I wouldn't dream of sending you into enemy territory. Your home is here now, and I do so want you to return."

Gashwrack's eyes darted from Arastha to the tired wolf at her side. The wolf let Arastha stroke his fur, and he stretched his neck out every time Arastha's fingernails scratched him between his ears.

"I don't understand."

"Aren't I wicked to tease and confuse him so?" Arastha said to the wolf on her bed as she stroked his long right ear. "I need you to return to the caern from which you came to us, Gashwrack. Temporarily."

"Why?" Gashwrack asked. He never wanted to think of that place again, much less return there.

"To act as my field commander," Arastha said. "And as an escort to an honored warrior. And to help you bond with your new pack."

"What warrior? And what pack? I haven't taken—"

"I know," Arastha sliced through his protest. "But you will. Tonight before you leave. Shrike's Thorn will perform the rite."

"Who?"

The wolf beside Arastha raised his huge head and regarded Gashwrack with clinical indifference. As the two males stared at each other, the dire wolf's body stretched, melted and drew itself out until only a naked man lay by Arastha's side. Tightly curled black hairs dusted his chest and shoulders, except for the bald patch of the spiral glyph on his right shoulder and the crescent moon patch on his opposite shoulder. Intense silver-white eyes continued to peer at Gashwrack, and silky, black hair framed his face on both sides.

"It's almost time," the man said.

"This is Shrike's Thorn," Arastha said. "He is newly arrived to our home from the Hive of Prisoners' Tears, and he helped overtake your former home. That victory cost him all of the beloved members of his pack. Yet he has very important work to do there, and he has joined us—he has forsaken his home Hive far to the south—to see that it is done."

Gashwrack tried not to wince at the phrase "forsaken his home."

"Therefore, you must take him through our tunnels and see him safely to your former home," Arastha continued. "He must be delivered there safely and allowed to conduct his work. You will see that he is."

"What work?" Gashwrack asked, trying to look both Arastha and Shrike's Thorn in the eye at the same time.

Arastha smiled with a lie in her eyes and said, "Clever Shrike's Thorn knows more about such confusing things than you or I. He is a visionary among us, given the most lavish gifts of insight by the Father. He can explain them along the way in less time than I could describe them."

"But first I'm to join his pack?" Gashwrack asked, trying not to growl. Back home—in his home from before—such decisions were not made for a werewolf without that werewolf's foreknowledge. "Why?"

"Not 'join,'" Arastha said, stroking the entire length of Shrike's Thorn's muscular back with her middle finger. "You will become a new pack. The two of you and one other. You will see each other safely and earn the Father's praise in pursuit of Shrike's Thorn's vision. You will be as one in this. And you, steadfast Gashwrack, have been alone among us for too long. Others in the Hive have begun to cast knucklebones over who will take you as their packmate. I would not have one so precious treated as wagers' stakes."

Gashwrack's face burned with muzzled rage, but he said nothing.

"We should begin," Shrike's Thorn said, rising to his knees and climbing down from Arastha's bed. When he did, Gashwrack saw a glyph scar depicting the coiled shepherd's crook of the Defiler Wyrm on his stomach. The head of the glyph encircled the man's navel, and the stem disappeared into his soaked and matted pubic hair. "I should collect the other before it gets late."

Making no move to put on any clothes, the black-haired man walked toward Gashwrack with a faint, absent smile. Gashwrack fought the urge to grab the man's shiny hair and smash him face-first into the floor. Instead, he only watched the man pass. A final glyph scar dominated the other's back. It was the whirling, chaotic glyph of the Black Spiral Dancer tribe. Gashwrack knew it well; a similar mark had been tattooed into the flesh between his right forefinger and thumb when he had come home to this Hive.

Before Shrike's Thorn left the room, Gashwrack asked, "Who is the other?"

"One like me and like you, and unlike either of us," Shrike's Thorn said. "Like me, he lost his other packmates in our war. Like you, he is an Ahroun. Unlike either of us, he was born a member of this tribe, rather than a convert."

"What else do you know about him?" Gashwrack asked.

"He is biddable and loyal," Shrike's Thorn said. "I only had to ask, and he agreed to stand watch outside the chamber door while Arastha and I waited for you. I told him to announce you once you arrived."

"Although you did take so awfully long getting here," Arastha said with a wicked smile. Her eyes twinkled in the torchlight.

"Surely you saw him," Shrike's Thorn said.

"I did," Gashwrack said, showing Shrike's Thorn his teeth. "You'll have to go find him if you want him here."

Shrike's Thorn glanced at Arastha, who only smiled back at him. "You should have little trouble following his trail," she said. "Go along and collect him, eager Shrike's Thorn. Gashwrack will wait with me for your return."

Shrike's Thorn looked at Gashwrack, smiled, then looked back at Arastha. "Of course," he said. "I'll take my time."

"Nonsense," Arastha said. "Hurry back here with your new packmate while Gashwrack is still ready." She turned her gaze on Gashwrack and said to him, "I'll help you get ready for the Rite of the Totem. You'll need all of the energy and inspiration I can give you once Shrike's Thorn and Splinterbone return. Once the rite begins, the three of you will have to decide who will be your alpha." Sitting on the edge of the bed, she stretched luxuriantly, exposing her neck and leaning back so that the tips of her three braids brushed the pillow behind her. Gashwrack's nostrils flared and his eyes homed in on her. "I can help you make ready if you're able, Gashwrack."

"Yes," he said. He knew about the type of pack rites that Arastha encouraged, but the thought didn't bother him. What mattered to him was what was in front of him. What she was offering him at that moment was more important than making himself alpha over Shrike's Thorn once the rite began

Chapter 5

Rain-Hunter left the lodge to rejoin her pack shortly after Karin Jarlsdottir excused herself, but Mephi remained behind a while longer. As the logs in the fireplace burned down, he looked over the topographical maps, crude star-charts and hand-written notes that had been left on the table, trying to instill in himself at least a passing familiarity with where he would be going tomorrow night.

But as his eyes drifted over the papers in front of him, his thoughts kept drifting back to Melinda Light-Finder. What was she doing here? When had she joined a pack, and when had it come across the Atlantic? How long had she been here? If she could still bring herself to speak to him the way she had when they'd been friends, he would have to ask her all these things and more. If not, which seemed more likely, he'd have to try to ferret it out of her pack.

As that thought occurred to Mephi, he paused with a troubled frown. Rain-Hunter had said that he was known to them because of what Melinda had told them about him. What exactly did that mean? If the emotional and spiritual ties that bound Melinda to her pack were as strong as the Rite of the Totem supposedly made such bonds, she'd probably told them everything about the time she'd spent with him since her First Change. If she had told them, Mephi would have a hard enough time even gaining their trust, much less pumping them for information.

He shivered in sudden discomfort. He was already at a disadvantage simply because he wasn't a member of the pack— or any pack, for that matter. He was well aware that the bonds of a werewolf pack were supposed to make the packmates closer to one another than family members, although his own familial experience hadn't set a very high standard. If Melinda had told her packmates the whole truth about him, he'd be lucky if Rain-Hunter's brusque treatment was the warmest reception he got from anyone in the Roving Wind.

"Hell," he said over his shoulder to his cobra-headed staff without actually looking at it, "I'll be lucky if they don't just kick my ass, no questions asked."

"Are you still carrying that around?" a familiar voice said from the doorway behind where Mephi sat. Startled, he turned around and stood up at the same time. "I thought you'd have ditched this by now."

Mephi drank in the sight of a woman he hardly recognized, but who had once been like a sister to him. He remembered her being two fingers shorter than him, but the heels of sturdy walking boots made up the difference. The long mop of tight curls that he'd once run his fingers through was now a halo of short, wavy hair that made her narrow face seem not so long as he'd once thought it was. A pair of tiny crescent-moon earrings decorated her earlobes, and the double claw-slash glyph of her tribe, the Shadow Lords, stood out on the back of each of her hands. The body fat that had once made her seem weak and in desperate need of protection had melted away, leaving only sleek feminine curves etched in the tight tones of hard muscle. She held his walking staff in front of her in both hands, pretending to examine the cobra head at the top. Her red-gold eyes peered at it, avoiding eye contact with Mephi.

"Hi," Mephi said.

"Hello, Strider," Melinda Light-Finder said with a faint trace of long-faded affection. Her voice was weary when she spoke, as if the modicum of affection was a heavy burden she'd carried until now, when she could finally let it go. It vanished as she met his eyes.

"You look great," Mephi offered, trying not to squirm.

"Walking," Melinda replied, looking back at his staff. "Second best exercise there is."

"So I've heard," Mephi said with a sad smile. "How are you, Lin?"

Melinda lowered her head and turned a gaze up at him that could have burned pinholes through glass. As she laid his staff back against the wall, she said, "Don't call me that."

"Sorry, Melinda. Or Light-Finder, if you like."

Melinda walked to the side of the table opposite Mephi and crossed her arms. She frowned down at the scattered maps and notes then said, "What are you doing here, Mephi? Of all the places in all the world…"

"The trial," Mephi began to babble. "Arkady, the Silver Fang. I heard he was still alive and that he was going to be on trial here."

"So?" Melinda asked. Her eyes remained trained on the tabletop.

"He's part of The Saga of the Silver Crown, remember? He tried to steal the birthright of the Silver Fangs' king, but he failed. Then, instead of being executed, he got sent back where he came from. Now he was supposed to be on trial here for conspiring with the Wyrm. Except he didn't show—"

"I know all that," Melinda snapped. "I've heard Arkady's story a dozen times. I asked why you're here."

"You know me," Mephi stammered. "I just wanted to finish the story. As The Saga of the Silver Crown stands, the villain just vanishes. But something's got to happen in a good story so the villain gets what's coming to him. I was hoping this trial would be it. The saga's just not satisfying the way it is with Arkady just…disappearing.…"

"You're right about that," Melinda said. "That's no way to end a good story. A guy just walking away, never to be heard from again. I see your point."

"Melinda, I—"

"Save it. Is that really the only reason you're here, Mephi?"

Mephi thought for a long moment, weighing the cost of confirming the truth. He could say that he'd come looking for her. He could tell her that he knew she'd come to this region and that he knew that she was going to be at this caern, surrounded by so many important werewolves. He could tell her that she was the only thread that could pull him so far away from his familiar stomping grounds. Some part of her might still believe such a thing. A part of him definitely wanted it to be true. In the end, though, he settled on the truth. She'd know if he were lying.

"Yeah," he said. "That's the only reason."

A roiling thundercloud passed behind Melinda's grim eyes, and silence hung thick between them. She shifted her weight from one foot to the other, then crouched down beside the low table. Glowering down at the papers there, she put her knuckles on the tabletop and didn't look up.

"I didn't know you were going to be here," she said finally.

"Me either, until the last minute," Mephi said. He looked down at the table as well, for lack of eye contact.

"I meant in here," Melinda said, rapping her knuckles once on the tabletop. "In this room. I didn't come to talk to you, if that's what you think."

"I didn't," Mephi said. "That Talon…Rain-Hunter said you didn't want to see me tonight."

"That's still right," Melinda said, making a show of rearranging the papers that were directly in front of her. "I came in here to make preparations for tomorrow night. If I'd known you were here…"

"Yeah," Mephi sighed. "I should probably leave you alone." He winced as soon as the words were out of his mouth.

"Go ahead," Melinda said, staring even harder at the tabletop than before. "You know what's best."

Mephi opened his mouth to reply, but no words came out. Instead, he clenched his teeth around a sigh of frustrated shame and turned to leave. He took up his walking staff from beside the door, dragging its ball-and-claw foot along the floor planks, and opened the door. Before stepping out into the cold, he turned back and looked at Melinda again.

"Light-Finder," he said over the sound of the skirling wind. "I won't pretend I still know how you think, but I do know how you must feel about me." Melinda's head turned so that she was almost looking at him. A look very much like hate curled her lips and creased her forehead. "What I don't know is what made you do it. What made you want me along on this quest? This 'mission,' as the Margrave calls it."

"I'm a professional," Melinda said. "When I think I might need some kind of help, I ask, even if it's easier to avoid the problem altogether. That's what you do when something's important to you."

Mephi's shoulders sagged, and he hung his head.

"Now go get some rest," Melinda said. "And get ready to leave tomorrow."

"I'll be ready," Mephi said.

"Good. Now you're letting the cold in."

Mephi nodded and backed out without another word. He pulled the door closed. When he couldn't see Melinda any more, he assumed his Glabro form once again and made his way back to the graveyard at the Hill of Lamentations. The dead could keep him company, he thought, until he once again had to face the ghosts of his past.

Chapter 6

With one final heave, Mephi tore himself free of the ossified Gauntlet and landed on his hands and knees on the forest floor. The gossamer webs that still clung to his clothes, his skin, and his hair burned off instantly in the crisp night air, sending blue-white threads toward heaven like altar flames. The wisps chilled him, and he shook himself to make sure that he was rid of the lot of them. He looked around the nighted glade to make sure that he had actually made it all the way back to the physical world, rather than snapping back into the Penumbra. He stood when he was finally convinced. "Now that utterly sucked," he said to everyone and no one. "One more trip like that, and I might just start sleeping in hotels from now on."

He turned to the corpse of the rabbit that was about to be his dinner and added, "I'm swearing off hammocks from now on, in any event. I blame you for the rocky discomfort that promises. I just want you to know."

Mephi smirked and started skinning the rabbit with his pocketknife. When that bit of work was done, he scrounged up a few sturdy sticks and set them up in a makeshift spit over his fresh fire pit. All the while he worked, he kept one ear cocked for spirits. He'd sent the rabbit's spirit off well enough with his quick thanks for its sacrifice, but that spirit wasn't the one he was worried about. He'd gotten stuck crossing back to the physical world from the spirit plane, and that sort of thing always attracted other spirits. As he got his fire burning and started to turn his rabbit over the blaze, his tension mounted. Whenever he got stuck in the Gauntlet, he had to deal with a spirit of some kind. It was never so much a question of if as a question of—

"When?" he asked aloud. "Say, Rabbit? Not many folks out here I noticed, but surely you saw somebody before I sent you on. Don't be shy; you can tell me."

"Dear God," a thin, hollow voice said behind him. "Dear God..."

Mephi snapped to his feet and spun around to face that direction. A man stood leaning over behind him, reaching toward the ground. The man was entirely bald, but a film of stubble mingled with several dozen pock marks on his cheek to give his face a decidedly unhealthy look. He wore rumpled hiking clothes and cracked leather boots, and his hands were clenched into fists about six inches from one another in the attitude of stretching out a cord or a bandage between them. The man's eyes crawled across the ground and took Mephi in from toes to eyeballs. Rather than stopping there, however, his gaze kept climbing until he was looking at a point almost three feet above Mephi's head. Mephi resisted the urge to look over his shoulder. When the man stopped moving, Mephi could see through four deep gouges that ran across his throat. If the man looked up any higher, his head would tip right down onto his back. Mephi recognized the shape of the wound without even having to think about it.

"Easy," Mephi said, raising his hands with his palms forward. "It's all—"

"Jesus God," the man said, not looking at Mephi. His hands popped open, and he thrust his arms out ahead of him. "I'm sorry, I'm sorry, I'm sorry!"

"Calm down now," Mephi said, taking a step closer. "I'm not the one who did this to you. Nobody's going to—"

Without even seeming to see Mephi, the man closed his eyes tight and turned his head. "Dear God, I'm sorry..." As the words left his lips, his head jerked backward, drawing the four wounds in his throat into straight lines. He bolted upright as some unseen force lifted him more than a foot off the ground. He hung there twitching like a bass hauled out of the water by a fisherman's line, until the invisible force that suspended him dashed him to the ground. He landed in a tangle of limp appendages and began to discorporate. Before he was gone, he managed to gasp, "I'm sorry..." one last time.

"And I'm sorry for you," Mephi mumbled. "Looks like you pissed off the wrong—"

An approaching sound cut the thought short, and Mephi turned back around to see his death barreling at him through the underbrush like a freight train. He registered black fur and red eyes zooming toward him behind a storm front of dripping claws, before he shoulder-rolled out of the way. A bloody howl split the relative peacefulness of the glade as a black whirlwind of snapping fangs, tearing claws and flying cloth tatters sailed just over him and slid headfirst across the leafy and root-knobbed ground.

Mephi sprang to his feet and simultaneously boiled up into his Crinos form. Letting a wave of battle lust and his self-preservation imperative carry him forward, he leapt onto the thing that had just missed eviscerating him. He landed knees-first on its back and leaned down to pin its elbows with his hands. The position gave him superior leverage, and his wealth of experience gave him the tactical advantage. The beast on the ground, the werewolf, was out of its mind with pain or rage or terror. It no more knew Mephi was there than the ghost of the man it had obviously killed did.

There was no fighting a werewolf in such a state, Mephi knew, but if you could get the drop on it and keep the advantage, you could keep the thing from getting itself into any more trouble than it already had. At least that was what Mephi guessed. He'd never fought a fellow werewolf in single combat before, much less one in the grip of a frenzy.

Fortunately, Mephi's half-baked theory proved correct in the short run. As he held the frenzied werewolf pinned beneath him, its struggles ceased and it began to shrink at last. In short order, it melted down from a thrashing, howling werewolf into a crying girl of about fifteen years of age. Letting his own excitement cool, Mephi shrank down beside the girl and held onto her in his Homid form. What remained of her clothes hung around her waist and shoulders, and blood smeared both of her arms to the elbows. None of it seemed to be hers.

"Easy," he said, letting the girl roll over onto her back, but not letting her go. Her eyes rolled, and she kept trying to pull herself away to go haring off to who knew where. "It's all right."

In answer, the girl lashed out and tried to bite him on the cheek. Mephi jumped back, and the girl scrambled away on her heels and elbows. As Mephi gathered his wits, the girl crouched up onto her toes and balanced on the tips of her fingers. A broken nylon cord dangled from her left ankle. The red fog was clearing from her eyes, but the terror was still the only light shining inside. Mephi stood up and held his hands out with his fingers splayed. The girl sucked ragged breaths in through her teeth and stared wide-eyed.

"Calm down now," Mephi said in a deep and even voice. He bent his knee to take a step, and the girl twitched backward as if she'd touched a live electrical wire. "I'm not the one who did this to you."

"Dear God," a small voice said behind him.

Without thinking, Mephi whipped around to see the same bald apparition half-crouching and looking up in dawning fear all over again. Mephi turned back around just in time to see the girl darting away. As the ghost went through his last motions once more, Mephi took off. The chase was short and no contest. The panicked girl made enough noise for three people as she tore through the darkness and tripped over every branch, rock and hidden depression on the forest floor. More used to traveling at night over broken terrain, Mephi caught the girl before she could cold-cock herself on a low limb or pitch ass-over-teakettle down an embankment. He wrapped his wiry arms around her and lifted her feet off the ground. She thrashed and kicked, but he opted to fall over rather than let her get away again. He held her until she wore herself out, and then a little longer until exhaustion finally settled over her. When she grew still, he lifted her and wrapped her up in his brand-new duster jacket. She curled against his chest like a baby as he lifted her, and he whispered to her as he carried her back toward his campsite.

"Nobody's going to hurt you now. Not any more. You don't have to be afraid."

When he returned to his trampled spit and his dirt-covered rabbit dinner, he laid the girl down in the light of the crescent moon and sat next to her. He noticed that she'd stepped on his thick oak walking staff and snapped it when she'd coming tearing through in her Crinos form.

"Nice going, kid," he whispered, pushing a long, matted lock of hair away from her forehead. "I just found that. Looks like we'll have to settle that up later. Right now, though, you look beat. And lost. Really lost."

The girl stirred in fitful sleep, and edged closer to Mephi. Mephi drew his coat more tightly around her and ran his fingers through her hair to push it back behind her ear. She craned her neck up and opened bleary, unseeing eyes.

"Don't worry, cub," he murmured, closing her eyes with a brush of his fingertips. "I'll be here when you wake. I'll get you through this. For now, just rest. Close your eyes and dream of home."

Mephi awoke disoriented on the cold, rocky ground in front of a graveyard. Lifting his head from his forepaws, he looked to the right, expecting to see Melinda lying there snuggled against him for warmth. Instead, only his cobra-headed walking staff looked back at him, and long shadows lounged all around him. Disappointment rolled in hand-in-hand with his sense of the present, and he huffed a sigh through his nose. He stood up, stretched deeply as if he were praying to the Graves of the Hallowed Heroes, then flopped back onto his haunches.

As hunger gurgled in his belly, Mephi licked his chops once then stretched out into his Homid form. The lack of fur and the extra surface area of his human shape did little to combat the cold, so he bulked up into his Glabro form in short order. That was a little better, if not enough to make him completely comfortable. It was still pretty early in the morning, judging by the direction and length of his shadow; maybe the day would get warmer once the sun was all the way up. Mephi certainly hoped so.

"I thought you Striders didn't feel the weather," a rich voice said just as Mephi made out the sound of footsteps coming up behind him. "I thought it came with the territory."

Mephi turned to see the familiar figure of the sept's Warder, Brand Garmson, walking toward him. The huge Get of Fenris stopped next to him and stared over Mephi into the graveyard.

"What territory?" Mephi replied.

The Get frowned a moment then said, "Right...I forgot you're all homeless."

Mephi bit back a growl, reminding himself that he was only a guest here. That and the fact that this sept's Warder would probably polish every stone in the bawn with him, then drop kick him into the next nearest protectorate. It couldn't hurt to mind his manners a little.

"You can adapt to this cold, Strider," the Warder pressed, still not looking at Mephi. "So, why don't you?"

"That's a Gift from merciful Gaia," Mephi said, trying to keep his teeth from clacking. "I don't like to do it unless I'm on the job. Seems wasteful otherwise. You know how it is. You don't use a rock to swat a fly. Plus, it isn't that cold."

Garmson snorted in amusement, then put his meaty fists on his hips. He favored Mephi with a quick glance then looked back out into the graveyard. Their breath misted, mingled and floated away on the breeze. As the white plumes disappeared, Mephi wondered if they were slipping across the Gauntlet into the Dark Umbra to tantalize the dead.

"The younger Guardians say you've been here all night," Garmson said after a brief silence. "Before and after the Greifynya sent for you."

"That's right," Mephi said.

"So what are you still doing here?"

"Research," Mephi said. "And getting some sleep. It's not so crowded here. Not so full of strangers."

"Everywhere you go is full of strangers," Garmson said without pity or humor. It was just a fact to him.

"Yeah," Mephi said. It was a fact to him, too.

"So are you finished then?" the Warder asked. "With your 'research' and your nap?"

"Uh-huh," Mephi said, cracking his jaws around a long

yawn. "It's time to Greet the Sun anyway."

"I thought so," Garmson said. "You've done the same every day since you got here. Today might be the last day you get that chance."

Mephi puzzled over that statement until he figured out what it was that Garmson had left unsaid. Although Greeting the Sun was a simple ritual paean to Helios—or Ra, as Mephi liked to think of it—it was a big deal to Mephi not to miss it. If nothing else, it kept his vocal cords in shape, but it was also a comfortable routine. Something to anchor him when all else was lost. Apparently Garmson had noticed, and he hadn't wanted Mephi to miss the sunrise on what might be his last day at the Sept of the Anvil-Klaiven.

"Yeah, maybe," he said, gathering his walking staff off the ground. Maybe he'd made more of an impression on the Warder here lately than he'd thought. "Thanks."

"You're welcome," Garmson said with a tiny nod. "Now go away. I want to be alone here."

Mephi's eyes widened in outrage, but he held his tongue when he realized what Garmson had been looking at all this time. The Warder had been staring at one of the newest markers in the graveyard—the one that bore the name and greatest deeds of his recently deceased son. Feeling like an intruder, Mephi turned and left the old man alone with his memories and his mourning.

Chapter 7

A sharp poke in the ribs woke Gashwrack some time just after sunrise. He grunted and swiped a lazy hand through the air in the direction from which the poke had come. Fortunately he missed, since it was Arastha who had poked him. He sat up on her bed, rubbing his face when he realized that she was there.

"Rise," Arastha said, walking to the other side of the bed to poke Splinterbone and Shrike's Thorn. "An eager generation of Galliards holds its breath, waiting for your work to begin."

Gashwrack groaned and extricated his legs from the tangle they occupied with Splinterbone's massive, hairy arm and the side of Shrike's Thorn's neck. Arastha herself was a Galliard, so he refrained from telling her where her eager generation could stuff its anticipation. His back hurt, his legs hurt, his throat hurt from an awful lot of howling. Every part of his body that he could reach with his hand, hurt. His hand hurt, too.

"Up, Shrike's Thorn," Arastha said, poking each of the others once. "Awake, Splinterbone. This new family has a journey to begin. All of you, come alive at once."

Splinterbone awoke next, and he wiped a mucoid film away from his large eyes with the back of his Crinos paw. Shrike's Thorn opened his eyes next, and he pulled himself up to his knees then stretched out on the bed like a dog. He didn't seem sore at all until he sat up straight and reached toward the ceiling. The grimace Gashwrack saw on Shrike's Thorn's face made all of last night worth the effort he had put into it.

"Lovely boys," Arastha said when everyone was awake. The tight leather outfit she wore creaked as she put her hands on her hips. "How darling you look. If I could but admire you all morning, I'd know the Father has truly blessed me."

Gashwrack picked up on the sarcasm, and he was the first to rise from Arastha's bed. The other two followed suit posthaste.

"We go," he said, crouching to pick up his neatly folded clothes from the floor beside the bed.

"Wait," Arastha said, urging him to rise with a long finger beneath his chin. "Answer this first. Who did you decide will become alpha?"

Gashwrack and Shrike's Thorn looked at Splinterbone, who looked at the floor and scratched his chiropteran nose.

"I will," the two of them said simultaneously while Splinterbone remained silent. They glared at each other, then looked back at Arastha.

"I see," Arastha said. "It was the same when you three drove me to delicious exhaustion last night. Did you commune with a totem spirit in my absence?"

"Hakaken," Splinterbone said. "They said it was Hakaken."

"'The Heart of Fear,'" Arastha said, scratching Splinterbone between his ears. Her eyes commanded Gashwrack and Shrike's Thorn to remain still. "From the Beast-of-War's brood, but no less noble for its heritage. Do you know Hakaken's history? He was a vainglorious Shadow Lord who sought to destroy the very heart of the Shattered Labyrinth by dancing the Black Spiral. He thought he could withstand the truth of what we are and the power of what we know. He even danced as deeply as the Eighth Circle of the Spiral, known as the Dance of Paradox. When the Bane of Enigmas asked him, 'What are you afraid of?' Hakaken's only answer was simply, 'The truth.' Our Father was so pleased that He made Hakaken into the Heart of Fear when the glorious beast passed the test at the Ninth Circle of the Spiral."

Shrike's Thorn nodded along with Arastha, and Splinterbone listened in wide-eyed wonder while Gashwrack merely waited. He didn't care as much about who Hakaken had been as he cared about what Hakaken could do for him and what he was expected to do for Hakaken in return.

"Which of you brave souls spoke to terrible Hakaken?" Arastha went on.

"I did," Gashwrack and Shrike's Thorn said. Splinterbone kept silent.

"Both?" Arastha murmured. "Not even he named one of you superior to the other?"

"No, Lady," Gashwrack said.

"And neither will submit to the station of the other?"

"All night long, they did not submit to one another," Splinterbone offered.

"Then if you will not heed each other," Arastha said with the first tinge of real irritation in her sweet voice, "or me, then you will heed the Dark Litany. Serve the Wyrm in all its forms. That includes the visions given to Shrike's Thorn. The three of you are tasked with making those visions a reality at any cost.

"Next, Respect all those who serve the Wyrm. You will work together, or the Eater-of-Souls will take all of you. Know also, The leader shall not be challenged in time of war. We are at war. From now until the Weaver's web falls. Finally, Beware the territory of another. In working together, you will not second-guess each other's strengths. Gashwrack, you will see that Shrike's Thorn lives to complete his visions. Shrike's Thorn, you will defer to Gashwrack in that. Gashwrack, when Shrike's Thorn arrives at your former home, you will do as he says. The Father has spoken to him, and you are not one to gainsay our Father. Splinterbone, you will do as you are told. Need I go on?"

The three Black Spiral Dancers shook their heads.

"Am I understood?" Arastha pressed. Her words simmered with anger, and the skin-tight leather she wore stretched against bulging muscles.

The three nodded.

"Your alpha will answer!" Arastha barked.

"We understand, Lady," Gashwrack said as soon as the word "alpha" was out of her mouth. Shrike's Thorn didn't challenge him or even make a move to speak. The Theurge had apparently started to realize, as Gashwrack had, that the Lady would not tolerate their snapping now that work had to be done.

"Then who are you?" Arastha said, turning on him and getting right in his face. Two lights burned in her eyes. One hinted at a reward far more satisfying than any teasing play she had engaged in with him last night if he gave her the right answer. The other made Gashwrack believe that Arastha would tear his throat out with her dull, Homid teeth if he spoke the wrong answer.

"I am Gashwrack," he barked back without fear or hesitation.

"Who are you?" Arastha demanded again, throwing her arms out in an explosive gesture that took them all in. One light in her eyes grew dim as the other flared. Splinterbone's hands began to shake, and his toe claws began to click against the hard stone floor. Shrike's Thorn tried hard not to squirm.

"We are a pack!" Gashwrack answered. "We are Our Father's Vision!" Shrike's Thorn smiled at that extemporaneous naming, and Splinterbone nodded so fast that a line of spit came out of his mouth and stuck in the fur on his chest. The bonds between the three of them resonated in harmony.

"Who are you?" Arastha screamed, putting her face less than an inch from Gashwrack's nose. Her chest heaved, and her breasts strained to be free of their leather prison. Red flushed her cheeks, and cords stood out on her neck. Thus far, she had been getting the answers she wanted. Only one kind of light glowed in her eyes. "Who?"

"Our Father's Vision!" Splinterbone howled, jumping to his feet and throwing up his hands. Shrike's Thorn began to growl as he caught a taste of Splinterbone's exuberance. Gashwrack's nostrils flared, and he breathed Arastha's excitement in.

Arastha looked at the overexcited Crinos beast, then cut her eyes to Shrike's Thorn. "Who?" she screamed at the Theurge.

"Hakaken's bastards!" Shrike's Thorn hollered, taking on the form of a wolf as he did so. The sound became a great howl that resonated in the chamber. Heat blossomed within Gashwrack's skin like an oil slick across crystal-clear water.

Arastha turned to Gashwrack with Balefire lust blazing in her eyes. The images of the Defiler Wyrm, G'louogh and Mahsstrac writhed in the bone mosaic above the bed. "WHO ARE YOU?" she screamed, grabbing Gashwrack's hair and lifting him from his seat.

"We are the Heart of Fear!" Gashwrack said, springing forward and grabbing Arastha to take her where she stood. "We are bastards of the Father! We are Our Father's Vision!"

Arastha danced back out of his grasp, but her eyes promised plentiful rewards for all three of them when they returned. As the fury and glory of the moment reached a long crescendo, she shifted into the full beauty of her Crinos form and let out a howl of orgasmic delight. "Be ready, poor fools," the howl said. "Be ready, for Our Father's Vision is at hand. Be ready and tremble, for they come!"

Gashwrack and Shrike's Thorn took on their Crinos forms alongside Splinterbone and joined the howl. "Be ready and tremble!" they howled to anyone who would stand in their way. "We come!"

Chapter 8

Mephi spent the rest of the day and the first part of the evening drifting from one pack shrine to the other at the Sept of the Anvil-Klaiven and then back to the Graves of the Hallowed Heroes. He spoke to no one, and he sought out no one's company in the long hours before his departure.

As the day grew dim, Mephi stopped dragging his feet and made his way to the barren peak of the Hill of Lamentations. It was there that the sept's Gatekeeper would open the moon bridge to the Sept of the Night Sky, and it was there that Mephi would meet the rest of Melinda Light-Finder's pack. When he did, he hoped, the werewolves' reaction to him would give him an idea of what Melinda had told them about him. Although he wasn't looking forward to it, it would be good to get it over with.

"Which you'll never do," he murmured, "if you stand here 'til moonrise. Pick it up, Strider."

At that half-hearted encouragement, he picked his staff up and jogged to where he was sure everyone was waiting already. His easy stride swallowed down the distance, and the rootless wandering he'd been doing since he arrived almost a week ago told him the way without question or deviation. He arrived in no time and found a group of five werewolves waiting for him.

He recognized only three of the werewolves, but all of them looked at him as he came up. Those he recognized were Brand Garmson, Rain-Hunter and the sept's Gatekeeper. Garmson and the Gatekeeper stood together talking and pointing in the direction from which the moon was about to rise. Rain-Hunter and the other two werewolves stood together opposite them. Various traveling bags and satchels lay on the ground between the Get and the "strays" who made up part of the Roving Wind.

Of the two werewolves that Mephi did not recognize, one looked like a local and the other looked like a college boy who had no idea where he was or how he'd gotten there. College Boy's hair was a deep auburn, and it was cut short. He wore a clean skiing outfit, black with a diagonal white stripe. His scarf and gloves matched, and his boots had hardly any scuffs on the toes. He had no weapons on him that Mephi could see, and the bright, eager look in his eyes suggested that he'd much rather talk than fight in the first place. Mephi wondered how long the kid had been with the pack if he could still display that kind of attitude.

In contrast, the other stranger's bulky muscles and dour expression more than made up for College Boy's seeming shortcomings. Although he was only an inch taller than College Boy, the other fellow was half again as broad in the shoulders. A heavy hammer much like Karin Jarlsdottir's weapon rested head-down beside the man, and his forearms—which were almost as thick as College Boy's thighs—seemed well up to the task of wielding it. His hair and beard were light brown, streaked with lighter gray. He stood with crossed arms, watching only his own thoughts. Mephi approached with caution.

"The Margrave has not come to see you off," Brand Garmson said without preamble once Mephi had joined the others, "but he wishes you success. He also bids you welcome to the Sept of the Night Sky in his absence. He asks that you not overstay your welcome once you arrive, and that you hurry back there when you have done your job."

College Boy snorted at that, but no one else offered a reply.

"You'll be moving through his territory, no moon," Garmson said. "Mind it."

College Boy nodded, but he didn't look particularly chastised to Mephi.

"It is almost time," the caern's Gatekeeper said, stepping up beside Garmson in the silence that followed. "Where is Light-Finder?"

Mephi, Garmson and the Gatekeeper looked around, but the other three werewolves did not seem put off by Melinda's lingering absence.

She comes, Rain-Hunter said. Soon.

"I'll make ready, then," the Gatekeeper said, turning and walking a short distance away. "But she taunts her unearned glory and honor by delaying this."

"She's on her way," the big fellow next to College Boy said. Neither the Gatekeeper nor Garmson argued the point with him.

"She does like fashionable lateness," Mephi said, mostly to himself. The three werewolves of the Roving Wind looked at him with unreadable expressions. None of them replied, but College Boy did offer a guarded smile.

"When she arrives," Garmson said, "tell her what I said. And you, Strider, you tell her what the Greifynya told you."

Mephi tilted his head with a questioning glance.

"Plenty of warning if you must return here with unwelcome guests," Garmson said. "If you bring them, let us be ready to welcome them."

"Right," Mephi said. "I'll tell her."

"Good," Garmson said. "Now make ready. These are good days to die."

"Good days," the Gatekeeper chimed in.

With that, Garmson walked away toward another part of the caern, leaving everyone waiting for the moon and Melinda. Mephi watched Garmson go, then turned to the three members of the Roving Wind. They were all still looking at him.

"I guess I should introduce myself," he said, trying to gauge their sentiments about him from their body language. "Seems everyone understands English. Would any of you prefer something local?"

"We've done a lot of traveling," College Boy said. His accent was pure Midwestern American. "English'll do, even though it's been a while for some of us."

"That works then," Mephi said. It hadn't occurred to him as such, but that simple touchstone began to set him at ease here among these strangers.

"You must be Faster-Than-Death," College Boy replied. "Melinda's told us about you. She described the necklace and the stick and everything. Right up to the pony tail and the goatee."

Mephi's fingertips brushed the front of his necklace and the golden plate there that had been engraved with the converging-wave symbol of his tribe.

"I'm Conrad DeSalle," the kid went on, "but my new name's Stone-Stepper. I'm still getting used to it, though, so you can call me Conrad or Stepper or whatever's easiest to remember."

"You have a preference?"

"Whichever," the young man said with a shrug. "They're all my name." Conrad paused and pointed with his thumb to the big fellow on his right. "This guy's Ivar Hated-by-the-Wyrm, and this short lady on my left is Rain-Hunter. They're Get of Fenris and Red Talon. Respectively."

"I gathered," Mephi said, nodding to the stony-faced Get then down to Rain-Hunter. "Rain-Hunter and I met last night. And something about you seems familiar," Mephi said turning back to the Get, "although I can't tell exactly what. You're a local? Maybe we've met elsewhere before…."

"I'm a prodigal," Ivar said. "And you don't know me. I don't spend time in the company of Striders anymore."

"Not that he's seen any as long as I've been around him," Conrad put in. "At least not so I'd recognize them, anyway. But then I'm still getting used to all of this."

"And what's your tribe, Conrad?" Mephi asked, changing the subject on purpose. "You forgot to mention it."

"I'm a Child of Gaia," Conrad said. As soon as the words were out of his mouth, he put his hands up and said, "But I'm not a hippie or anything like that. I know it sounds like it, but…" He shook his head.

"Don't worry about it," Mephi said. "I know some Children of Gaia who'd pull your tail off and make you smoke it for calling them hippies."

"Harsh," Conrad said with a wide grin. Mephi agreed.

"What's everyone standing around for when the moon's coming?" Melinda Light-Finder said as she approached from around a bend of stone several yards away. "I told you all to be ready by now."

Melinda walked up just as the first sliver of the waning gibbous moon broke the horizon and cast pale light on the stony flat. She was dressed as she had been the night before, and she'd packed as Mephi had taught her so many years ago. She had no more than one bag, and it was slung over her shoulder to her opposite hip so it wouldn't get in her way if she walked or ran with it on. Mephi smiled at her, remembering old times.

When Melinda had joined them, her packmates came alive. The two men hoisted their satchels onto their shoulders and stood ready to move at a second's command. Conrad smiled and looked to the Gatekeeper, and even Ivar's eyes widened a fraction in anticipation. Rain-Hunter stood up with her ears forward and pawed the ground. Each member of the pack stood facing the three others, and they checked each other to make sure that they were indeed ready to go. Melinda's expression softened a little as she scanned her packmates for loose satchel straps, worn-out shoes, dark eye-circles of fatigue and whatever else she ritually checked for when the Roving Wind was about to move out. Standing outside the tight circle, Mephi smiled with pride at the way Melinda's presence turned the pack into an efficient, organized unit. He was still smiling when she turned her gaze on him.

"You, too," she said, sparing him none of the subtle good humor she had shown the others. "Get your things together and come on. I don't want you slowing us down."

Mephi's smile turned into a grimace, and he squeezed his fingers around his walking staff in self-conscious discomfort. "I'm ready to leave," he said.

"I should have guessed." Melinda said. She glanced once at his staff then turned her back on him. To her packmates, she said, "Let's go, everybody. It looks like the Gatekeeper's ready."

The Roving Wind did as Melinda said, and Mephi followed them over to where the Gatekeeper was, indeed, waiting. She stood before a shimmering disk of mist and silver light. The disk was the opening of the moon bridge, and Mephi could see farther along its shrouded path as the gibbous moon rose higher above them. The air around the portal shimmered as if the portal gave off its own heat haze in the frigid night. The spirit half of Mephi tugged toward the portal and the Umbra beyond in the same way that iron filings would orient themselves toward a magnet.

"They're waiting at the Sept of the Night Sky," the Gatekeeper said to Melinda. "Pay your respects there, then be on your way."

"We will," Melinda said.

"When you've stolen the pathstone out of the Wyrm's mouth, they'll be waiting for you," the Gatekeeper replied. "As will we to hear of how it was done. Good luck, Roving Wind. Gaia's grace. May Luna guide you and Fenris guard your back."

Following their alpha, the Roving Wind stepped through the portal and onto the moon bridge. Mephi followed a step behind them all, but the Gatekeeper stopped him with a hand on his elbow.

"I know your kind, Silent Strider, and I know the realms you may try to visit," the grizzled old werewolf said. "You must beware the Dark Umbra. A great storm has been loosed there, and its devouring winds blow faster than even you can run."

"I know well, Gatekeeper," Mephi said. "I've seen this storm at its weakest, and only Owl's grace delivered me to safety. We don't plan to go there, but I'll pass your caution on to the others. Thank you."

The Gatekeeper nodded and let him go. Before he could go on, though, the Keeper said, "Strider, if you must go into the Dark Umbra, remember this: These are still good days to die. The best to be had before we all journey to Battleground and the Plain of the Apocalypse to fight the last battle."

"They are," Mephi said with little conviction. "I'll remember. I'll see the others remember as well."

"They will, Galliard," the Gatekeeper said. "And you will sing to us of your exploits when you all return, no matter what road leads you back."

"I will," Mephi said. "I look forward to it."

When nothing more seemed forthcoming, Mephi turned away from the Gatekeeper and jogged through the portal onto the moon bridge to catch up with the Roving Wind.

Chapter 9

After a brief stopover at the Sept of the Night Sky, Mephi and the Roving Wind set out east across the Mätra Hills of Hungary in the direction of the Tisza River and the caern at Owl's Rest. They walked to the hills in the physical world, avoiding all signs of human construction and habitation as they went. Several hours after they first came among the hills, Melinda decided to make camp in a nicely secluded grove of tall trees that was well away from roads or hiking trails or any other means by which curious humans might stumble upon them during the night.

Once her packmates had made camp, Melinda arranged the watch rotation and informed them that they would be leaving after noon the following day. Mephi dug a shallow fire pit while Ivar and Rain-Hunter checked the immediate area one last time for interlopers or signs of an impending ambush. Conrad gathered firewood, and Melinda stepped sideways to lay down a protective spirit ward. When everyone returned and began to get settled for the night, Conrad broke out some provisions. As the Child of Gaia passed them around, Mephi made a fire.

"Listen up," Melinda said as everyone ate and warmed up. "I know you all remember what Tisza and the park was like when we found Owl's Rest. Thick with Weaver webs. Surrounded. I know you all remember what it was like the night the Elders awakened the caern's spirit. They still sing about the way we and the other packs stood vigilant while the spirits closed in."

"We kicked ass," Conrad said around a cheek full of hard bread. Ivar smiled wryly and snorted.

"We did," Melinda nodded. "But now is not then. The Wyrm has come to that place and fouled it. Packs of heroes—some of whom were more powerful than all of us put together—died fighting to save that place, and they all failed." She turned to the Get of Fenris, who crouched on the balls of his feet and gnawed on a rabbit bone. "Ivar, I think only you've seen places so terrible as the one we must go to. You and the Strider."

"I have," Ivar said.

"When we get there," Melinda continued without so much as glancing in Mephi's direction, "there's something I want you all to remember. We don't go there to do battle. We don't go there to die. When you see what Tisza's become, when you see the Hellhole for the first time, remember that we have a mission to accomplish. Don't let your rage overtake you. And believe me, it will try."

Mephi knew that Melinda spoke from experience. In the time they'd spent together, he'd taken her to see a Hellhole that had formed around an illegal toxic-waste dumpsite. He'd done it to show her what she and all other werewolves were up against not only in the physical world, but on the spiritual plane as well. Although the two of them had fought Banes and fomori together, the sight of that place had affected her more strongly than Mephi had anticipated. She'd flown into a berserk frenzy more severe than even the one she'd been in when the two of them had met.

"Hey, can I cut in here for a second, Melinda?" Conrad asked, raising his hand and grinning in embarrassment. "I have a question."

"What?"

"Well, this Hellhole's just in the Umbra, right?"

"Penumbra," Ivar corrected. He crouched with his hammer balanced head-down before him, and he stared into the fire.

"Okay," Conrad said. "But it's not all that bad here in the real world. Sorry, the physical world."

"Not exactly," Melinda said. "But I know what you mean. It will be worse there than here, yes."

"So why do we even have to go see it?" Conrad asked. "Why not just sneak up on the caern in the dead of night, get the pathstone, then cut and run across the good, solid ground?" He stomped his booted foot once for emphasis. "It seems a hell of a lot safer to me."

Mephi leaned forward at that as well.

The pathstone, Rain-Hunter answered.

"Yes," Melinda said, nodding to the Red Talon. "I've been talking to some of my local...cousins...since the caern fell. Their Stormcrows report that the last survivor—the Gatekeeper—took the pathstone into the Penumbra to hide it there. He tried to run with it from the caern, but he was already seriously wounded. The Stormcrows don't think he made it very far before his wounds took him."

"How far did he get?" Mephi asked. "Was he able to hide the stone?"

Melinda regarded Mephi with flat, cold eyes then looked back at Conrad. "The crows that survived to relay the news found only his trail before they had to flee the Wyrm spirits that are thick in the region now. They think he didn't make it as far as the river, but he definitely made it south into the Hellhole itself."

"What about the pathstone?" Mephi asked, trying to maintain his cool despite the snub.

"No word, Strider," Melinda said, still facing Conrad. "That's what we're here for. To find it."

The other members of Roving Wind stole glances at Mephi, but none of them said anything.

"Now," Melinda went on, focusing on her packmates once more. "The reason we're not sneaking in overland on this side of the Gauntlet is twofold. One, the Weaver's webs are thick and plentiful around where we're going, thanks to human habitation and development around the Tisza."

A menacing rumble came from Rain-Hunter, and Ivar scowled in sympathy.

"I know," Melinda said to them. "What that means, though, Conrad, is that we might have trouble getting back and forth across the Gauntlet in a hurry if we need to. If we get caught up, we fail our mission, and we're as good as dead.

"Second, just trust me. You don't want to step sideways straight into a Hellhole. We'd be surrounded and get picked off the second we crossed over. If we were lucky. It's not like parachuting in behind enemy lines, like in those war movies you're always going on about."

"Oh," Conrad said in a small voice. "Well then, what's the plan for getting in and out?"

Sneak in, Rain-Hunter answered.

"Carefully," Mephi added, trying to give the kid a reassuring smile.

"We're going to sneak in," Melinda confirmed, speaking over Mephi. "This is the plan Rain-Hunter and I have been going over with the other leaders back at Anvil-Klaiven. We're going to step sideways tomorrow before we're all the way out of the Mätra Hills. We're going to go through the Penumbra to where the Stormcrows found the Gatekeeper's trail." She nodded toward Mephi but didn't look at him. "The Strider's going to help us navigate the webs between the Hills and the hole itself, and he's going to help guide us around with our heads low. Like I've told you guys, he's done this before—and worse—so don't second-guess him. He knows what he's doing. A lot of what I learned about the Umbra I learned from him."

Mephi looked for some sign of affection or even appreciation on Melinda's face as she said that last bit, but he saw none. All he saw was the leader of warriors who knelt by the fire and gave her pack its marching orders.

"Once we find the trail," Melinda went on, "the operation's all search-and-recovery. Conrad, I want you to be the one doing the Rite of the Questing Stone for the Gatekeeper so we'll have some idea where to start. We've all got more experience than you, so we'll all need to be free and ready if something goes wrong while we're searching."

"Sure," Conrad said. "You don't want your heavy gunner lugging the radio, and you don't give the heavy gun to the RATELO. I understand."

"And when we have it?" Ivar rumbled. "The pathstone."

"If we haven't been detected, we'll try to step sideways right there, and we'll take our time about it so we don't get tangled up. If we attract pursuit, we'll go back the way we came and try to lose our pursuers in the webs farther away from the river."

"Those webs aren't going to be empty when we get there," Ivar said.

"And I didn't say this was going to be boring, did I?"

Ivar smiled grimly and set his war hammer down in front of him.

"If worst comes to worst," Melinda added, "we'll try to find a moon path out of the Hellhole and look for a safer way back to the physical plane."

We will return here, Rain-Hunter said, picking up Melinda's explanation. Next we will go to Night Sky.

"Ah, that all doesn't sound so hard," Conrad said with a cavalier disregard for the truth.

"Right," Melinda said, smiling at him through the hard expression that did not fade entirely. "Why don't you run ahead and take care of that for us then, wise guy?"

"Hey, packs are supposed to share, right?" Conrad joked back. "The glory, the honor, the danger. I'm all about sharing the danger with you guys. I'm not selfish, believe me. I'm here for you guys on that."

"You're here to get fat while we protect you, little one," Ivar said, poking Conrad in the side with a meaty finger. "Our little baby fostern."

"Knock it off, you gorilla," Conrad said, swiping at Ivar's hand.

You break every twig and crunch every leaf in the forest, Rain-Hunter said, swishing her tail with relaxed good humor. Stone-Stepper.

"Oh, now that hurts," Conrad said. "You know that's not how I meant that name."

"How did you mean it?" Mephi asked, trying not to intrude but curious nonetheless.

"Oh, it comes out of the way wolves talk," Conrad explained. "Not the Garou language, but just regular lupus talk. It's how the first real wolves I ever spent any time with came to think of me. I was 'the wolf who wanted to step on every stone in the whole world' to them. It's 'cause I like to travel around and see the world and I don't really call any one place home anymore. I think of this whole green planet as my home."

"That's a nice sentiment," Mephi said without conviction. "How long have you been doing what you're doing now?"

"Not long," Ivar said.

"Yeah," Conrad said. "Not long. Since a little after I got to Europe. That's when I had my first time. When I Changed. You know?"

"Yeah."

"Yeah," Conrad went on. "Well, I was over in Prague with some other spoiled American kids after college when it happened. I was running from the folks back home and the software company that wanted me to manage it once my dad kicked the bucket. After the Change, I stopped calling home and e-mailing, and I headed out for the hills in a real panic. Luckily for me, these guys—" he indicated his fellow pack members "—heard about the mess I made, and they came looking for me. I've been with them ever since, and that's been a couple of years now.

"It's funny. At first I just wanted to see the world. Now here I am supposed to save it. How's that for a kicker?"

"You get used to the feeling," Mephi said.

"Yeah," Conrad said. "So anyway, I was trying to describe the traveling bug to these wolves the first time the guys showed me I could talk to them, and the wolves came up with the stepping-on-every-stone-in-the-world bit. When that idea went to the Garou language and then over into English, it got turned into Stone-Stepper. I like it."

"And you're lucky we like you, motor-mouth," Melinda said, pushing Conrad off balance with her boot. "You should have been a Galliard if you're going to talk so much."

"He could do worse," Mephi grumbled.

"Now if you're through relaying the history of this pack according to Stone-Stepper," Melinda said to Conrad as he sat back up and crossed his ankles, "the Strider's got first watch." She turned in Mephi's direction and said, "Come on. I'll show you how far my spirit ward goes. We'll call that the camp perimeter."

"Sure," Mephi said.

The two of them stood, and Melinda addressed her pack once again. "Try to get some sleep everyone. Ivar, you're next, then Rain-Hunter, Conrad and me."

"Graveyard again," Conrad groaned.

"Just be ready when it's your turn," Melinda said. "I'll be right back. Let's go, Strider."

Mephi picked up his staff and walked off after Melinda as she headed away from the camp. He caught up and followed her, waiting until they were out of easy hearing range to speak.

"Light-Finder, hold up a sec," he said. "I want to ask you something."

Melinda stopped but didn't look at him. "What?"

"How long have you been here? In Europe, I mean."

"Seven years."

"That long?" Mephi said. "I had no idea. What about your pack? Did they come with you, or did you meet them all here like you did Conrad?"

"Here and there," Melinda said. "Ivar's from here, but I met him in the States. Conrad's the other way around. Rain-Hunter's from here, too, and I met her once Ivar and I got here. We all sort of fell in together one way or another."

"You guys must work well together."

"Yeah, we do. Thanks."

"I don't get it, though," Mephi pressed on. "What made you come here in the first place?"

Melinda turned around at last, and Mephi was taken aback by the look of seething fury on her face. She'd kept any clue that the sentiment was there out of her voice. He was also surprised to see a single tear track on her cheek. The light through the trees from the waning gibbous moon colored the single line bright silver.

"Ask me one you don't already know, Strider," she growled. "Better yet, keep your questions to yourself."

"Melinda," Mephi sighed, "what happened happened a long time ago."

"Not long enough," Melinda spat back. "Not if you ask me. Not if you wake up like I do having to remind myself that you're not there. Even when I'm glad you're not, it still hurts to wake up like that."

"You know I couldn't stay," Mephi said. "Staying with you like I was was wrong. Somebody has to have explained that to you by now."

"Sure they did," Melinda said. "But it doesn't matter. It didn't change anything except make you look like even more of a creep."

"Lin, I wanted to come back," Mephi said. "Every day, I wanted to come back. Some days, I didn't even care that it would have been wrong."

"So why didn't you?" Melinda asked. The tear trail had vanished, and the edge was disappearing from her anger. However, it was dulling back into resentment rather than forgiveness.

"Because it would have been wrong," Mephi said. "And because I just couldn't. Every time I thought about coming back, I could just imagine you with a pack or breeding a family. I imagined you finding your place in the sept I took you to, and I figured you wouldn't...I didn't think you'd want to go. Or worse, you would go if I asked, but you'd resent me for wanting you to."

Melinda remained silent for a few minutes, digesting all that. Finally, she crossed her arms and sighed.

"You've always been so stupid, Mephi," she said. "I waited for years to form my pack, and I'm still not part of any sept. What I resented was you leaving me with those people and that life right when I was just getting used to what I thought was going to be my new life with you."

"That wouldn't have worked out," Mephi groaned. "The Litany—"

"The Litany piss! I didn't want to mate with you, for Gaia's sake, I wanted to work with you. We were doing good together, and I wanted to keep that up. I liked the traveling and helping put ghosts to rest and scouting against the Wyrm and Weaver. I was happy. You were, too."

Mephi didn't say anything.

"But that was your problem, wasn't it? It took me a long time to figure that one out. You were just too used to being on your own. You let me get too close, so you panicked and ran away."

Mephi hung his head and remained silent. Melinda stayed silent for a few long minutes herself, waiting for some response—any response. The two of them stood facing each other, surrounded by the sounds and smells of the Mätra Hills in the chilly fall night.

"But whatever," Melinda said at last, throwing up her hands. "That was a long time ago, right? Water under a bridge you burned. Whatever."

"Light-Finder, I can explain," he said. "You just won't like what I say."

"Whatever," Melinda said again. "Don't bother. I'm going back, and I'll send Ivar when it's his watch." The anger disappeared from Melinda's face by degrees, and smooth professionalism took its place. Only the tightness in her voice betrayed any hint of her emotions. "Keep your eyes open, Strider. And try to get some good rest once you get back. We've got hard work ahead."

Without waiting for a reply, Melinda turned and headed back to camp. Mephi stood alone watching her go.

Chapter 10

When Ivar came to relieve him on watch several hours later, Mephi padded over in his Lupus form to meet the Get of Fenris. Ivar propped his hammer on the ground head-down and crossed his arms over the expanse of his chest. Mephi unfolded into Homid and stood up to give his report.

"All's quiet thus far," he said.

"Didn't fall asleep?" Ivar rumbled as quietly as it seemed he could. "Didn't run away?"

"Of course not."

Ivar grunted and made to walk past Mephi without another word. Mephi stood his ground, and Ivar's shoulder jolted his since the big man didn't step far enough aside. Mephi grabbed the man's elbow as he passed and tugged him around until they were eye to eye. A fire burned deep within Ivar's gaze, but Mephi didn't back down.

"What?" he growled.

"Go to bed, Silent Strider," Ivar growled back. "Go to sleep."

"What is it with you? Have you got a problem with me?"

"Not you," Ivar snarled. "Just your kind."

Mephi's blood started simmering, and he kept a tight leash on his Homid form. "If you've got a problem with my 'kind,' you've got a problem with me, Get. Cough up."

"I've known Striders," the Get rumbled, careless of how loud his voice was growing. "One was even my friend. She was a packmate. I trusted her. Everyone in my last pack did."

"And?"

"She betrayed us. She'd led us far out into the Umbra, right to the gates of Malfeas—"

"Malfeas? What were you doing there?"

"It doesn't matter," Ivar snapped. "The point is, we were there and we had to go in for our own reasons. But before we found what we were looking for, the Strider abandoned us. She got scared and couldn't take being surrounded by the Wyrm. She just ran away, leaving us stranded there with no idea how to get back. All of my packmates died trying to escape that place. Even Parts-the-Water herself."

"Parts-the-Water?"

"That was the traitor's name," Ivar said, glaring down at the ground. "I found her dead at the gates of the Gardens of Nightmare."

"Wait," Mephi said. "Parts-the-Water—I know that name. And yours. You were looking for the Wyrm's last shed skin, weren't you? You all figured the Wyrm hadn't shed his new skin, so that was why he couldn't get out of the Weaver's web and why he was so angry all the time. Set's forked tongue, I knew I recognized your name! You were one of the Screaming Trailblazers."

"How do you know that?" Ivar demanded, taking a step toward Mephi.

"You're a part of The Saga of the Silver Crown. You and the rest of the pack. You helped out Lord Jonas Albrecht's pack on a quest to get the Silver Crown. I've told your story to dozens of people. You didn't know you were part of it?"

"No."

"Well, you are. I always wondered what happened to you guys."

Ivar's eyes thinned to knife blades, and he said, "So now you do. And now you know why I have a problem with your kind. I only got out of Malfeas by losing myself in the Garden of Nightmares and watching my packmates die again and again while I stood powerless. I escaped that nightmare into Atrocity where finally I, too, had to die as my brothers in arms stood over me and laughed. That's what happened to the Screaming Trailblazers. That's why I can't even look at one of your kind without thinking of her."

"Sweet Gaia," Mephi said, looking away in shame. "Ivar, I'm sorry. I didn't know Parts-the-Water personally, but I can tell you this: Not all of us are like her. Most of us are better. All of us know better."

"Don't tell me that," Ivar spat. "Light-Finder and I talked about you. I know you better than you think. Rain-Hunter may think you did the right thing when you walked away from Melinda, since you shouldn't have spent so much time alone with her in the first place. I don't agree. Don't tell me you're better than Parts-the-Water, with only the story of how you abandoned a lonely cub to prove it."

Mephi felt the change coming, and red haze swelled at the edges of his field of vision. It took every ounce of effort to restrain himself from leaping for Ivar's throat. Only the fact that the hulking Get was right forestalled any such rash action. Mephi closed and opened his eyes, willing himself to calm down. As if he were made of wire-bound wood, he turned around to go back to camp. Ivar didn't stop him or challenge him.

"Whatever Lin's told you, I'm not like what you think," Mephi said over his shoulder as he left. "Maybe once, but not anymore. I've grown up since then."

The Get simply snorted in disgust, and Mephi walked on.

Chapter 11

"You don't like it, do you?" Melinda said, scuffing her boot in the dirt like a child. Mephi had never seen such an adorable display of disappointment in all of his life. "You hate it."

"I don't…'hate' it," Mephi said. "I've just never seen anything like it. I certainly wasn't expecting it."

"Well, I wanted to get you something after that talk we had last week," the girl said. "Remember? You told me you had your First Change on today's date. I figure that's kind of like a birthday for us, right?"

"I suppose. It's just…"

"What?" Melinda asked. "I didn't break some weird werewolf taboo, did I?"

"No, Lin," Mephi said, chuckling. "We're not Jehovah's Witnesses. We can give each other presents."

"Well, is it too tall? Too gaudy?"

Mephi held out the present that Melinda had given him. It was a seven-foot-tall walking staff with a hooded cobra's head hissing at the top and a golden owl's claw holding a golden sphere at the bottom. The staff was stout and sturdy, good to lean on after a long walk. Plus, it was wrapped so tight from head to foot that it could break a fomor's neck without snapping in half like his last one had.

"It isn't too tall or gaudy," he said. "Where'd you get this?"

"A craft shop between Bodine and here. I went last night while you were asleep. This was the best one in the shop. Most of the other ones had Indian heads on them or tigers or other stupid stuff. One had a wolf, but it didn't look like you. I liked this one. I thought you might like it, too, since you've got all this other Egyptian stuff." She shrugged and scuffed the ground again. "It looked kind of Egyptian. I don't know."

"Yeah," Mephi said. "It does. No worries there."

"So what's wrong with it? You're frowning."

"Well, it's great, don't get me wrong. I could walk a million miles with this thing. It's just the head. It makes me think of Set. Have I ever told you about Set?"

Melinda shook her head.

"All right, then, listen up. Today, people think Set was the Egyptian god of evil. He killed the god Osiris a couple of times and took over all of Egypt. What people don't know is that Set was real. He's an ancient evil spawned from a demon and the Serpent from the Garden of Eden. He was an unstoppable terror back when the world was smaller, and he did rule all of Egypt for a while. He was in power long enough to exile all of my people from there when we tried to stand up to him. Even today, we can't go back because of what Set did to us."

"I didn't know that," Melinda said in a small voice. With her head down, she held out her hand and said, "Here, let me have that back, then. I'll take it back to the shop right now. I'll trade it for the one with the wolf. It sort of looked like you, I guess."

"Well, no, hold on," Mephi said, pulling the staff back. "You don't have to do that."

"No," Melinda said, "I didn't know it was going to upset you. I'm sorry, Mephi. Let me take it back and get you another one."

"No, look, Lin, it's all right," Mephi said. All things considered, he was more upset seeing Melinda so embarrassed than he was at the staff. The staff wasn't even that bad. "I like it. Really. Like I said, I just wasn't expecting it. Plus, it was nice of you to remember what I said about my First Change. Doing something like this wouldn't have even occurred to me."

"You're just saying that because I'm embarrassed," Melinda said.

"Okay, partly," Mephi admitted. He laughed in equal parts exasperation and amusement at how silly this whole exchange had become. "But I do like the staff. It's sturdy and plenty tall enough. It's balanced. It'll take some getting used to, but it's neat. I like it."

"What about that stuff about Set?" Melinda asked, coming around out of her disappointment. She was even beginning to show her own smile.

"He and I'll work something out, I guess," Mephi said. He twisted the staff so that cobra head seemed to be looking at him. When he spoke next, he addressed the gleaming snake in a sibilant whisper. "What do you say? I'll sacrifice the little one to you, and you stay off my case after that. Deal? Deal." He looked back at Melinda and turned the staff so that it seemed to do the same.

"Dork," Melinda said, rolling her eyes.

"Sorry, kiddo," Mephi grinned. "Looks like you're outvoted, according to my latest staff poll."

Melinda groaned and punched him in the shoulder. Hard. "I'm just glad you like it, dork."

"Guess it's growing on me. Kind of like the one who gave it to me is."

Melinda smiled at him and waved the endearment away. "Yeah, I wonder about that sometimes with all the running you make me do to keep up with you. That and all the weird werewolf rules that don't make any sense. And don't even think I can't tell you're probably keeping a lot more from me."

"Some," Mephi admitted. All of a sudden, he felt the light leave his eyes, and his smile felt decidedly pinned on. "Nothing important. Nothing you need to know out here where it's just you and me."

"Yeah," Melinda said, "that's something I've been meaning to ask you about, too. Why is it just you and me all the time? I like it, don't get me wrong, but I still wonder. You talk about all these werewolf rules, and you say we've got this mission to fix what's wrong with the Earth, but I've never even seen another werewolf but you. What gives? I mean, how many of us are there?"

"We don't have to talk about this now, do we?" Mephi asked, walking away from Melinda to the fire she'd built earlier. He sat down Indian-style and began to poke the fire with a long twig that had been sitting just outside the circle of stones. "It's getting late."

"Well, I want to know," Melinda said, turning around as he passed and coming to stand next to him. "It always seems like you're so close to telling me really big things about being a werewolf, but you never do. Like when you mentioned Egypt before. You said your people were kicked out. Do you mean werewolves? Is that where the first of us came from? How long have we been here in the Americas, then?"

"Slow down," Mephi said. "Yeah, you're partly right about Egypt. I was talking about werewolves when I said 'my people,' but not all werewolves came from there. Just my tribe—the Silent Striders."

"That's a pretty name," Melinda said. "But how do you mean tribe? Werewolves have tribes like Indians do?"

"In a sense," Mephi said. "That's pretty fitting where my tribe's concerned, actually."

"So, if you're a Silent Strider," Melinda went on, "does that mean I am, too?"

"No," Mephi said, shaking his head. "Not exactly. You could be if you wanted, but you don't have to. It's more a matter of your lineage and who your parents are."

"Were," Melinda corrected him.

"Right. Anyway, a cub usually chooses her parents' tribe. Or her grandparents' tribe if it skipped a generation. You don't have to, but that's the way it's usually done."

"But by who, though?" Melinda said. "You say this like it's some ancient tradition. Are there places where people from the same tribe get together? Do people from other tribes get together somewhere?"

"Yeah," Mephi said, still staring into the fire. "Those kinds of places are out there."

"Are they like us?" Melinda asked. Excitement was growing in her eyes, and she plopped down on the ground next to Mephi. "Do the other werewolves have the same mission we do?"

"Yeah."

"How many are there?"

"We're our own whole culture," Mephi said. "We aren't as

many as we should be, but there are a lot of us. Maybe even enough to survive what's coming."

"Well that's great!" Melinda said, transported beyond Mephi's glum words by her growing excitement. "A whole culture. Can you take me to meet some of the other werewolves you know?"

The stick that Mephi was using to poke the fire broke in half in his fist. He hadn't even realized that he was squeezing it.

"What do you say, Mephi? Take me to meet some of our people. Please."

"Yeah, sure," Mephi said, dusting off his hands and throwing the broken stick into the fire. Never once did he look in Melinda's eyes. "I know of a sept less than a week from here over the line in New Mexico. I'll take you to meet some other honest-to-God werewolves I know. It's probably something I should have done before now."

"So why didn't you?" Melinda asked.

Mephi looked at the ground, hoping that the colored light from the fire hid the color in his cheeks. His eyes fell on the cobra-headed walking staff that Melinda had just given him.

"I was holding out," he said, manufacturing a grin to go along with his words. "Waiting 'til after you got me my First Change present before I foisted you off on the rest of the Garou nation."

"Well, if they're all like you," Melinda said with a mischievous grin, "then I'll be surrounded by dorks who think they're funny." She pushed Mephi over with the ball of her foot, then pounced on him.

"Cut it out!" Mephi laughed, trying to wrestle himself into a better position, despite his lack of leverage. "I'll take you to the sept over my shoulder in a sack if you—ow!—if you want to act like a wild animal."

"Half wild animal," Melinda said, trapping Mephi's legs with her crossed ankles and poking him in the ribs. "The other half's all-American teenager!" She punctuated the sentence with another poke, this one in the side just below his ribs.

"Same difference!" Mephi said, howling with laughter and trying in vain to roll free. He could almost get free, but Melinda had wrapped him up like a blanket, and she kept poking him every time he either cracked a joke or tried to flip her. He was just laughing too hard to put any real strength into the effort. He didn't want to get away from her any more than he wanted her to get away from him.

Of course, now that he'd started to tell her about the other Garou out there, she was going to start asking more questions. He might still be able to stall her, but not for very much longer. He'd been keeping her to himself, when what he really should have done was take her to the sept near where she'd lived before and introduced her to the werewolves there. Although he'd waited this long, he was going to have to do it soon now. Melinda would insist, and she wouldn't leave off about it until he relented. And like an idiot, he would take her there. When he did, she'd like what she found and want to stay, even though he needed to move on. Then, like so many people Mephi had cared about, Melinda would be out of his life except for the rare times when he made it back to her sept's protectorate. It was just a matter of when she decided to insist....

A rough shake woke Mephi to sunlight and birdsong. He opened his eyes and lifted his head to find Ivar squatting beside him. The Get's war hammer stood head-down on the ground, and Ivar kept his balance with one hand on the end of the haft.

"Up, wolf," Ivar said with a sleep-scratchy voice. Whitish gunk clung to the beds of his eyes, and his breath was a hellish wind. "It's morning. We're leaving soon."

Mephi stood up on all fours and stretched. Once he'd limbered up a little, he stood up into Homid form and wiped his eyes. "Did I miss dawn?"

"By a couple of hours," Ivar said, rising to his feet. "Light-Finder's still on watch, and Rain-Hunter's gathering breakfast. Come make us a cook fire."

"Sure," Mephi said, frowning. He headed past Ivar toward the center of the small camp. A few yards away, a bright, exuberant Conrad was already laying out a small bundle of fresh firewood. The kid waved. Mephi nodded with little enthusiasm and scratched his armpit.

"Strider," Ivar said before Mephi got out of earshot of his low voice. "Answer this."

Mephi looked back at him.

"Did they find it?" the Get asked. "Albrecht and the two who were with him. Did they find the Silver Crown? I didn't ask last night."

"Yeah," Mephi said. "I thought you'd have heard before you left the States." Ivar shook his head. "They did. That's why Arkady came home in disgrace. That's partly what that concolation at Anvil-Klaiven was about. I thought you'd made the connection yourself."

"It didn't occur to me," Ivar said. "It's a small world."

Mephi nodded. "Maybe once we're done here and we get back, I can tell you the rest of the story. I can tell all the Roving Wind The Saga of the Silver Crown."

"Don't get ahead of yourself," the Get said. "You may die today."

"Death won't catch up with me before this quest is over," Mephi said with a smirk. Ivar only shrugged. Mephi turned halfway back toward the fire pit then looked at Ivar again as a thought occurred to him. The Get stared at him without expression.

"Say, Ivar, tell me this," he said. "Did you and the Screaming Trailblazers find what you were looking for? The last cast-off skin of the Wyrm?"

"It wasn't out there in the Umbra to find," Ivar said, looking away rather than into Mephi's eyes. "We thought we'd figured out where it is, but it wasn't out there."

"Where then?" Mephi asked. "If you don't mind me asking."

"I'm looking at it," Ivar said. "So are you. That's what my dead friend Jack Wetthumb figured before we set off for Malfeas."

"I don't follow."

"Follow this. Every one of us Garou knows that Gaia created us. She made us spirit and flesh, fury and wisdom, man and wolf—all in balance. What no one's thought to wonder is exactly what Gaia made us out of."

The large man shrugged again, letting Mephi's mind do the work.

Mephi stood stunned at the insane possibility. "Do you really believe that?"

Ivar's eyes narrowed, and he put himself in Mephi's face before Mephi could even react. "My best friend crashed the gates of Malfeas because he believed it. I followed him, and there he died. Don't ask me that again."

"I'm sorry," Mephi said, tilting his head and sticking out his chin. He backed off a step and waited to see what Ivar would do. When the Get regained the composure he'd lost, Mephi turned back toward Conrad and the circle of stones. "I'll get the cook fire started."

Chapter 12

"You must feel like you've come home, Brother Gashwrack," Shrike's Thorn said as the two of them stood in the heart of what once was the caern of memory known as Owl's Rest. "Care to show me around?"

"I'm not home," Gashwrack snapped. "You can look around well enough yourself."

"Yes," Shrike's Thorn said. "It's most impressive. The Hive will be pleased by what progress is being made here."

Gashwrack concurred and took a slow look around. The physical half of the area had always been left well enough alone by the park officials who had marked this territory off as "protected." Here, the marshes that bordered the Tisza River had given way to grassy flatland and light forest. Birdcalls chased each other in the trees above and off in the distance, interrupted only by the sounds of passing vehicles on the nearest road. The place smelled of earth and water and exhaust. The smell of blood and the stench of decay lingered under everything else, but without the same power it had had when Gashwrack was here last. The bodies of the werewolves who had contested this caern had been removed and prepared for what was to come, and the land had already reclaimed what little evidence of their short reign here had remained. From a physical perspective, the place was ready to be consecrated in the Father's name.

The spiritual reflection of the place was a different story, though. Here at the caern's heart, Gashwrack had no trouble peering through the Gauntlet into the Penumbra, and he was annoyed by what he saw. Too little progress had been made since this caern had been won. Thick Pattern Webs still draped the bounds of the caern on three sides and piled up at the perimeter in an insanely complicated design. Although Banes and corrupted Weaver spirits worked tirelessly, and Wyrm tunnels undermined the Penumbral ground beneath the heaviest webs, the Pattern Webs still bore down and threatened to overwhelm the place at any moment.

Only the state of the fourth, exposed side of the caern gave Gashwrack any hope. That side faced the glorious Tisza Hellhole, which other brave soldiers had helped create in the Father's name. The Webs were thin, fraying things in that direction, and Gashwrack could see almost to the river itself. As nearly as he could tell, the slow tide of corrupted marshland had actually advanced since last he was here. That was something at least. Gashwrack shifted his perception back to the physical plane and found Shrike's Thorn speaking to him.

"—e've found it finally," the Theurge was saying.

"What?"

"The pathstone," Shrike's Thorn said. "The reason we're here. I was just explaining it to you, Gashwrack."

"I was looking across the Gauntlet," Gashwrack said. "What about the stone?"

"I said we've found it," Shrike's Thorn said. "A Scryer for one of our packs of Ooralath discovered it between us and the river. This caern's former Gatekeeper didn't hide it very well."

"That's why we're here? Your visions were leading you to the pathstone? We'd all thought it was lost or carried to another sept for safe-keeping."

"It was not lost," Shrike's Thorn said. "And finding the pathstone is only part of what I have been commanded to do in my visions."

"Right," Gashwrack said. "When we return it here, you'll activate it and renew its connections to the other local caerns. I'll send Splinterbone back through the tunnels to have Lady Arastha ready our forces for—"

"You won't," Shrike's Thorn said, staring in the direction of the Tisza without really seeming to see anything. "That isn't part of our Father's vision. It is not what he would have of us."

"But we have the warriors! They're ready and able to launch a surprise attack. What's the matter, can't you do it? Can't you even use the pathstone for its intended purpose?"

"Don't bark at me, Ahroun," Shrike's Thorn growled, glaring at Gashwrack and daring him to do something ill advised. "While alpha acts, beta learns, and I am alpha now."

"But we'll have the advantage," Gashwrack insisted. "With enough forces, we can cut a bloody swath through this entire region, just like Tisza did."

"We don't have the standing forces ready to leap to rash commands," Shrike's Thorn said. "Every pack, every Hive, is engaged with local septs or tearing down the Pattern Web already. If we pull those forces too early, we lose what they're poised to gain."

"It's simple, Theurge," Gashwrack said, crushing his fist into his open hand in frustration. "We withdraw our warriors so the enemy pursues to finish us. Then everyone falls back here, scorching the earth as we go and luring our opponents on. We gather here, and they'll gather around us expecting a showdown. But once our enemy's over-extended, we use your pathstone's connections to attack their caerns while they're unprotected. It's a simple strategy."

"My visions and the Father's commands do not pander to your concerns of strategy," Shrike's Thorn said without anger. "We're not here to realize your fever-dreams of battlefield glory. Our Father has given us another mission that's more important than a single conflict. It may be more important than any single battle before the Apocalypse itself."

"Bullshit," Gashwrack sneered. "One pack of three for something so important? Now you're having fever-dreams of glory."

"Maybe," Shrike's Thorn said. "But I'll act on them as our Father commands. And you will follow your alpha and do the same. This is a time of war, and I will not be challenged."

"Fine," Gashwrack spat. "If we're giving up a strategic gem like this, what we're giving it up for better be as important as you say."

"It is," Shrike's Thorn said with a distant smile. "From what I've seen, it truly is. It's something that will cut out our enemies' spirit and devour it while they wail in terror. If we're successful here, we'll win our Father's war."

"All because of one captured pathstone?"

"Every whirlwind begins with a single breath," Shrike's Thorn said. He clapped his hands on Gashwrack's shoulders and squeezed. "You'll see."

Gashwrack looked into Shrike's Thorn's silver-white eyes and saw both zeal and madness swirling within. The Theurge's words weren't just rhetoric to him—Shrike's Thorn believed. Gashwrack had never known such conviction in either this life or the one that had come before. That strength of faith was comforting.

"If you say so," he said, "then I'll believe you."

"Excellent," Shrike's Thorn said, releasing Gashwrack and turning away. "Then let's go. We have to ready the bodies of this caern's fallen and take them to where the Ooralath discovered the pathstone. Splinterbone is there already, waiting and making the area secure."

Gashwrack nodded and followed, wondering just what his pack was about to engage in.

Chapter 13

Just after nightfall, Mephi and the Roving Wind slipped through a thinning tangle of Pattern Webs to crest a Penumbral rise. From the top, they caught their first glimpse of the Hellhole that the Tisza River had become. A single, unifying chord sounded within each of them, and a tide of rage tried to drive them forward in a frenzy. They were each filled with the unreasoning urge to charge down the hill and tear apart the ones who had done this thing to one of Gaia's rivers. They would destroy the Wyrm's petty servitors in the river basin below. They would rip the throats out of the humans who had caused this accident. They would tear and kill and roar until this place returned to the way it should be. They were Garou; thus would they take vengeance for every torture that Gaia had endured.

Only an effort of will and rational thinking forestalled this deadly and likely suicidal urge. Melinda marshaled her wits first and began to back away from the rise. The other members of her pack did the same, turning away from the disgusting, horrifying view below. Only Mephi remained, and he had to back away a few steps himself.

"Jesus Christ," Conrad said, with a weaker rein on his emotions than those his fellows enjoyed. "Did they do that? Did the Wyrm do that?"

"Yes," Melinda said. Her voice was calm, but her red-gold eyes were ablaze. "I told you it would be like this."

"No, you didn't," Conrad said. As he spoke, his voice grew thick and deeper. His muscles began to bulge, and his body hair became dark and coarse. He'd begun to puff up into his Glabro form. "You just said it would be bad. That isn't just bad down there! It's the end of the fucking world! It's all going to look like that if we don't do something right now!"

Hush, Rain-Hunter warned. Be calm. Her raised hackles, wide-open eyes and thrashing tail made the statement seem hypocritical. She pawed the ground and looked over her shoulder in the direction of the Hellhole.

"Don't tell me that," Conrad thundered. "Did you see what I saw down there? Somebody has to pay for that! Those things down there are going to pay on the ends of these!" He lifted his hand with his claws pointing up. His Glabro claws were not as long or strong as his Crinos talons would have been, but they were thick and sharp enough to get the idea across.

"They will pay," Melinda assured him. "All of them between now and the Apocalypse. But not tonight."

"Are you afraid?" Conrad yelled, turning almost inhuman eyes toward her. Already, he was growing larger, shifting without thought into the half-man, half-wolf warrior form. "Why are you afraid? Because there are only four of us?" Mephi's eyes narrowed at the unintentional slight. "You make me sick, you coward bitch! I'll lead us myself!"

"Boy," Ivar said. "Look here."

When Conrad jerked his head left to look at Ivar, the barrel-chested Get of Fenris punched Conrad in the jaw. The Get was as tall as Conrad's Glabro shape, and the two of them were almost equally broad in the shoulder, but the punch wadded the Child of Gaia up on the ground like an empty sack. Melinda winced, and Rain-Hunter merely cocked her head and looked down at Conrad. Mephi also winced. He was glad he hadn't driven the Get to anger when the two of them had first talked.

Still sitting on the ground, Conrad assumed his Homid form once again and put a hand to his red and swollen cheek. A glassy mist rose in the boy's eyes, and he glared up at Ivar.

"Jesus Crap," he said in a small voice. "What was that for?"

"Making up my mind," Ivar said. "I couldn't tell if you were ready to rage or if you were just reacting."

The second, Rain-Hunter answered. Her tail swung low in disappointment.

"You needed it, kiddo," Melinda said, reaching down to pull

Conrad to his feet. "Ivar's right, and you ought to thank him."

"Maybe I could if my jaw wasn't on the back of my head," Conrad said after a long, thoughtful pause. He dusted himself off and stood up straight. He was in control of himself once more, but he had to make an effort not to look toward the Hellhole again. "Man, Ivar, you did that in Homid?"

Thank him again, Rain-Hunter told him.

"It felt like you slugged me with a sack of golf balls." Conrad worked his jaw up and down then from side to side. The swelling was gone, and none of his teeth seemed to be dangling. All that was left was a light flush of embarrassment. "Guess I was kind of losing it, though, huh?"

"It's natural," Melinda said. "You're right to feel the way you did. It's how we're made. Our rage was given to us by Luna, it's blessed by Gaia, and it's feared by the Wyrm." As she spoke, Mephi thought the words along with her. He'd given her this same speech more than once. "It's a part of who we are, and it's wrong to deny it its release. You just can't let it rule you. Use it, but only use it the way you want to use it. Otherwise it'll get you killed."

"Like down there," Ivar said, pointing toward the Hellhole with his thumb.

"I think I got it," Conrad said. "Tell me this, though, Ivar. If I'd have jumped on you a minute ago, would you have gone down into that with me?"

"Yes," Ivar said. "All of us would, if it came to that."

"Well," Conrad said, "all things considered, I guess I'm glad I didn't. Next time, though, just flip a coin."

Ivar favored the kid with a smile and shrugged.

Melinda slapped Conrad on the back and said, "No way. You got a good head for taking punches, kiddo."

Learning lessons, Rain-Hunter amended.

"I won't forget it," Conrad said, working his jaw one more time. "But can we make a promise? All of us?"

Mephi didn't even turn around to see if he was included. No one so much as mentioned his name.

"Sure," Melinda said. "What?"

"We're going to do something about this," Conrad said. "After we get the pathstone back to Konietzko, we'll stop wandering the damn countryside and make this place our protectorate. If it's my life's work, I want us to clean up this mess. I want us to take the caern back and rebuild the Sept of the Owl's Rest."

Ivar, Rain-Hunter and Conrad looked at Melinda, who peered at Conrad. She searched his eyes first, and then those of her other pack members. "Would you stay?" she asked the three of them.

It isn't right to wander without territory, Rain-Hunter said.

"We've been traveling too long, Light-Finder," Ivar said. "You and I especially. We'll come back and plant our standard here."

"I don't care what it takes or how long," Conrad said. "If I can't die of old age here with this place the way Gaia created it, I'll die trying to fix it."

"We're one mind and spirit and body," Melinda said. "We're a pack, and we're decided. We'll return and reclaim this place. By our honor, we're bound."

The others echoed the last sentence, then stood together sharing a solemn moment of silence. Standing alone near the edge of the rise overlooking the Tisza Hellhole, Mephi gazed up at the moon and thought about what he'd just heard. The words sounded sincere as they were spoken, but he just didn't believe that they would come true. The five of them, he knew, would be lucky to make it back to the Sept of the Night Sky alive with the Owl's Rest pathstone.

Plus, from what Mephi could see, the land was already too far gone to be saved by any single pack. The place was beset on two fronts by the mad excesses of both the Weaver and the Wyrm. Before the river was polluted, the Weaver had been strong here. Man had carved irrigation channels and built dams to direct and leech off the river. Man had built roads along the river's sides and bridges across it. Man had strung telephone wires and power lines over the area in precise formation. Man had imposed his order on this wilderness, and the Weaver had grown strong. Pattern Webs lay everywhere, just under the Penumbral surface. The moon shone on snatches of that webbing here and there all throughout the region, wherever man had touched and claimed and built. The web persevered even in the diseased and ravaged stretch of land below. But where the Weaver had once been strong, the Wyrm now ruled. The polluting sludge that had oozed down this river's physical body in months past had poisoned and corrupted its spiritual counterpart seemingly beyond salvation. The flood plains alongside the river's banks had been affected as well, as had the marshes that fed from the river in the distance. Despite the best efforts of the ubiquitous Pattern Webs in this region, the Penumbral landscape had become a nightmarish plane of festering decay and filth.

Land that was unbroken and grassy in the physical world was a fetid bog in the Penumbra, and toxins bubbled to the surface. Some bubbles belched their filth into the air to rain down in noxious showers, while others simply deflated and leaked their putrescent cargo along the ground in slick, steaming pools. What had once been the spirits of sky-defying trees had either fallen or been twisted beyond recognition. The tree-spirits that remained had been warped into gnarled and knobby mockeries. They looked like the grasping claws of long-dead giants that had sunk into this nauseous quagmire ages ago. Fat scuds tried to block out the moon and threatened to vomit acid rain at any second. Dim moon paths led away to Scar, Atrocity, and possibly even Malfeas. Raised welts that criss-crossed the ground marked the presence of Wyrm tunnels just beneath the surface. Further off in the Penumbral distance, the land simply curled up at the edges, walling this defiled patch of ground off from the rest of the spirit world.

The river itself was the centerpiece of the Hellhole. The viscous, brackish fluid crawled along much more slowly than water should have, making a sound like a plastic-enshrouded corpse being dragged through a vale of sucking mud. It seeped and oozed forward in sections as if it were a leprous serpent creeping away to die. Unidentifiable scraps of solid filth and colloidal glops that shimmered like oil drifted and sank in the water making its way toward the Penumbral reflection of the Danube. Eddies swirled and died in the flow, and some crosscurrents even managed to carry themselves several yards upstream before breaking up and heading back the right way. Bones and bodies of dead fish littered the sides of the river, as did the corpses of several birds that had eaten too many of the poisoned fish too quickly. No Gaian or Wyld spirit could survive in such a place on such a bounty.

The spirit servitors of the Wyrm, however, were legion, and they were foremost in Mephi's attention. Broken, mutated bird spirits flapped spastically through the air on asymmetrical wings and picked through the detritus that littered the riverbanks. The malformed tree-spirits that still dotted the landscape trapped these bird spirits in poorly woven nets of Pattern Web scraps. Warped Pattern Spiders with too many eyes and uneven, multi-jointed legs repaired these makeshift nets, then disposed of the captured spirits according to whatever mad whim had been built into them. Some carried the bound and wriggling spirits to other nets in other trees, some dumped their burdens into the river, and some simply devoured the spirits on the spot for their Essence.

Elsewhere, spirits more dangerous or more disgusting carried on their ugly business. Mephi saw nauseating H'ruggling sludge Banes crawl up out of the river, leaving slimy trails behind them. He watched purplish Wakshaani toxin Banes shift along the ground in blotchy, thick-veined sheets. Packs of armor-plated Ooralath slogged through the mire as if on patrol. Vicious Psychomachiae prowled in search of signs of human habitation that might have a reflection here. Huge, razor-clawed Scrags bathed in the foul river, then emerged, baptized by the filth.

Uncorrupted Weaver spirits tended the Pattern Webs at the edges of the Hellhole, but their every attempt to repair what damage had been done met with failure. The river was thick with Banes as far as Mephi could see, and those Banes crushed any Weaver incursions. The Weaver spirits hemmed the corruption in so that it spread no further than it already had, Mephi saw, but the territory that the Wyrm had claimed would not be won back easily. Yet the Roving Wind had promised to do just that. Shaking his head, Mephi wished them luck and Gaia's grace.

The sound of footsteps behind him caught his attention, and

he turned to find Melinda coming up to stand next to him while the rest of her pack congregated several yards away, attending to their own business. From the way they made a point not to look this way, Mephi guessed that Melinda had asked them to leave her and him alone for a few moments. She stopped at his side and looked down the rise at the Hellhole below. Her face was smooth and expressionless, but Mephi read the tension in her shoulders. He saw how her hands were clutched into fists. Her nostrils flared as if she were drawing breath for a furious howl. Mephi braced himself for something unpleasant.

"We wouldn't be here if you hadn't come, Strider," Melinda said as she scanned the abused landscape. "I wouldn't have to expose my people to that down there."

"What?" He looked back at the other members of the Roving Wind and saw them breaking out provisions for their last reasonably relaxed meal. Conrad looked up, then made a hasty study of the contents of his satchel.

"None of this was here when we found Owl's Rest. Just Pattern Webs and Wyld spirits. Now look at it. Look at what the Wyrm's done."

"I know," Mephi said.

"Ivar's seen worse than this," Melinda went on. "I've seen places this bad. But Rain-Hunter and Conrad are in over their heads. They don't know how to get around in something like that, and I don't have enough experience to lead them safely myself. Maybe if I were back home in the States, I'd give it a try, but here's still just too alien to me. If I hadn't seen you at Anvil-Klaiven, we would have just left. There are other places that need our help these days. Ivar's got a brother he hasn't seen since before the Shadow Curtain fell. Rain-Hunter's afraid for the wolf cubs she left when she joined us. We have plenty of other responsibilities...."

"Melinda, you volunteered for this," Mephi said. "It sounds like you're holding that against me."

"I am," Melinda said, turning to him at last. She kept her voice down so that her packmates couldn't hear her. "If I hadn't seen you—if you hadn't been there—I wouldn't have volunteered. I knew how bad this place had to be, and I know that my people aren't equipped for it. And I know I don't know enough what to look for out there to keep them all safe. Not in a place like that."

"But I do," Mephi said, completing the thought before Melinda spoke it. "Right?"

"You do," Melinda admitted, although the confession only made her more upset. "Everything I learned about staying safe in the Umbra I learned from you."

"But by now, you must have learned enough to—"

"You can run from hell to breakfast in the Umbra without snapping a twig or making a Bane's nose twitch," Melinda said. "With you along, we actually have a shot at doing this and getting back safely. Since I knew that, I had to volunteer us, and I had to include you. Otherwise, we'd have had to mobilize a larger force and weaken some other sept by having some of its warriors cut us a swath through that mess. Now that you're here, we might be able to get in and out without bringing all those monsters down on us."

"You're holding that against me?" Mephi asked. "It's not like you to be that irrational, Melinda. What's really bothering you?"

"You're bothering me," Melinda said. "Your being here. I don't really blame you, I guess. It's not your fault we ended up at the same concolation. I just wish you hadn't picked now to magically show back up. Everything would have been so much easier. But you did, so I couldn't pass up the chance to get this mission done right. You didn't do it on purpose, but you obligated me to volunteer for this mission."

"What if I hadn't wanted to go with you?" Mephi asked. "I could have told you no when you asked."

Melinda snorted. "Right. I still remember everything I knew about you, Strider, and I doubt you've changed very much. You don't like going places for no reason. After a week sitting around useless at Anvil-Klaiven, I could tell you were either ready to get involved with something important here or go back to America where you could do some good. When you found out I was doing something important and dangerous, I knew you'd stay. You feel too guilty not to offer to help."

Melinda had wagered her pack's good name and likely its

safety on her impression of him as a fool who'd come to rescue her from danger without considering the consequences. "I guess you know me pretty well," Mephi snarled.

"Yeah," Melinda snarled back at him, letting old anger take the place of her nascent worry. "Pretty well, considering how long it's been. What is it now, ten years? Or don't you even remember anymore?"

"All right, look, Melinda," Mephi barked, "there's only so many times you're going to be able to make me feel guilty about that. Now quit throwing it in my face!"

"Or what?" Melinda spat. "You'll run off and strand me again? Well, now's your chance. It should be second nature to you by now."

Mephi threw his staff down on the ground and grabbed Melinda's shoulders. "Knock it off, Light-Finder," he said. "Or I will leave. The hell with your pathstone and your mission. And you. I'll leave!"

The emotion that had been rising in Melinda's eyes grew in a flash, and her shoulders went rigid in Mephi's hands. She jerked back a step out of his reach and stood looking down at the staff that divided the world between them. None of her bitterness remained now. Only hurt shone in Melinda's eyes. The hurt of a little girl who'd lost her best friend and big brother and surrogate father all at once. Shocked at his own outburst, Mephi stuffed his hands in his coat pockets and looked down as well. For a long moment, neither of them spoke.

"Melinda, listen," Mephi finally said without looking up. "I still know you fairly well, I think, and I know what's happening here. You're scared. You're right to have a grudge, and you might be right never to forgive me for leaving you when you were still a cub, but nothing's going to get resolved like this. Especially when that's not all you're upset about. I can see how much you care about your pack, and you're scared you're going to lose them when we go into that Hellhole. If you've got any sense, you're probably scared you won't come back yourself. You're trying to be tough and in charge, but you're hanging on to too much other baggage at the same time. If you don't get it out before we go down there, you're going to get distracted. You won't be any kind of a leader then."

"I know," Melinda said. "I just know I'm going to get distracted some time when the others need me. More than anything, that's what I'm holding against you. I realized a few years ago—once I stopped being constantly pissed at you—that I needed to deal with you. But you just weren't around. I couldn't yell at you or talk to you or forgive you or tell you I hate you or anything, because you just weren't there."

"I'm here now," Mephi said. "I know that's not worth much, but I'm here. If you're going to bottle your fear up right and live through this, we've got to settle up."

"Yeah," Melinda said. "I just hope it hasn't been too long."

"Me too," Mephi said. "Now how do we start? I've always had a speech in the back of my head for in case you and I ever met again, but it always sounded pretty weak."

"Let's talk about why I get scared when the Roving Wind takes on something important or dangerous, Mephi. Like it or not, that's been your legacy to me more than anything else,"

"All right," Mephi said. He had trouble keeping the shame out of his voice, but part of him was relieved that this confrontation had finally begun.

"I wasn't afraid when you first showed me what a Blight looked like," Melinda said. "When we had to edge through a Hellhole for the first time, I wasn't afraid either. The first time I got stuck in the Pattern Web trying to cross the Gauntlet and I was face-to-face with that Pattern Spider, I wasn't scared. All because I knew you were there for me.

"And then one night you weren't. You were gone, and I had to be the leader and take care of myself. Even though I knew I could do it, there was always that fear I had to swallow before I could do what I had to do. And now here it still is, even though you're back. Why? Why can't I just be strong and be the leader without that fear? Even when I'm feeling it, I know I'm stronger than that. But then...I'm just not."

Mephi shook his head and looked up at Melinda with weary eyes. "You always were, Lin," he said. "As long as I've known you, you've always been brave and eager. I don't know where in your head this feeling you're talking about comes from, but it's a good thing I left you when I did. A werewolf's got to be tough and self-reliant, or he's not going to survive out here. Since your First Change, you were never alone. You never learned how to take care of yourself because I was always there taking care of you. Even after all that stuff I taught you, you'd have been helpless out there if something happened to me. You were depending on me too much."

When Melinda looked up at last, hurt still clouded her eyes, but she wore a bitter smile. "Are you saying I was clingy?"

"No, Lin," Mephi said. "Soft. That time together was making you too soft for the work we have to do. Your rage wasn't building. You were having too good a time with me, and that isn't the right attitude for a werewolf to have. I did what was best for you before it got too late."

"Is that so?"

"You know that fear you swallow?" Mephi answered. "If we'd stayed together longer and something happened to me, that fear would be even bigger and harder to swallow. That, or your grief would have paralyzed you or pushed you into Harano."

"Well, someone's a little full of himself."

"It's true," Mephi said. "It happens all the time to Silent Strider cubs who stick with their mentors too long after their Change. When I saw it happening to you, I did the only thing I could think of."

Melinda frowned, looked away, scowled, then looked back at Mephi at last. "Couldn't you have just told me all this back then, Mephi? I was a smart kid. I would have understood."

"I wish I could have," Mephi said. "But if I explained it to you and dropped you off at a caern, you'd always have been waiting for me to come back. Some part of your mind would always expect it. My way was better. I wanted you to be strong, and nobody gets as strong as somebody who's been abandoned."

"Is that what the werewolf who brought you up told you?"

"No," Mephi said. "I learned that one from my parents. But it's right. Look at what you've done since then. Look where you are, for Gaia's sake. You've made a home for yourself halfway around the world from where you started out. You may be right that you wouldn't be here in this place tonight if I hadn't come to Anvil-Klaiven, but you wouldn't be half the Garou you are if I hadn't left you way back then."

Melinda thought about that for a long time, looking around at anything but Mephi. She looked at her packmates, who were still graciously minding their own business just out of earshot. When she finally met Mephi's eyes again, the hurt was fading, and she no longer even looked angry. Now, she just looked older and sadder. The last clinging wisp of childhood innocence had dissipated, leaving only the hardened adult. In all this time, Mephi guessed, Melinda had really just wanted an explanation for why he had left her. She wanted closure. Whether she understood his reasoning or ever agreed with it remained to be seen, but she accepted it.

"Didn't you ever think about a pack, Mephi?" Melinda said. "Everyone in the Roving Wind is stronger for the bond we share. In our pack, there's no such thing as depending on each other too much."

"Yeah," Mephi said. "That's the way a pack works. That wasn't like what you and I had together, though."

"So why didn't we ever become a pack? When we were together, I always thought it was kind of weird that natural wolves ran in packs but werewolves didn't seem to."

"It wouldn't have worked out," Mephi said. "I'm not the type."

"Is that a Strider thing?" Melinda asked.

"Partly. It's mostly just me, though. I can't really explain it."

Melinda shrugged and turned back toward the rise and the Hellhole. A slow change worked over her features, tightening her jaw line, drawing her chin a little higher and hardening the gleam in her eyes. Mephi kept silent and let it run its course. He bent down to retrieve his walking staff from the ground. It didn't seem to be cracked or any more scuffed than it already was when he'd first set off with the Roving Wind.

"I'm glad you kept that," Melinda said as Mephi planted the staff between them and stood beside her. "After you disappeared, I honestly thought you'd get rid of it."

"It never even crossed my mind," Mephi said. "I didn't want

to forget about you, Lin. That'd be a worse thing to do than leaving you behind. People are always out there somewhere to find again if you lose them, but once you forget about them, they're gone for good. That's the last thing I wanted to do."

"Good," Melinda said. "Because if you did, I'm afraid I'd have to hunt you down just to kick your ass."

"And, 'Who's this kicking my ass?' I'd have to say," Mephi said with a tentative grin. "'What's the meaning of this, ma'am? Who are you?'"

A small smile shone on Melinda's face, and Mephi secretly rejoiced to see it. It was not the same smile he remembered from all those years ago, but it was genuine. It was the first genuine smile he'd seen from her in ten years.

"Look at that down there, Strider," she said, after a long moment of peace between them. "Can we really make it through that?"

"Yes we can, Lin," Mephi said. "Between the two of us, we'll get this done."

"We'd better," Melinda said. "But, Mephi, before we get started, let me ask you one favor."

"What's that?"

"Don't call me Lin. It's not who I am any more. I'm Light-Finder now."

"All right, Light-Finder," Mephi said. "Fair enough. Now let's talk about how we're going to get this pathstone out of that mess down there and get home safe."

Chapter 14

"Friend of yours?" Shrike's Thorn asked Gashwrack as the two of them joined Splinterbone.

"He was a packmate once," Gashwrack said. "It's hard to recognize him now."

"What was his name?"

"I don't remember," Gashwrack lied.

On the ground between them lay what was once the body of the Gatekeeper of Owl's Rest. Now, it was a Homid-form shell that had been torn open and defiled by Ooralath and Scrag, and quite likely by Splinterbone as well. The least serious wound on the dead man's body was the ragged hole in his stomach that peered into the hollow cavity of his abdomen. In the bottom of that open pit lay what appeared to be a flat pearl with the tiny mark of a wolf's paw on one side. The Gatekeeper had apparently swallowed it in desperation as he ran from Owl's Rest.

"Ooralath found him this morning," Splinterbone said, squatting down beside the body. He plucked at the corpse's dangling lower lip with a long talon. "He's still got it."

"Yes he does," Shrike's Thorn said as he knelt down in the Penumbral muck beside Splinterbone and reached into the Gatekeeper's open stomach. He pulled out the small pathstone and wiped the blood on it more evenly across its flat sides. It glowed with a wan red light.

"Good," Gashwrack said. "Now what do we do with it?"

"Take it home?" Splinterbone suggested. He pulled the Gatekeeper's lip completely free of the body and held the fleshy strip on his palm like a leech. "Give it to Arastha."

"No," Shrike's Thorn said. "I have a vision to make real here in this place the Father has touched."

"What do you want to do?" Gashwrack asked.

"A ritual," Shrike's Thorn said, gazing into the middle distance. "A special ritual the Father has given me. It's time."

"What do we do?" Splinterbone asked. "How can we help?"

"The warriors' bodies," Shrike's Thorn said. "How many were salvaged from the caern?"

"Four whole," Gashwrack said. "The rest were divided up among the packs that helped take the caern after the Tisza was polluted. And we've got this one."

"Four whole will do," Shrike's Thorn said. "Bring them here, the both of you. And set them up as I tell you."

Gashwrack and Splinterbone hurried away side-by-side to collect the fallen Garou warriors' bodies as Shrike's Thorn asked.

Chapter 15

"Our Father who art imprisoned," the tall Black Spiral Dancer intoned behind his makeshift altar of Garou corpses, "hallowed be thy name. Thy freedom come, thy duty be done on Earth, in the Umbra and all throughout Creation."

"This is not good," Conrad murmured, edifying no one.

He, Mephi and the Roving Wind all lay flat in the concealment of an eroded ridge only a few hundred feet from where the Dancer was speaking. Once the Child of Gaia had performed the Rite of the Questing Stone at the edge of the Tisza Hellhole it hadn't taken long at all to find the body of the Gatekeeper of Owl's Rest. With Mephi in the lead, the pack had navigated the Hellhole without attracting attention and even found a reasonably safe place to cross the Umbral reflection of the Tisza. Now, however, they were more or less pinned down.

"Give us this day your grace and power," the Black Spiral Dancer went on, "and punish our transgressions as we punish each other for the same."

The object of the Roving Wind's attention was one of three Black Spiral Dancers who stood together around a vile altar, and who were themselves surrounded by a host of Ooralath and Scrags. The altar that was the center of this fell congregation consisted of four corpses sitting back-to-back on the ground, and bound together by each other's braided intestines. Each corpse's head hung down against its chest, and a fifth body had been laid across their shoulders like a tabletop. That corpse's wounds gaped open toward the patchy, cloud-marred sky, and a sickly light shone from somewhere within its ravaged stomach.

"What is he doing?" Conrad whispered, fighting to maintain control of himself. "Those are the Guardians and the Gatekeeper of Owl's Rest. What is that son of a bitch doing to them?"

Everyone looked at Melinda, but she only shook her head. "I don't know. Some kind of rite, but I don't recognize it."

"He has the pathstone?" Ivar murmured.

"That body…on top of that…thing is the Gatekeeper's," Conrad said, swallowing hard and looking away from the Spirals' altar. "If they've got that, they must have the stone, too."

"Lead us not into weakness," the Spiral continued, "that we may yet deliver you from evil."

"He must be trying to connect to our other caerns," Mephi said. "Just like the Margrave said."

We're too late, Rain-Hunter said. Her tail drooped, and she hung her head.

"No," Melinda said. "He'd do that at Owl's Rest. That's where the moon bridges go, not here. Plus, this doesn't look like the right kind of rite. It's an invocation. I can tell that much."

"For thine is the wisdom and the honor and the glory forever and ever," the Spiral concluded at last. "In nomine vermiis." The other two who were with him lifted their heads from what appeared to be an attitude of reverential prayer and looked around. The orange werewolf in Crinos form glanced around and turned back to the speaker. The other Spiral remained in Homid form, and he looked around more carefully. He did not see the Roving Wind, but he seemed tense and suspicious nonetheless.

"I don't believe it," Melinda said, barely able to get the words out in a sudden surge of anger. "He's still alive."

"Traitor," Ivar spat.

"Who?" Mephi asked.

"The one on the right," Conrad said. "His name's Eric Fire-Stealer. He's a Guardian for the Sept of the Owl's Rest. He was. Now, it looks like he's—"

"Dead," Ivar said. He squeezed the haft of his war hammer so hard that the wood creaked. "He died the day he let his caern be violated."

Not first, Rain-Hunter growled low. The pathstone.

"Right," Melinda said, glaring at the traitor's back. "Whatever those three are doing with it is something we should stop."

"But what are they doing?" Conrad asked. "And how do we get up there through all those Banes to stop it?"

"Father," the tall Spiral said, holding his arms toward the sky. In his right hand, he held a blackened wedge of something that the silent observers couldn't make out against the night sky. It might have been the scale from a dragon or a tooth from the largest and oldest shark in the ocean, and a hole had been cut into its blunt side so that the Spiral could hold it like a punching dagger. "Your Forgotten Son lies imprisoned and asleep in the land far to the south. Yet, despite all your power and presence there, that Forgotten Son cannot wake."

Mephi looked at Melinda with a questioning frown, but she just scowled in confusion and shrugged.

"How long are we just going to sit here?" Conrad whispered hoarsely. "Light-Finder, come on...."

Hush, Rain-Hunter growled.

"No," Melinda said, looking out over the terrain that separated them from the Spirals and the pathstone that they'd come to collect. "He's right."

"But now," the Spiral continued, "you have shown us the way. You have given us your vision, and our eyes have been opened by it. Burn away our ignorance, oh Father, and let us remember your Forgotten Son. We offer these unhallowed souls. We commend them to your service."

As the Spiral spoke, the gruesome altar at his feet began to writhe. The eyes of the bodies that made up the base jerked open, and an unearthly wail tore free of their mouths. The fallen werewolves' legs began to drum on the ground and their arms lifted like the limbs of marionettes with tangled strings. Each seated corpse took hold of one of the Gatekeeper's limbs, pulled it taut and hoisted the Gatekeeper's body into the air. The corpse balanced there between their outstretched arms, seemingly ready to fall apart under its own weight because of the severity of its many wounds. The sickly red light emanated from it with more intensity, and the ghostly wail issued from the fallen Garou's mouths without a break. The two Dancers who were not speaking dropped to one knee, and all of the Banes in the immediate area began to sway in place.

"Help us remember, Father," the Spiral said, holding his dagger above his head in both hands. "Give your Forgotten Son the strength to rage against his prison walls! Show us the chains that bind him, that we may set him free!"

As he spoke, a green glow emanated from the point of his dagger and bathed him and his two packmates in its ugly light. The light grew brighter steadily as his volume increased.

"What's your plan, Light-Finder?" Mephi asked, trying to keep the tone of desperation out of his voice.

"There," Melinda said, pointing to a space just beyond where the three Black Spiral Dancers stood. "You see that raised line running from over here to behind them?"

"I see it," Conrad said. Mephi saw it, too. It looked like nothing more than an earthen speed-breaker, except that it ran almost two hundred yards across the open ground before it disappeared. Similar lines welted the rest of the Hellhole's skin. From atop the rise that had given the Roving Wind its first view of the Hellhole, Mephi had recognized those welts. They were the mounded tops of Wyrm-tunnels. The one that Melinda was pointing at missed the sickeningly animated altar by no more than three yards, and ran in a straight line to a point just beyond the edge of the ridge behind which the Roving Wind was now hiding.

"Good," Melinda said to Conrad. "Then you're with me. Take your Lupus form and hold that thread."

"Light-Finder, have you lost your mind?" Mephi said.

"Ivar, Rain-Hunter, you know what I'm thinking," Melinda said, ignoring Mephi's protest. "And you know what I need."

"A distraction," Ivar said, stone-faced.

"A damned good one," Conrad said. He hadn't yet changed forms, and his skin was decidedly more pale than it had been mere moments ago. "Jesus, Melinda..."

"There's too many eyes to distract," Mephi said. "What you're thinking is suicide."

"Don't talk to me," Melinda said. She pointed at Ivar and Rain-Hunter. "Help them figure out how to get all those eyes pointed somewhere else."

Twenty long breaths to cover the distance, Rain-Hunter said.

Then grow, then come out of the ground. Do not stop.

Melinda nodded and looked at Conrad. "Get all that?"

Conrad nodded.

"Good," Melinda said. "Now don't panic. It's a short hop, and all the Banes look like they're on the surface. This won't get scary until we come out on the other side. Ready?"

Conrad steeled himself, took a deep breath, clamped the twine with its crystal pendant in his teeth and folded down into Lupus form.

"Die well," Ivar said to the two of them. "Or not at all."

Melinda nodded solemnly, then turned to Mephi. She squeezed his shoulder and looked deep into his eyes. "We don't need long, Strider," she said. "Just give us a distraction and make it good. We're counting on you."

Mephi swallowed his final protest, knowing that it would do no good anyway. He only nodded and said sadly, "I won't let you down."

Melinda flashed a fearless smile and turned to Conrad. "This way, Stepper," she said, pointing to the edge of the ridge closest to the near end of the Wyrm-tunnel. "We'll dig in here."

Chapter 16

Shrike's Thorn held his dagger high over his head in both hands as the radiant ball of energy at its tip grew. His packmates stood frozen in awe, and the Bane servitors who attended them had all but collapsed in reverence. The sacrifices that made up his altar shrieked. It was time.

"Now, Father!" he howled, rising up into his Glabro shape in exultation. "Now, give your Forgotten Son strength! Drive him against the bars of his prison! Give him your torment! Give him your power!"

That power coursed through Shrike's Thorn, driving him upward even higher into his Crinos form, and it coalesced in a blinding, Balefire sun above his upraised dagger. Waves of invisible energy blasted outward from it, obliterating lesser Banes, tumbling the more powerful spirits to the ground, and even forcing his packmates to their knees. But even still, Shrike's Thorn remained standing. He was the eye of the storm. He was the voice in the whirlwind. For one glorious, excruciating moment, he was the Wyrm, the Unmaker, the Balance. Then with a tortured, rapturous howl, he drove the blazing dagger in his hand down onto the blood-soaked pathstone that lay in the center of his altar.

When the Wyrm's power crashed into the pathstone, a single harsh, discordant note rang out across the Pattern Webs and the very surface of the Gauntlet, rippling the spirit world like a sheet of stagnant water. Neither the stone nor the dagger shattered, but the vile altar beneath them blew apart and was no more. Even the hardier Banes in the immediate area were destroyed, so that only the strongest Ooralath and Scrags remained whole. Splinterbone and Gashwrack were thrown to the ground, and the closest exposed Wyrm-tunnels collapsed. The shriek and whine of rising power vanished, leaving the Hellhole and the surrounding Penumbra eerily silent for miles in every direction. Of Shrike's Thorn, there was no sign.

Chapter 17

Somewhere far to the south, something stirred. It was a being long imprisoned like the elder entity that had given it birth, but possessed of a much more active malignance. This being saw pinprick silver-white eyes and heard a faint and reverent voice exhorting it to rise. The tiny voice called it to wake and do its father's bidding as it had once in a time long forgotten. It extolled, insisted and commanded, did this tiny voice. Enraged that this insignificant thing would demand from it the impossible, the entity devoured it. Yet, when the voice was silent, the entity could not return to slumber. It knew once again that it had been imprisoned and that it had been forgotten long ago.

These revelations incensed the entity, and it began to flex its sleep-weakened limbs. When these exertions gained it nothing, the entity heaved with all its might and rage against its bonds. The bonds flexed and threatened to give, but at last held firm. Blinded by frustration, the entity threw itself at the bars of its prison, determined to gain his freedom in escape or self-destruction. Even this effort proved fruitless, however, and the entity collapsed.

At this point, the entity would have eaten its own tail and given itself over to the bliss of forgetting, had not a sudden jolt against one of its prison bonds far to the north renewed its hope.

Chapter 18

A long moment after the explosion of energy, Mephi finally climbed to his feet blinking back white afterimages, and he shook his head to clear it. Stinking mud stuck to him, and the cobra head of his walking staff was chewing a mouthful of muck. Clinging to the staff, he surveyed the field quickly looking for survivors of…whatever had just happened. Ivar stood as proud and steady as a mountain several yards away, and Rain-Hunter was regaining her feet not far beyond him. The two of them looked at Mephi, then the three of them looked in the direction of the three Black Spiral Dancers.

Almost all of the Banes who had been within fifty yards of the Spirals were disintegrating to re-form elsewhere, and the ones that remained were scattered and confused. Two of the Spirals seemed unhurt, but the third was lying flat in his Homid form. The other two looked at one another as if they each expected the other to give a command. They seemed to have no better idea of what had happened than Mephi did. They had all been standing, there was an explosion, then… nothing.

As Mephi's thoughts raced, he noticed Ivar and Rain-Hunter looking back toward the Tisza River. Mephi looked there as well, and what he saw served only to confuse him further. From somewhere far to the south, a brilliant beam of light now lay stretched along the Penumbral earth to a point several hundred yards north—presumably as a result of whatever rite the Spirals had been conducting. Squinting his eyes, Mephi saw that the beam appeared to be made out of a dizzyingly complicated braid of Pattern Web strands. It disappeared into the distance, but it hummed with tension, as if whatever was on the southern end was pulling against it with all its might.

What Ivar and Rain-Hunter were looking at, Mephi realized, was the point at which the taut beam bisected the Penumbral reflection of the Tisza River. The toxic water crackled and spat as it flowed beneath the beam, and something at the very bottom of the riverbed began to stir. The water churned and sloshed, and a great striped and blotchy tail thrashed a spray of filthy water dozens of yards through the air. Then, as the thing's tail flopped back into the water, its head rose just shy of the beam that crossed its home.

The beast was unlike any Mephi had ever seen, and he felt he should look away lest he go mad with fear and fury. The thing was toxin and sludge and pollution given form, and it excreted H'rugglings and Wakshaani from dozens of puckered orifices that speckled its oily hide. This malformed thing, Mephi guessed, was what had become of the Tisza River's once proud and beautiful spirit when the river had been polluted and poisoned. Its maggot-white eyes rolled, and a wave front of prehensile vomit-water surged from its mouth. When that searching tendril found the braided beam of light, it wrapped around several times, pulling the disgusting beast forward. Driven by hunger or design or mad whim, the corrupted spirit began to gnaw on the beam of Pattern energy.

When Mephi was finally able to look away from the insane display, he turned to see the two remaining Black Spiral Dancers standing just as rapt as he had been. They stared transfixed at the erstwhile spirit of the Tisza River as it set to its task. What they did not see was a pair of long, hairy arms punching up through the ground only a few yards behind them. Hands with long talons dug frantically at the mud until Melinda emerged in her matted and disheveled Crinos form. It was not until Mephi saw her that he realized that the tunnel through which she and Conrad had been traveling had collapsed. Where the ground had once been mounded and relatively smooth, there lay only a shallow trench. And, although Melinda had somehow dug herself out, Conrad was nowhere to be seen.

Mephi looked one more time at Ivar and Rain-Hunter, but he found them both staring in horrified fascination at what was going on in the river. Neither of them realized that Melinda still lived or that the Roving Wind still had a mission to accomplish. Miraculously, Melinda still had a chance to find the pathstone as long as she had a distraction. The river creature's emergence had served briefly, but the Spirals' shock was wearing off just as Mephi's had.

Taking all these factors in at once with his life and those of the Roving Wind hanging in the balance and no time to spare for thought or planning, Mephi did the first thing that occurred to him. He jumped up into plain view of the Roving Wind and the Spirals, boiled up into his Crinos form, threw his head back and howled as loud as he could. Standing tall like legendary Anubis, with his staff planted at his side, Mephi bellowed a Cry of Elation that he hoped would not be his last.

"Look at me!" he howled to the Spirals. "I am Mephi Faster-Than-Death! Come to me when you're ready to die! I'll spit you both on this staff and serve you to the jackals of the desert! If you run, I will catch you! I am faster than Death, but Death comes with me!"

The howl shook the Spirals out of their stupor, and they looked at him as if he had lost his mind. Even Melinda froze behind them. The Spiral who was still in Homid form shifted into a haggard, white-streaked Crinos form. Before he or his partner could come running to answer Mephi's cry with their claws, however, another howl broke out from a few yards to Mephi's left.

"Cowards!" Ivar shouted, leaping up the ridge in one fluid motion and bursting into his Crinos form at the same time. "I am Ivar Hated-by-the-Wyrm! I have killed your brothers in your own hall! I have seen the worst your master can dream of, and I have lived to tell my story!" He waved his enormous war hammer over his head in one hand. "Your story ends on the head of this hammer!"

Before Ivar had finished, Rain-Hunter had already climbed up beside him in her Crinos form. When his words ended, hers began right away, in the traditional Garou tongue rather than simple wolfspeak. "I am she who hunted a man for three days through the pounding rain because he trespassed!" she howled. "It is not raining now! You are easy to find!"

The two Spirals exchanged a look then lifted their heads in unison. "We are Our Father's Vision! We come! Rally, children of our Father! We go to war!"

As the Spirals howled, the slouching, razor-clawed Scrags, the armored, four-legged Ooralath, and the tall, chittering Psychomachiae who remained alive began to converge. As one, they charged the three Garou who had dared to challenge them.

Howling their fury, the Garou ran forward to meet the coming rush.

Chapter 19

Melinda Light-Finder came out of the ground blowing mud out of her nostrils and spitting what she could out of her mouth. Wiping her eyes proved almost useless, since her hands and forearms were as coated as her eyelids. She expected to be gutted any second for not being able to see, hear or smell, and she welcomed the sensation. A quick and painful end would take her mind away from poor Conrad. When the Wyrm-tunnel had begun to collapse, her first instinct had been to change forms and begin digging before she was completely buried. Conrad, however, had panicked, and he'd started running the other way. The last sound Melinda had heard was Conrad's pitiful cry for help as the walls had collapsed. She had finally freed herself after what had felt like an hour digging, but she now had no idea where Conrad was. She couldn't go back to save him.

After a long moment of wishing for one of the three Black Spiral Dancers who were nearby to tear her throat out had passed, Melinda finally managed to get enough mud out of her eyes so that she could see. She was more than a little surprised to find herself relatively alone in roughly the position she wanted to end up and with a battle about to begin of which she had no part. Two Crinos Spirals and maybe a score of Banes were moving away from her toward Ivar, Rain-Hunter and Mephi, and the third Spiral appeared to be dead. That one lay face down in the mud in front of the blackened circle on the ground that had once been his vile altar. The wicked glyph scar that covered most of his back had begun to fade and flake like a scab.

She also noticed the braided beam of energy and recognized it at once as a single strand in an enormous binding pattern that connected the caern at Owl's Rest to the surrounding caerns.

She didn't remember any old stories about imprisoned spirits or beasts in this part of the world, but the evidence stretched out before her. And with that thing in the Penumbral Tisza gnawing mindlessly on the strand, what she'd heard or hadn't heard didn't matter a damn. She had to get word safely to another sept of what was happening here so that someone would have a chance to deal with it. That and she had to find and return with the pathstone as she'd been charged by Margrave Konietzko.

Putting first things first, she melted down into her Homid form and searched the blasted altar site for the lost pathstone. She found the crude and ugly ritual dagger that the Spiral had used sticking out of the mud point-down, and she used it to dig. She drove the knife down right in the center of where the Spiral's altar had been, and immediately came up with a lump in the shape of a flat pearl. She wiped the lump as clean as she could with her dirty thumb. When she did, she saw the etched paw print of a wolf on a white stone, and she knew that she had indeed found what she and her pack had come so far to find. She dropped the stone into her pouch, sealed the pouch tight and began to rise.

Still partially deafened by the mud in her ears, she did not hear the previously insensate form behind her begin to stir. She did not hear the Spiral rise from the ground, wipe mud from his eyes and grow into his shaggy Crinos form. She did not hear the beast's slow steps coming toward her through the greedy mud. Only when she stood and turned around did she realize that her death was looming over her.

Without preamble or emotion, the Spiral put all five talons on his left hand through Melinda's abdomen and held them there. His eyes were vacuous white orbs, completely devoid of intelligence. Despite the grievous wound he had dealt Melinda, he hardly seemed to know she was there.

"What's happened?" he whined, looking in Melinda's direction, but not directly at her. "Where is my Father? Can you help me?"

Tears welled in Melinda's eyes, and she spit out a mouthful of bile and blood. She could see the glyph scars on the Spiral's shoulders glowing and shifting as if a Balefire burned inside his skin, and she felt every millimeter of his claws as they ate her alive from the inside out. She couldn't wrench herself free.

"Help me!" the Spiral whined, flexing his hand. "I am lost."

As he spoke, Melinda could feel the unwholesome radiance that burned in his scars traveling down the length of his arm and into her. She grabbed his shoulder and screamed as burning black lines began to intertwine and draw a hideous Wyrm glyph on her wounded and blistering skin. Through a wave of pain like none other she had ever experienced, Melinda remembered the Black Spiral's dagger which still dangled from her fingertips. She made a weak fist and tried to lift her arm.

"Please," the Spiral begged, putting his dirty face very near hers. "I don't know where I am."

Melinda gagged up another mouthful of blackened blood and said, "You'll be...home...very soon." The Spiral tilted his head slightly, and Melinda made a fist around the handle of his dagger. With a wrenching, defiant scream, she slammed it into his eye up to the hilt. With a howl of agony and fury, he staggered backward and let her fall to her knees in the mud.

Chapter 20

Mephi and Ivar heard Melinda's scream at the same time, as did the two Black Spiral Dancers who loped behind the first ranks of Banes. The Spirals turned just in time to see Melinda stab their newly risen comrade in the eye and to hear him yelp a piteous Call for Succor. As Melinda fell away from the Spiral, Mephi and Ivar saw the red, ropy mass fall from the Spiral's hand. The Spirals halted immediately and began to charge back up the hill toward their injured packmate. Mephi and Ivar made eye contact only briefly, but that quick glance transmitted their intent to each other clearly enough. They both looked to Rain-Hunter, who was in the process of tearing a leg off an Ooralath that had gotten too close. The Red Talon nodded at them, slinging sinew and blood in a tight arc.

With a vicious sideswipe, Ivar crushed the skull of the first Ooralath to reach him and sent the beast crashing into its next nearest compatriot. With the ball of his staff, Mephi swept the legs out from under the loping Scrag that came at him, then vaulted over the three Ooralath that were closing in on him behind the Scrag by planting his staff in the back of the Scrag's neck and pushing off. As the Scrag's neck snapped under the sudden pressure, Mephi invoked a Gift taught him by a jackrabbit-spirit. Rather than simply leaping over the approaching Ooralath, he sailed over them and cleared several dozen yards of the field before he hit the ground running. All but surrounded by another pack of Ooralath, Rain-Hunter headed into the thick of the wall of flesh that blocked her way.

Having made significantly more progress already, Ivar closed in. He ran at the two retreating Spirals as fast as he could, all but ignoring the Banes that tried to block his way. His war hammer cleared the larger obstacles in his path where a stiff-arm or a backhand claw rake would not suffice. Scrag claws and Psychomachia teeth tore away strips of his flesh in passing, but he paid those minor wounds no mind. His eyes were fixed on Melinda and the Black Spiral Dancers.

Mephi too was focused, for the Spiral that Melinda had wounded was coming shakily toward her again. Melinda fell onto her back and was trying to crawl away, but her wounds made a quick escape impossible. The Spiral looming over her tried to jerk the dagger from its eye socket. With its right hand engaged thus, it reached for Melinda again with its bloody left hand.

Rain-Hunter broke free of the first three Ooralath that blocked her way, and barreled into a pair of approaching Scrags. She knocked the right arm off the one on her right, and her fangs dug into the left knee of the other, but her foot slipped in the treacherous muck. She fell behind, surrounded.

Thinking a quick prayer to Gaia, Mephi called on the Gift that a sly cheetah-spirit had taught him and began to run at the speed of thought. Time seemed to blur around him, and he bolted past a pack of charging Ooralath before they could tell that he was changing directions. He arrowed for Melinda, praying that he could be fast enough to save her.

At the same time, Ivar put on a burst of speed born of his rage, and he overtook the two Spirals who were still slogging through the muck side-by-side trying to answer their packmate's Call for Succor. However, rather than attacking either one of them, he shouldered them both to the ground and charged between them. His baleful gaze was leveled at the Black Spiral Dancer whose hand was raised to finish off Melinda Light-Finder.

Rain-Hunter disemboweled the Scrag on her left, but the one on her right pinned her to the ground with a long claw. The Ooralath she had eluded moments before closed in on her from behind.

Mephi and Ivar arrived at the same spot on the battlefield with only a split-second's margin between them. Throwing a short plume of mud behind him because of how fast he was going, Mephi crouched low and scooped Melinda up in a sliding dive that became a sliding tackle that then became an ungainly tumble of arms and legs that carried the pair of them out of harm's way. As they rolled, Ivar leaped forward and brought his war hammer down as hard as he could on the wounded Spiral's head. The ritual dagger in his eye burst through the back of the Spiral's skull and stuck in the ground like an arrow. The Spiral's body melted into a ruined Homid shell and collapsed on top of the knife. Ivar brought the war hammer down on the misshapen skull once more for good measure. With blood and chips of bone stuck to his chin and chest, he turned to see where Mephi and Melinda had ended up. Still in Crinos form, Mephi got to his feet with Melinda and his walking staff in his arms.

"Alive?" Ivar growled. His eyes found the two remaining Spirals where they were just coming up out of the mud. He also looked beyond them at where his fallen packmate had been.

With a pained expression, Mephi shrugged. "I can't tell. Where's Rain-Hunter?"

Without taking his eyes off the pair of Spirals, Ivar shook his head. "Overrun. Too many, too fast."

Near the ridge where Ivar had been, Mephi saw a knot of at least three Scrags and an entire pack of Ooralath gathered as if they were a murder of starved crows. One of the Ooralath fell backward out of the cluster and collapsed, but then the rest dove in. Closer up in the field, though, the two Spirals and the remaining Banes began to close in with slow ease. All Mephi or Ivar could do for Rain-Hunter now was mourn. And avenge.

"What now?"

"Failure," Ivar said, setting his shoulders in resignation. "We make our stand here."

Gauging the forces that were arrayed against them, Mephi could only agree. But as he moved to lay Melinda's body on the ground and join Ivar, Melinda clutched the golden band around his bicep and forced her eyes open.

"I have it," she whispered. "The stone."

"Set's teeth," Mephi gasped. He looked up and said, "Ivar, she's alive. She's got the pathstone."

Ivar spared Mephi and Melinda a hopeful glance, then sighed. He turned back to face the advancing rank of Wyrmspawn and said over his shoulder, "Go then, before they close you in. Take her home."

"You can make it, too," Mephi said. "This doesn't—"

"I stay," Ivar growled. "While I breathe, they will not pursue you. Go!"

Mephi clamped his teeth around another protest and turned away with Melinda in his arms. He knew better than to push a hopeless subject. "You won't be forgotten," he murmured. With that, he called on the cheetah's Gift once again and broke for a gap between a Psychomachia and a Scrag that approached from the rear.

When they were gone, Ivar invoked the terrible visage of Fenris and let out a vicious snarl just as the wolf-spirits of his homeland had taught him. The snarl promised visceral agony and a slow death to everyone in reach. The two Spirals paused in their approach momentarily, cowed by the ferocity in the lone warrior's bearing, but their superior number and the presence of their Father's touch in this ugly place bolstered their courage. With a singular howl to match Ivar's defiant snarl, they charged him, leading a phalanx of Banes.

Chapter 21

The moon path that led Mephi away from the Tisza Hellhole was a narrow and treacherous one that was broken and partially obscured by cloud cover, but Mephi did not slow down as he traveled on it. Carrying Melinda like a broken doll, he passed Lunes as if they were standing still, and fled deeper into the Umbra with biting, slavering Ooralath hot on his heels. In no time, dense mists swirled into place on either side of the path, and the foulness of the Hellhole fell mercifully behind.

Some of the following Ooralath stumbled from the winding path and disappeared in the mists—perhaps snapped up by the dire creatures that lurked just out of sight. Others were intercepted by the Lunes that tended the path. Still excitable and riled by the recent passing of the full moon, the Lunes set upon these trespassers with insane zeal. The only one that got within reach got Mephi's d'siah blade through its eye before it stumbled off the path bellowing in pain.

Mephi's subconscious registered this information, but he ignored it. He ran carelessly, clutching Melinda to him and remaining on the moon path more by old habit and luck than concerted effort. His long strides carried him within mere miles of the Scar—a bizarre industrial hell of Pattern Webs, Balefire smoke and grinding metal gears. His long strides carried him within earshot of desolate and blood-soaked Battleground— where the crunch of bone clubs mingled with the echo of cannon-fire. His long strides even carried him almost to the perimeter security of the CyberRealm—where information was the coin of the realm and the dreams of the Machine Incarna hummed in the air like electrical currents. But Mephi avoided each of these places, knowing that he and Melinda might never return if they sought solace within.

He ran between long strands of Pattern Webs, over hills made of shadow and through smoky veils of spirit gossamer that disappeared like the music of a waking dream. He climbed a stairway made from the backs of Pattern Spiders and splashed through a stream of ice-cold noise. The land around him blurred and folded along multiple axes, then froze in geometric perfection for a sublime instant with every step. He plunged ahead, losing his pursuers one by one, until he was hopelessly lost in the trackless realm of dream and spirit and creation that was the Umbra. Only the path remained constant.

Yet Mephi could not run forever. Finally, even his prodigious stamina wore away, and he staggered. Exhaustion forced him to his knees, and he thumped to the ground at a strange junction in the path that seemed to be made entirely of corners. He set Melinda down gently on her back, then slumped next to her on his hands and knees trying to catch his breath. He had run farther and faster in his life, but never while carrying a burden so important. His huffs and puffs swirled the mists alongside the path.

When he no longer felt ready to pass out, he melted down into his Homid form and sat up on his heels. He looked at Melinda to find her trying to focus on him through fluttering eyelids.

"Lin," he said with a sinking stomach. "Light-Finder. Can you hear me?"

"Mephi," Melinda said in a thread-thin whisper. "I got it. I did good, didn't I?"

Mephi opened her bag and found the Owl's Rest pathstone inside, stuck by blood and mud to a poorly folded topographical map. "Yeah," he said softly. "You did good, Light-Finder."

Melinda nodded weakly, then grimaced and coughed up a black dribble. "Something's wrong," she gurgled, swallowing down half of what had come up. "I can't heal."

Mephi lifted the tail of Melinda's torn shirt and saw just what the Black Spiral Dancer had done to her. Melinda cried out through gritted teeth as the fabric clung to the sticky wound and only came free reluctantly. Five ragged holes had laid waste to her stomach, and their edges were a gangrenous blue-black. An unnatural black scar wove around and throughout the grave wound and glistened like a leper's gums.

"Bad."

Mephi nodded, not looking Melinda in the eyes. "Really bad."

"Then here," Melinda said, pushing her bag toward him along the ground. "Take the stone. Keep moving."

"Don't say that," Mephi growled desperately, planting his fist on top of the bag. "You carry it. I'll carry you."

"No," Melinda said. She lifted her head and forced her eyes open wide. "You can't carry me any more."

Despite his exhaustion, Mephi closed his eyes and shook his head.

Melinda grabbed one of his bracelets and said, "Don't argue. You won't be safe here very long once the moon goes down. You'll be stuck. You've got to go."

"No, Lin. I'm not leav—"

"People—" Melinda began before another wet, choking cough cut her off. "People are counting on this pathstone. People are counting on you."

"I need to get you to safety."

"We'll both die," Melinda said. "If those Banes don't find us, others will. Or worse things from deeper out. Don't be stupid."

"I've been stupid already," Mephi said, brushing Melinda's hair out of her face with one hand and clawing the ground in impotent frustration with the other. "Melinda, what I told you before about why I left you was a lie."

"Mephi…"

"I didn't leave because I was afraid you were too dependent on me, Lin," Mephi continued over Melinda's increasingly weak protests. "I left because I depended on you too much. I knew I'd lose it if I stayed and something happened to you. I was right, Lin."

"I don't believe you," Melinda whined. "Mephi, go."

Mephi clamped his eyes shut and shook his head. "No, Light-Finder. I can't. But don't worry. I'll be here when you wake. I'll get you through this. For now, just rest. Close your eyes and dream of home."

Careless of what might befall the two of them, Mephi Faster-Than-Death lowered himself to the ground beside Melinda Light-Finder and let exhaustion take him. Just before he surrendered consciousness, he heard Melinda whine one last time, and he felt her put her arm around him.

Chapter 22

Mephi closed his eyes and dreamed himself into a hell of his own making that he had visited many times in the last ten years. He stood alone on a long, empty stretch of asphalt somewhere out in the middle of New Mexico. The gibbous moon hung almost near enough to touch, and a million stars winked to each other in the sky. A dozen miles behind him was the Painted Coyote caern and Melinda, whom the locals had taken to calling Light-Finder because she always seemed to wake up with her nose pointing toward the rising sun, no matter what position she was in when she went to bed.

Many nights since he'd been in this place physically, Mephi had dreamed himself back here to relive the same fateful moment and make the same painful decision time and again. He wasn't that far away from where he'd left Melinda snoring. If he turned around now, he could still make it back to her side before dawn. In the morning, he could join her in her (and his) first Rite of the Totem, which would join them together as a pack. If he went back now, he and Light-Finder could leave the caern together and carry on as they had been for so long already. Yet in all the dreams he'd had up until now, Mephi had just sighed and kept on walking, convinced that he was doing the right thing for both of them.

Now, however, the dream was different. His dream self was the same age and had the same demeanor as his waking self. His clothes were filthy with detritus from the Tisza Hellhole, and his entire right side stung from where some Bane had apparently taken off a piece of him when he'd gotten too close. His walking staff was coated with grime, and Melinda's travel bag (which now hung from his shoulder) was smeared with filth and blood. He knew without looking that the pathstone from the caern at Owl's Rest was still inside. It pulled the bag down with the weight of four headstones.

"Well, just what the hell is this?" Mephi said, turning to face the cobra atop his staff.

"This is your home," a voice said behind him. He turned to see a large, snow-white owl perched on a rock beside the road. The owl looked at him with ancient, sagacious eyes. Every star in the night sky reflected in those eyes. "Your memory."

"How did I get here?" Mephi asked the owl. "What am I doing here?"

"You had a dream," the owl said. "A powerful dream that brought you here from where you were."

Mephi realized what the owl was saying, and he didn't like the sound of it. Somehow, he'd been moved from the moon path he remembered into the Dream Zone, which touched every layer of the Umbra. "I don't want to be here," he snarled.

"Of course you do," the owl said, "or you wouldn't be here. You're a more accomplished traveler than you think."

Mephi grumbled at the compliment then said, "Where's Melinda? Light-Finder. Where is she?"

The owl turned its head slowly in the direction of the Painted Coyote caern and said, "That way. Dying. Probably dead already."

Mephi looked back down the road and saw that that path disappeared into a bank of swirling mist. He took a determined step in that direction.

"You have something she gave you," the owl said. Mephi stopped.

"Yeah, and I'm giving it back to her," Mephi said, staring down the road.

"That isn't why she gave it to you," the owl said. "She wanted you to pass it on to someone. Someone in that direction." The owl looked down the road the opposite way, and Mephi could just see the shimmering mouth of a moon bridge that led to the Sept of the Night Sky.

"No. I'm going back."

"It isn't your way to end a journey where it began," the owl chided him. "You wouldn't have found this place if it were."

"What do you know about it?" Mephi snapped, turning back to face the owl.

"I know it's your way to remember rather than revisit," the owl said.

"I'll remember as much as I want in the time I have left with Light-Finder," Mephi said. He took a half-step back toward the Painted Coyote caern.

"And when you have no more time," the owl said, "who will remember you? Who will remember Melinda Light-Finder and Ivar Hated-by-the-Wyrm and Conrad Stone-Stepper and Rain-Hunter when you die in Light-Finder's arms? Will you take their memory with you when you throw your life away?"

Mephi knew that the owl was right. He drove his staff downward hard enough to crack the dream-woven asphalt. "Damn it! God damn it! I just found her! Why do I have to leave her again? Why?"

"Because you must remember her," the owl said. "You must remember them all. Your destiny is no light one, Mephi Faster-Than-Death. When the Last Battle comes and the Serpent rises from its slumber, you must remember all the fallen heroes whose stories you've ever heard. To fail in this—to forget even one—is to take the Wyrm into your body and destroy the world yourself."

Mephi ground his teeth and looked again toward the Painted Coyote caern. "Can't I even say good-bye? I'd like to at least do that right this time."

"You will," the owl said. "Every day from now until the last. But not there. That way lies the end of days. Only in going forward is the future always ahead of you."

Mephi stood still, doing nothing but looking back toward where Melinda lay dying. If he ran one last time, he could make it to her before she died. He was faster than Death; he could arrive at her side and usher her into the next world with the knowledge that he had not abandoned her. He would only be abandoning himself. He thought about it for a long time then finally turned once again to regard the cobra head atop his walking staff. Melinda might be able to die in peace if she saw it in his hands one last time. She'd realize why he'd kept it for all those years even though he'd abandoned her. She'd know that he'd never forgotten about her.

"But what good would it do?" he asked the snake. "None I know of. None at all. It's just wishful thinking."

The snake didn't answer, and when Mephi looked at the rock where the owl had been perched, the spirit was no longer there. Mephi turned down the road toward the Sept of the Night Sky. If he hurried, he could drop off the pathstone and take another moon bridge back to the Sept of the Anvil-Klaiven the same night. If he hurried, he might still have time to warn Mari Cabrah and Brand Garmson before they set off south toward Serbia that a new kind of trouble was probably waiting for them there. If he hurried, he could still make it. So, alone with only his memories, Mephi started running toward the Sept of the Night Sky without looking back.

Epilogue

Gashwrack stood alone in the Penumbral morass alongside the Tisza River. His left shoulder still refused to budge where the bastard Get's cursed hammer had knocked him flat. Sitting up had blinded him with beautiful explosions of colorful pain, and standing had almost driven him into a frenzy of ecstatic agony. Balancing uneasily now and staring out over the field told him that all the pain was worthwhile and temporary. Splinterbone lay dead with his head knocked almost all the way around backward, but the bastard Get lay dead on top of him, surrounded by the half-dozen Banes he'd taken with him even in his death throes. The Get lay on his face in Homid form with his back still torn open and lightly steaming from the double claw slash Gashwrack had given him. His body lay trampled on the ground, and his mighty, rune-carved hammer was stuck headfirst in the mud. That the Get had managed to transfix a clawing, screaming Scrag on the hammer's protruding haft before he'd finally fallen only made Gashwrack snicker.

What filled Gashwrack with true elation, however, was the greater state of the battlefield. The new and beautiful spirit of the Tisza River had moved on downstream toward the Danube, for its work here was done at last. Where once a bright strand of braided chains had stretched across the river toward the caern that had once been Gashwrack's home, now only broken, scattered links remained. Those links cooled and steamed where they'd fallen, and as they disintegrated, new Banes arose from the filthy ground.

Gashwrack couldn't remember ever having seen such Banes before, but then again, it wasn't the duty of his auspice to keep up with such things. What's more, it didn't matter what kind of Banes they were. All that mattered was that the chains from which their substance derived had been broken in the Father's name. Whatever it was that those chains had bound—whatever the "Forgotten Son," as Shrike's Thorn had called it, was—was now a step closer to being free than it had been since time out of mind.

Gashwrack rejoiced and headed for the Wyrm tunnel that would take him home. He had good news to tell Arastha and all the denizens of his Hive. And woe be unto any fools who would go south toward where the Forgotten Son's prison was no doubt beginning to unravel.

BLACK FURIES

Chapter 1

L una's glow cascaded over Mari like the massaging waters of a welcome shower, cleansing her, invigorating her. Luna Crescent. The Theurge's moon. Through Luna's eyes, just over her shoulder, Mari watched herself: hair plastered to the side of her face, beads of perspiration speckling taut muscles, sweat-stained T-shirt, hands and feet taped, striking at the bag that hung with the weight of the world, punching, kicking, punching, kicking. She paused, silencing the sharp report of her blows, and strained to hear a peculiar sound, gradually rising.

As she listened, the light changed, and Mari peered again through her own eyes. She turned, slowly—so slowly; slowly as only possible in a dream, a vision from beyond; her body sluggishly responding to her will, moving as if the air were water, heavy and suffocating—to gaze upon Luna. The Sister's face was red, and her light shone upon Mari like a sheen of blood. The Red Star. Where was it? Mari could feel its malevolent presence, but the glaring beacon was hidden from her.

Screams. The sound that had caught her attention was more clear now—or was it? The bleating of humans, or the howls of suffering wolves? Every time Mari thought she was sure, the tenor shifted, becoming something different, like an endlessly swirling wind, turning back upon itself, ever changing.

Whatever the source of the noise, the anguish given voice tugged at Mari's insides, roiled her gut to the point that she could not idly listen. She turned back to the punching bag to vent her welling rage, sparked by uncertainty, helplessness—except the bag was gone. And where before her every movement had fought an ocean of inertia, now her fist carried her like mighty Mjölnir, costing her balance. Falling. As dark wings blotted out the red glow of defiled Luna, Mari was falling, falling…falling until she woke.

"I would have words with you, woman!" called the Get warrior across the Aeld Baile of the Sept of the Anvil-Klaiven. His heavily accented English careened off the snow and ice of this sea-side caern and cut a deep, dissonant swath through the ever-present whistling of the wind.

Mari kept walking. She pulled together the collar of her coat against the cold. Irritated by the Get's bombastic pronouncement, she wondered at what pig-tailed little Kinfolk he was hollering, but resolved not to get involved. This was the Get's caern. If some Fenrir delinquent on steroids wanted to verbally abuse an unenlightened girl who didn't have the sense to go find a tribe that would treat her decently, then…well… Mari gnashed her teeth. She'd long since learned that there were too many wrongs in the world for her to be able to right all of them. She knew that in her head, but her heart still had trouble with it.

"Let him try talking to me that way," she muttered under her breath, pressing onward. Not until she heard the heavy, snow-crunching footsteps drawing closer did she begin to suspect that the Get was talking to her.

"Woman! Don't walk away from me."

She knew he was going to grab her shoulder. She just knew it, and only that expectation allowed her to clamp down her rage and negate her trained response: to whirl in the direction he spun her, using his own action against him; elbow to throat; crushed windpipe; roundhouse kick to the head; assailant down. When he did grab her shoulder, she merely slapped away his hand and turned to face him.

"Woman, I would have—!"

"Keep your hands off me."

Mars-Rising glared down at her. Even in his man-form, he was at least a foot taller than Mari, and he seemed not to have imagined that she would do anything other than bow her head before his tirade. He was practically bare-chested, a time-worn fur draped from his shoulders. Running downward at an angle across his bulging pectorals and rippled abdomen was an ugly green-black burn scar. Mars-Rising wore the mark as a badge of honor, a memento of his pack's recent tangle with a brash trio of Black Spiral Dancers. To Mari's way of thinking, the scar meant he was either not fast enough or not smart enough to get out of the way.

"Don't interrupt me, woman," he snarled.

Mari forced herself to take a deep breath. Without shifting her eyes from him, she could feel the attention of other Garou around the Aeld Baile drawn to his bluster, but she tried to rein in her temper. No point in letting this brute's boorishness escalate into an intertribal incident. Besides, she was going to have to work with this jerk. "You got something to say, then say it. And, yes, I am a woman, as you have so observantly noticed, but my name is Mari. I suggest that you—"

"I hear tell, woman, that you think to challenge the Warder for leadership of our mission." Mars-Rising chewed the words like gristle.

"You hear wrong, buddy. I'm not—"

"We have no need of you, woman. You will endanger the pack. Providing for your safety will be a distraction."

"My safety?" Mari felt her restraint beginning to crumble. "Look, you don't have to worry about—"

"We are the IceWind Pack," Mars-Rising insisted, edging closer. "There is not Wyrm-beast spawned that can stand against us."

Mari breathed deeply again. She let the insults roll off her back, trying to hold her pride, as well as her rage, in check. Albrecht hadn't been overjoyed about her coming to this moot in the first place; he didn't have great confidence in her skills of diplomacy. An unfortunate side effect of belonging to King Jonas Albrecht's pack was that Mari became a de facto ambassador every time she stepped beyond the boundary of his New England protectorate. Mindful of, if aggravated by, that constraint, she decided that reasoning with the hulking Fenrir was worth a bit more patience. "How many Theurges you got in

your IceWind Pack?" she asked, fighting a losing battle to keep
her voice calm. "Any? Or is it full-moon fever?"

Mars-Rising, whose face had been jutted out toward Mari,
now stood to his full height. He seemed affronted that she would
dare talk back to him. "We do not fear the spirits," he said.

Her patience extending only so far, Mari jabbed a finger at
his chest. "You wouldn't know a spirit if it bit you on the ass."

Mars-Rising grabbed her wrist. "We are the IceWind Pack,"
he said, as if repetition and increased volume would prove his
point. "There is not Wyrm-beast spawned that can stand against
us. And if you think this little hand can best Brand Garmson..."
Mars-Rising squeezed Mari's wrist.

She had been fine up to that point, resigned to an argument
with this lout. Even when he grabbed her wrist, she'd held
herself back. She had poked him, after all; she had initiated the
physical contact. All he did was respond in kind. But Mari's mind
was always racing ahead, taking in the details of the situation,
formulating plans of action to get her out of a tight spot. She
noted the strength of Mars-Rising's grip, the set of his feet, his
center of gravity. Nine times out of ten, if it came to violence, a
palm-heel to the nose or a kick to the groin would do the trick.
Mari's intuition—along with Mars-Rising's considerable heft—
told her that this was not one of those nine times. The Get was
simply too massive, too strong and battle-tested. He could take
a broken nose, a shot to the 'nads, or lose his feet without ever
loosening his grip. He would just take her down with him, and
in a wrestling match, his brawn would be tough to overcome.

All that had run through Mari's mind before Mars-Rising
squeezed her wrist, before hot-blooded rage got the best of her.
So much for patience and reason.

While Mars-Rising was still listening to himself talk, Mari
stepped to her left and swept with her right leg, taking his right
leg out from under him. It was a close thing. She hit him as hard
as she could and, solid as he was, he barely went down. But fall
he did, like a hundred-year-old fir tree crashing to the ground.
As Mari had suspected, even surprised he didn't let go of her
wrist. But that was okay.

She launched herself with him, in the direction of his falling momentum, so he didn't yank her arm out of its socket. Instead, she somersaulted and rolled as he struck the ground. He hit hard with an audible ufff, the wind knocked out of him. Mari was back on her feet, twisting Mars-Rising's arm above his head, and landing a kick against his wrist. As the bone snapped with the sound of an ice flow breaking free of a glacier, he did let go of her.

To his credit, the Get Ahroun bounced to his feet more quickly than Mari would have guessed he could, but she was already several feet away, crouched and ready for any attack he might launch. She was ready, too, to match him Crinos for Crinos, should he give license to rage and begin to shift. It was a touchy thing. Mari didn't want to take the fight that route, but neither was she about to back down in the face of this overgrown collection of muscle and testosterone.

Mars-Rising, though he held his arm to his body, didn't appear hindered overly much by his broken wrist. Rage smoldered in his eyes. Mari could see that one snide comment was all it would take to push him over the edge into full battle frenzy—a sound strategy in some cases, but not what she wanted here. Maintaining her defensive posture, she held her tongue. Mars-Rising held his position as well and his glare, still angry, was more wary now. He didn't seem inclined to go berserk on her. The shock of being taken down by a woman half his weight had taken the bluster right out of him.

I should have crushed his knee instead of sweeping him, Mari thought. By trying not to hurt him more than necessary, she might have extended the fight—a disadvantage for her. Mars-Rising regarded her with a rewarding amount of contempt, but he wasn't rushing to attack. He learns, she thought. Who woulda thunk?

For a long, tense moment, they matched gazes, neither one flinching, neither backing down.

"And what is this?" came another gruff, hearty voice from the crowd of onlookers that was beginning to assemble.

"Mars-Rising seems to have taken a fancy to one of the guests," said another.

Mari recognized the voices—packmates of her opponent.

That could turn into a problem, and fast. They wouldn't join in the fight—that would be dishonorable, especially against a lone female—but they might egg on Mars-Rising, encouraging his rage and natural bloodlust. Or they might—

"Now we know why Mars is always Rising," said the first. "He's constantly getting up after being knocked on his ass!" Great guffaws and deep belly laughs followed from many of the spectators.

But not from Mars-Rising. His ears pricked up—quite a neat trick for a Homid. The fair skin of his cheeks, already red from the cold wind, reddened further.

"Are you all right?" the second packmate asked him through a gap-toothed grin. "It's your turn to stand guard...at the nursery." The renewed laughter did nothing to improve Mars-Rising's mood. An angry growl rose from deep in his throat.

Mari flinched as the Get, broken wrist and all, sprang to the attack. But the packmates were his target, and all three went down in a heap of curses and flailing limbs. Within seconds, they had slipped into Crinos—over a ton of snarling and thrashing fur, muscle, claws, and teeth. The form shift came to them more easily than breathing. Or thinking, Mari muttered to herself.

She was quickly forgotten as the assembled crowd cheered and jeered the new trio of combatants. Shouted odds were proffered and accepted. The circle tightened around the melee. Mari slipped beyond the ring of onlookers, gripped the collar of her coat again against the wind, and continued on her way.

Chapter 2

As she entered the low, three-walled structure known to the Get as the Icehouse, Mari made the mistake of letting her hand brush against the frosted black metal of the old forge. The silent monstrosity, its once legendary blistering fire having died, now radiated cold. Not until Mari pulled her hand away and a patch of flesh the size of a quarter stayed behind did she realize that her skin had frozen to the forge. She cursed under her breath. Leave it to the Fenrir to guard a caern in such a barren, inhospitable—some would say uninhabitable—locale. Even the Scandinavian humans had shunned this place, with its desolate ice packs and bald hillocks unceasingly swept by frigid arctic seawinds. But the Get thrived here.

This was about as far from New York as Mari could go—not in miles, but in spirit. In the city she called home—and which also some would call inhospitable and uninhabitable—the Weaver held sway while the insidious Wyrm determinedly tried to core the Big Apple from within. Just enough of the Wyld remained to keep the whole mess from collapsing in on itself. Just barely. There, if Mari ventured into the Penumbra, that shimmering reflection of the mundane world was thick with Pattern webs, the most noticeable exceptions being the not uncommon areas where Wyrm-spirits had destroyed or reworked the strands to their own malignant designs.

Here, on the other hand, Mari would be hard-pressed, if she stepped sideways and scoured the Penumbra, to find the first sign of Weaver or Wyrm. This was generally considered a testament to the fidelity and zeal of the Get, though Mari, in times of aggravation at their wrong-headed air of superiority, or at having herself ripped a raw patch on her hand, wondered if safeguarding a patch of ice that no one else wanted was really that difficult.

Edging past the forge, she found the open stairway to the cellar. Her eyes took a few moments to adjust to the shift from the near-blinding ice-glare of the surface to the dim recesses beneath. Left unprotected after, no doubt, some ale-muddled Fenrir had ripped the cellar door from its hinges, the steps down were coated with a thin sheen of frost, so Mari stepped carefully. The rich scent of cured meats was strong, as was the sharper odor of ale and spirits. The cellar floor proved no less slippery than the steps; in fact, it was a solid sheet of ice. So too were the walls and ceiling, from which hung sides of beef and venison. The wind, seeming angry that Mari had escaped its most direct buffets, whistled and moaned about the doorway in the ceiling, but could muster no more than a chilling draft down here.

From one of the dark back corners, a shape stepped forward from the deepest shadows of stacked wooden barrels. "What in the Nine Hells were you thinking?" asked the woman, who stood several inches shorter than Mari. Stepping more fully into the scant light cast through the doorway, the woman looked as if she'd been plucked from the midst of a raging tempest. Her eyes were hard, desperate, almost panic-stricken. The wind had turned her hair into a tangled mess of rat's nests and dramatically straying strands. Then again, every day, wind or no wind, was a bad hair day for Kelonoke Wildhair.

"Nice to see you too," Mari said. "Thanks for not sneaking up on me—not trying to sneak up on me—this time. Sorry I'm late. I had an unexpected…um, discussion with—"

"I wanted you to come with me back to Greece," Kelonoke insisted, still overwrought and refusing to be drawn into friendly banter. "How could you volunteer to go investigate in the Balkans with Brand Garmson?"

"Same neighborhood."

"No," said Kelonoke. "There's nothing the same about them. Nothing. They're worlds apart."

Mari couldn't understand why her friend was so agitated. On the final night of the concolation, the elders had decided that three packs should investigate happenings of dire portent in the Balkans: one to infiltrate a fallen caern in Hungary; a second to investigate the disappearance of earlier packs sent into Serbia; and a third...well, Mari wasn't completely clear on the role of the third pack, but Antonine Teardrop had been fairly insistent that it was necessary, and she had sought help from the old Galliard enough in the past not to doubt him now. But none of that explained Kelonoke's ire. Somebody had to go on these missions.

"Look," Mari said, more seriously, "if it's as bad as what you've told me, then I want to help do something about it. What doesn't make sense about that?"

"It is as bad as I've said, Mari. No, it's worse. And we've sent packs into Serbia. Most of them haven't come back. You know Diana Howl-Strong. She and her pack have gone missing. And too many others."

"But you wanted me to help!"

"We're not talking about traipsing around New York!" Kelonoke fumed. "This has gotten so bad, it's not just a local thing anymore."

Mari ground her teeth together. She was growing angry, but she couldn't figure out why they were arguing. "I believe you! Like I said, I want to do something—"

"I wanted you to help convince others how bad it's gotten, not run off and..."

"And what?" Mari demanded.

Kelonoke opened her mouth but stopped; she held back whatever she was about to say. "It's not what I meant," Kelonoke said finally. "You shouldn't go with them."

Kelonoke was so emphatic, Mari didn't know what to say, so instead of responding she made a show of casually surveying the contents of the cellar. The Garou gathered for the recent concolation must have consumed an enormous amount of provisions: Many of the gleaming meat hooks were vacant, and a bit of tapping on random casks found more empty than full. "You thirsty?" Mari asked, sensing that her friend had vented a bit of her tension and decompressed somewhat. "That why you wanted to meet here?"

"No," Kelonoke said softly. She suddenly seemed tired, defeated. The fire was gone from her voice and eyes. "It seemed a good bet that it wouldn't be in use. Most of the guests of the caern have departed, and the fosterling is recuperating under the care of the jarl in Spearsreach."

"The fosterling," Mari said. "From Dawntreader's sept. What's his name?"

"Cries Havoc."

"Cries Havoc." Mari pondered that for a moment. "I wonder if he realizes how lucky he is that Karin Jarlsdottir didn't bust his head wide open."

Kelonoke nodded, but clearly she was still distracted, still struggling with whatever had led her to be angry with Mari just a minute before. "Yes," Kelonoke agreed. "Sometimes the blood price and the blow are construed to be symbolic. Cries Havoc has been adopted by the Get, his life paying the debt for the death of Arne Brandson, known as Wyrmbane."

"And sometimes..."

"And sometimes," Kelonoke continued, "the blood price is taken quite literally."

"Some of the Get are grumbling that Cries Havoc surviving the blow proves that Jarlsdottir isn't Garou enough to wield the hammer of the Lawgiver," Mari said. The conversation seemed to be calming Kelonoke, which was good, because Mari had some questions of her own.

"Jarlsdottir is a woman, and so the Fenrir grumble whenever they can," Kelonoke scoffed. "You know how she came to lead the sept?" Mari shook her head. "When her father, the Old Jarl, was ambushed and killed by Black Spiral Dancers," Kelonoke explained, "there was no lack of claimants to succeed him. The elders decided that whosoever could move the Anvil of Thor to the Old Jarl's grave on the Hill of Lamentations would be fit to lead the sept."

"Anvil of Thor?" Mari asked. She had heard the name before, probably during one of the countless marathons of storytelling during the concolation, but she couldn't remember any details.

"For years and years, it was the fire at the heart of the forge above our heads," said Kelonoke. "The Fenrir Galliards say it fell from the sky, a blazing gift from Sister Luna—"

"From the... You mean a meteorite." Mari said.

Kelonoke nodded. "It was larger than three men and full of celestial fire. The sept formed around it. The Forge Masters and Spirit Crafters saw to it that the Anvil never grew cold. Generation after generation, mighty weapons were forged here, and always the fire burned hot and true...until the death of the Old Jarl. The Anvil's fire died with him. The forge produced no longer. And so the elders set the task for the succession: that the Anvil should join the Old Jarl on the Hill.

"Ahroun after Ahroun tried to move the Anvil. One after another, the greater Fenrir warriors failed. One each day. In the morning, the claimant would drag or push or roll the massive stone. By early afternoon, he would collapse from exhaustion, and the rest of the day would be spent by an entire pack returning the Anvil to the forge, so that all who strove would face the same challenge. The next morning, another claimant; the next afternoon, another failure, so on and so on. Warclaw Silverfist, the most determined of them, made the best showing. His strength lasted until after sundown.

"After weeks of this, the Get began to grow restless as well as derisive of those who stepped forward to prove themselves. After all, the mightiest heroes had all failed already. This was the mood on the morning Karin Jarlsdottir, woman, half-moon, approached the forge. Many of the warriors scorned her and laughed. They may well have bitten off their own tongues when she raised the grand klaive of her departed father and with one almighty blow struck the Anvil in two."

Mari laughed. "Eeeww, I bet they hated that."

"Many howled in protest," Kelonoke continued, "but the elders ruled that she had broken no rules of the test. Even with the Anvil sundered, though, the task was not easy. Karin was not so huge as many of the Ahroun. She grappled with the first half of the Anvil throughout the morning, and the afternoon, and into the evening and night. At midnight she dragged the first half onto her father's grave. Again the warriors howled: again that she had failed, this time because the day was over. But the elders had set no time limit, and so Jarlsdottir staggered back down the Hill and began her struggle with the second half of the Anvil. The rest of the night passed with her striving, as did the whole of the next day. But at the next midnight, both halves of the Anvil of Thor rested with her father, and Karin was leader of the sept—now called Anvil-Klaiven."

Mari was shaking her head. "And a lot of them are still pissed off." She gave her friend a long look of mock scrutiny. "Are you sure you're not a Galliard?"

"We Furies admire wisdom wherever we find it, Mari Cabrah. Is there no love of stories and history in your America?"

"Well, you know...I end up hanging out with my pack more than with the sisters...."

"Learn what you can of the stories, Mari. Our past is part of our present is part of our future. You asked about Karin Jarlsdottir. Her past tells us that she is more than strong enough to have crushed Cries Havoc's skull, but wise enough not to."

Mari considered that, nodded assent. "But I still don't get him wanting to pay the blood price. I mean, he couldn't have known that she wasn't going to kill him. All the Get were screaming for blood."

"He thought his sacrifice would heal the schism between the tribes, would unite them," Kelonoke said dourly.

"Killing him wouldn't have served any purpose," Mari insisted.

Kelonoke's reply was interrupted by a shadow that suddenly fell over the two women. They looked up to the doorway and the dark figure that blocked out almost all of the exterior light. Mari shifted so that the blinding ice-glare from beyond didn't frame him in such ominous silhouette. Only slowly was she able to discern his granite-like features, his fair and windburned face, the layers of rugged cloaks hanging from his shoulders.

"Brand Garmson," Kelonoke said respectfully, her years as ambassador from the Sept of Bygone Visions taking over instantaneously. "Come in out of the wind."

Mari tried to affect the same confident poise, but she felt on edge. Brand Garmson, he whose son had died while under the protection of the Sept of the Dawn, and he who had called for the blood price against Cries Havoc. How much of their conversation had Brand heard? Mari did not fear him, but neither did she wish to provoke him. She had felt the weight of his grief for the loss of his son. One could not help but sense it in the droop of his proud shoulders, in the set of his jaw, in his pale eyes: the resignation that no wound of claw nor klaive could ever hurt him more than that which had already befallen him. And those eyes didn't seem to take in Kelonoke; they latched upon Mari and would not release her. He did not descend into the cellar, but stood there above them, impassive, as the wind whipped his cloaks about his legs.

"Mari Cabrah," he said, his voice filled with a sorrow as deep as the sea, "you have had time to reconsider. Do you still wish to accompany the IceWind Pack upon our quest to seek out this great evil far to the south?"

Mari stiffened. How dare he question her courage? Though, in truth, his manner and words were too full of...of, again, resignation to be an actual challenge.

"The IceWind Pack's quest is my quest also," Mari said. "I have committed myself, and Karin Jarlsdottir has given her blessing."

Brand nodded ever so slightly. "Come, then, so we might prepare ourselves."

Kelonoke stepped forward, refusing to be ignored. "Mari must come to Greece first, to the Sept of Bygone Visions. Our elders will have wisdom to help you on your quest."

Now Brand's eyes did take her in, and they were as cold and inexorable as a glacier. "We have lost too much time already," he said. "I have completed my tasks as Warder and now leave the caern in safe hands. Otherwise, I would have preferred to have left with the other pack. We have lost much time."

"I know a way that will not take long," Kelonoke said. "And why rush into the unknown when our elders will be able to arm you with knowledge?"

Mari observed this exchange with interest: Kelonoke speaking in her most reasonable, diplomatic cadences; and Brand, his face set in a scowl, but his heart not truly in the argument.

After a moment, he sighed, not happily. The sound was lost

to the wind, but the rise and fall of his wide chest was visible. "We leave in three hours," he said at last. "Make sure you are both ready." And then he turned and left them.

Chapter 3

Mari had just finished stuffing her sparse traveling gear into her backpack when a quiet knock sounded at the door. She'd been using the small room, now that most Garou had departed the concolation, and the Hall of Spearsreach was not so completely overcrowded, but few individuals would have known to find her here.

"Yeah?"

Karin Jarlsdottir poked her head into the room and offered a faint smile. "The others are on the Hill."

Mari frowned and glanced at her watch. "Brand said three hours. It's barely been one."

"I'm not trying to rush you," Karin said disarmingly. "Just letting you know." She slipped into the room and leaned against the wooden chest that, aside from the hard wooden pallet that served as a bed, was the only furnishing.

"Well…thanks. I get the feeling Brand is in a hurry to get where we're going," Mari said, tightening the straps on her backpack. She hadn't planned on being away from New York for more than a few days, so a couple changes of shirt and underwear would have to do.

"I think," Karin said, "that Brand is in a hurry to be…away."

Mari nodded. That sounded right. In a hurry to be away from the place that held the most memories of his dead son. Mari set down her bag and regarded this peculiar woman who had won the grudging respect of the Fenrir; who seemed so astute, so…unlike a Get. I guess even they have their half moons, Mari thought. "Do you think Brand is all right to go on this mission?" she asked.

"I don't think there was any other option," Karin said. "If he is to continue after Arne's death, then this is the first step. Is he the best one for the job?" Karin shrugged noncommittally. "But the job is best for him."

Again Mari found herself nodding. "So you think he'll either get over it or go down in flames. What about the rest of us who are with him?"

"The others," Karin said stone-faced, "they are his pack. Where he goes, they go. As for you..."

"No, I'm not changing my mind," Mari snapped. "Brand already tried to get me to back out."

Karin wore the same faint I'm-not-trying-to-tell-you-what-to-do smile as when she'd entered. "Good," she said. "A crescent moon will be a great help to them. The IceWind Pack has normally guarded the caern, and there was no shortage of Theurges here. You will make a good traveling companion." Karin folded her arms and watched Mari closely. The Jarlsdottir's eyes took on a harder, more scrutinizing aspect. "I was surprised," she said. "You didn't speak out against Lord Arkady during the moot."

Here we go, Mari thought. This is what she wanted to know, not what I think about traveling with her old Warder. "Surprised? How come?"

"Your King Albrecht has denounced Arkady."

"Yeah, well you know those Silver Fangs," Mari said. "They're either mating with their cousins or denouncing somebody as Wyrm-tainted. I think it's part of the job description." She returned Karin's amused smile, if a bit more sarcastically, while picking up the backpack and slipping it on. "I was more interested in what was going to happen with the fosterling."

"Cries Havoc," Karin said.

"Yeah. I figured if anybody would be stupid enough to execute him, it would be the Get." Mari watched Karin intently. The comment was the sort that would drive Mars-Rising, or most any Fenrir, into a snarling fit.

The Jarlsdottir, though no longer amused, did not, however, fly into a raging frenzy. "I did my duty, Mari," she said. "As did Cries Havoc."

"That's what Kelonoke said too. Heal the schism, and all. I still don't see it. If you people hadn't been rabid for blood over something that, from all tellings, was a case of Garou-killed-in-action, then there wouldn't have been a schism."

Karin shook her head, tolerant but disappointed. "There's too much of America in you, Mari. I know. I've spent enough time there. But what good is all that rugged individualism if it's not directed to a greater good, something larger than yourself? If we do not keep faith among the people, then we are nothing."

"Yeah, whatever. And eating our young serves the greater good?" Mari felt a full-fledged rant working its way to the surface, like those with which she'd blistered Albrecht on many an occasion. But she held it back. Why I am having this argument? she wondered. It's Evan's fault. Heals-the-Past. He was her friend, her packmate, and he was rubbing off on her more than she liked. He was the one who went in for philosophical debates. Mari was more for taking action, correcting the problems that she could affect in some tangible way: Get this woman away from an abusive boyfriend, and make sure that he stays away; help that kid find his way out of a gang, and if the leader interferes, hand him his balls; teach women how to defend themselves. Empowerment, Evan called it. Survival was more like it.

"Kelonoke tells me that you need to visit the Sept of Bygone Visions before venturing into Serbia," Karin said, shifting the conversation to a less contentious topic.

"Seems to make sense," Mari said. "If the elders can help us, it's worth the quick stopover."

"Brand will not be pleased by the delay."

"Brand isn't pleased by much of anything, far as I can tell."

Karin smiled again. She was so young, yet her expression at the mention of Brand was almost motherly, proud and slightly indulgent. "Kelonoke is very persuasive," she said.

"What's that supposed to mean?"

"Simply that she has argued fiercely for these expeditions to the Balkans," Karin said. "Is the need suddenly less urgent?"

"Is whatever's wrong going to go away?" Mari countered. "Are we going to miss anything if we take an extra day or two to make sure we have every advantage we can?"

"I'm sure you're right," Karin said, conceding a bit too

quickly. "And I don't imagine the margrave would object."

The Margrave Yuri Konietzko, Shadow Lord and leader of the Sept of the Night Sky in eastern Hungary. Why did she bring him up? Mari had wanted to ask Kelonoke a few questions about Konietzko, but Brand's appearance at the Icehouse had circumvented that. On the final night of the concolation, Kelonoke had seemed surprisingly willing to leave preparations for the expeditions to the margrave. I am content to place this matter in his hands, she had said.

As if she already knew that was going to happen, Mari thought. In fact, the only development that seemed to have caught Kelonoke off guard was Mari's volunteering to accompany the IceWind Pack. How much of the whole arrangement, Mari wondered, had been worked out in advance, behind the scenes? And by whom?

But what difference does it make? Mari then had to ask herself. If the Wyrm was running rampant in the Balkans and the expeditions were to help figure out what was going on and how to combat it, then what difference did it make who came to that conclusion?

"I shouldn't keep you any longer," Karin Jarlsdottir said. She bowed slightly as she slipped out of the room. "I trust to the spirits for your safe return."

Chapter 4

The others were waiting on the Hill of Lamentations when Mari climbed the slope. Kelonoke and Karin Jarlsdottir were speaking with Brand Garmson, who towered above them and stared down, glowering. For Mari, whatever the two women were saying to the obviously disgruntled warrior was lost to the wind which determinedly whipped about their hair, even the thick braids of the two Get. The rest of the IceWind Pack was nearby. Mars-Rising, his broken wrist completely healed, was assiduously checking his gear, probably for the twentieth time. His studied indifference to Mari's approach was impressive, considering the enthusiastic elbowing of his gap-toothed companion who was whole-heartedly attempting to point out Mari. Three other Fenrir were gathered about, variously double-checking gear, sharpening klaives, and listening to the exchange between their pack alpha, the Jarlsdottir, and the wild-haired Fury.

"So it's settled," Karin was saying, as Mari drew closer. "You'll travel by moon bridge to the Sept of the Dawn, and from there Kelonoke will lead you to the Sept of Bygone Visions."

"We'll consult with the elders," Kelonoke added, "and then you can head north into Serbia along one of the routes we've mapped out."

"One of the routes from which your packs did not return?" Brand said. "Perhaps there are better routes."

Mari saw Kelonoke stiffen at that, but Wildhair played the diplomat and ignored the slight. "You are certainly free to choose what path you will."

"The decision," Karin agreed, "is, of course, yours, Brand... but the Fury elders may have wisdom to contribute."

Brand nodded curtly. He turned, looked at Mari, then started toward the other members of his pack. "Let us go, then."

"Who are the others?" Mari asked him, walking very quickly to keep up; she had seen all of them over the course of the past days, but not caught all their names.

Without slowing, Brand pointed them out to her, one at a time: Aeric Bleeds-Only-Ice sat apart from the rest and watched Mari skeptically; then there was Fangs-First; Jorn Gnaws-Steel, who Mari had noticed before was missing several teeth; Fimbulwinter, alone among them darkly complected, and named for the final dark season before the Last Battle, bore a gruesome round scar, fresh, on his bare chest. "And you've met Mars-Rising," Brand said dryly. His sharp gaze silenced a sudden bout of snickering from a few of the others.

"Thank you," Mari said.

Brand regarded her silently for a long moment, then nodded, nodded likewise to the Jarlsdottir. As Karin raised aloft the hammer of the Lawgiver and began to speak the ritual words, the wind picked up on the hillside. Mari brushed her hair back from her face. In the motion of the air, she could feel the suddenly active spirits, guardians and servants of the caern. They whistled past her, obscuring the Jarlsdottir's voice. Not for the ears of an outsider were the words of Opening at the Sept of the Anvil-Klaiven. With a blinding flash, a streak of lightning hung in the sky as if frozen...then lowered slowly to the earth, taking on the form of a wide moonbeam leading away from the hillside. Brand took the lead, as was his due. Mari and Kelonoke followed and they, along with the rest of the IceWind Pack, stepped away from the earth and climbed the bridge of light into darkness.

Walking upon a moon bridge, in her earlier days, had made Mari uncomfortable to no end. The bridge was not a solid glassy surface, as it appeared from a distance. Instead, the shaft of moonlight, redirected by the spiritual energy of the caerns at either end and the Garou who protected them, was diffuse, like the beam of a flashlight on a foggy night. Mari and her companions didn't walk on the bridge as much as in it. With each step, an illumined mist swallowed her feet, her knees— sometimes rising above her waist and giving her the unnerving sensation that she was sinking through the porous bridge. Could she fall through the bottom and down into...into what? Unlike a mundane bridge, she could step off this path and not "fall." Gravity was not necessarily the culprit here in the Umbra. The moon bridge did not traverse an actual chasm as much as it distinguished the route between two places. Stepping off, Mari wouldn't fall; worse, she'd be lost.

A Glass Walker, Chani Deep-Byte, had once tried to explain it to Mari in terms of optics: reflection, refraction, the Umbral environment responding predictably to the stimuli of Garou spiritual manipulation. Of course, Chani had disappeared into the Umbra shortly thereafter and not been heard from since. *I could have predicted that,* Mari thought. In her experience, the only certainty about the Umbra was that it would raise more questions than any Garou could ever hope to answer.

As the travelers climbed the gently rising arc of light, Mari glanced back at the Hill of Lamentations. The mound seemed even larger in the Penumbra, that shadowy realm so close to the mundane world, yet so different in many respects. Graves that to Mari's eyes before had been covered by many years' worth of packed earth and snow, here were open—open, and empty.

"Always gives me the shivers," said Jorn Gnaws-Steel. "The empty graves."

Aside from Brand, who strode onward in the lead, and Mars-Rising, who immediately feigned indifference once he noticed Mari looking, the other Fenrir were gazing back toward the Hill as well.

"Their spirits have departed for Valhalla," Fimbulwinter said, "waiting there until Ragnarok, when they will return to fight with us against the Wyrm."

Something else from the Hill caught Mari's notice: the Anvil of Thor, its halves burning fiery red here in the Umbra, beside the empty grave of Karin Jarlsdottir's sire. When the graves and even the blurry outline of the Hill itself were lost to sight, even then the klaiven stone glowed through the Umbral mists like the ever-watchful eyes of the legendary Fenrir Wolf. Mari repressed shivers of her own, but not for the same reason that Jorn felt them.

She turned and looked far into the distance, peering, straining to see what, suddenly, she knew had to be there. She couldn't be sure that she actually saw it; perhaps it was just beyond the scope of her vision, hidden in the mysterious Deep Umbra, but she sensed it: the gleaming Red Star. Anthelios, those who knew such things called it. In New York City, the tightly knitted construction of the Weaver blotted out the celestial realm. But now Mari experienced the Red Star, a beacon shining as if in response to the red wolf eyes below. And signifying what? The Final Winter and Ragnarok of which the Get spoke? That seemed to fit with the warnings of the prophets and the eldest storytellers; they said that the star heralded the End Times, the culminating battle between the warriors of Gaia and the Wyrm, the outcome of which was far from certain. And so Mari and her kind were left to do what they could in the meantime.

She tried to shake off the chill, but whether the others saw the Red Star or not, its ominous pall hung over the party. Or perhaps it was Brand's grim determination that brought down on them grief-hardened silence, thicker, heavier, more oppressive than the swirling Umbral mists. Or maybe it was her own presence, and Kelonoke's, outsiders to the pack, which set the Fenrir on edge. Glancing around, though, Mari sensed resentment only from Mars-Rising, and he didn't seem interested in another confrontation, which was just as well with her.

Mari did not often travel without her pack—Albrecht and Evan—and she noticed their absence in much the way a child cannot ignore a recently lost tooth. Kelonoke's presence was a welcome distraction; the two women shared ties that, if less personal than the bond between packmates, were on a different level equally as fundamental. The common sisterhood of the Black Furies was not to be underestimated. Mari might not buy into the most anti-male sentiments of the tribe's extremists—not completely, at least; yes there were scum among them, but it seemed to her that to deny categorically the basic dignity of men was the flip side of the oppression men, unchecked, would heap upon women—she did, though, as a Theurge and as a woman, recognize the special affinity that females shared with Gaia, mother of all. It was a relationship that the few, best males could appreciate, but none could understand. For men, violence was an end to itself; for women, destruction was a means of preservation.

As a result of this unequal burden of enlightenment, the Furies counted few males among their number, mostly a few metis, who were equally as subject as women to the patriarchal prejudices of most of the Garou tribes and the majority of the human world. Among the Garou, the Get were by far the most destructive, the least attuned to the special relationship of women and Gaia. And it was the Get with whom Mari and Kelonoke found themselves on the first leg of this long journey.

Thankfully, travel in the Umbra was expeditious, and the Garou covered in a matter of hours what in the mundane world would have taken days. They followed the arc of the moon bridge to its peak. Gradually, the upward slope grew slight, then the path leveled, and soon they began the descent. Mari let her thoughts wander among the celestial bodies that sparkled beyond the mist, some of which she had visited with her own pack. Kelonoke, seeming pensive, kept her own counsel as they progressed, as did the Get, none more palpably silent and brooding than Brand. Luna had not yet reached her apex when the travelers finally stepped from the moon bridge and found themselves beside a clear spring and a willow that sprawled above and around them, encompassing much of the glade with its drooping branches.

A huge man stepped toward the Get and Furies. He was as tall as Brand Garmson and twice as broad—Mari had not believed such possible until she'd seen Sergiy Dawntreader at the concolation.

"The Sept of the Dawn welcomes you," he said. "Our hospitality is freely and gladly availed to you." His flaxen mane reflected the bright flash of the moon bridge winking out of existence until the next time it was needed, while his deep rumbling voice resonated in Mari's chest and seemed to fill the entire clearing. He wore a long robe, which Mari guessed to be the hide of a bear. "Quench your thirst," he said, "with water from the Spring of Gaia's Tears." A darkly complected youth stepped forward bearing a tray crowded with earthenware mugs.

A woman stood to Dawntreader's side. Like the youth, she was dark, and Mari could not deny her beauty, the strength of her features, the nobility of her bearing. She seemed almost in miniature standing there, but most would next to the Dawntreader. Mari had seen the woman, too, at the concolation, and the same as there, the woman's demeanor tonight was guardedly neutral. The Fenrir were less guarded. Fangs First rubbed his hands together and reached for one of the offered mugs—until checked by the voice of his alpha.

"We have no time," said Brand. "To satisfy the women, we are journeying far to the south of our object. Every hour squandered is not to our credit."

Mari started to say something—anything, to soften the impact of Brand's rudeness, but she was tongue-tied. Of course, Brand knew that the group's route via the Sept of the Dawn was chosen for a specific reason: to symbolize the healing of the schism between the Get and the Children of Gaia, the easing of the tensions caused by the death of Arne Wyrmbane. Arne Brandson. But Brand was not healed, nor was there any easing of the tensions, of the all-pervading sorrow that tore at his insides. And he would accept no comfort from those he felt had contributed to his son's wrongful death.

Fangs First furtively drew back his hand and skulked back among his comrades—as much as a Fenrir warrior is capable of skulking.

"Many thanks for your gracious hospitality," Kelonoke Wildhair said at last, waiting just long enough not to step on Brand's refusal and slight him, but speaking quickly enough to minimize the embarrassment caused the Dawntreader by the Get's refusal. "But we are upon urgent business and have far still to travel tonight."

"May we aid you in some other way?" asked the woman beside Sergiy. She was a Shadow Lord, Mari remembered, an advisor.

"You have done enough," Brand said flatly, and his words struck the woman like a slap to the face. She recovered quickly, masking her hurt as the diplomat she was—as Kelonoke might—but with the Garou every slight was a blade across flesh, and rage was the blood flowing through the offended veins.

Even Kelonoke was at a loss this time, but Sergiy Dawntreader placed a meaty hand on the shoulder of the Shadow Lord. "Peace, my child, Oksana," he said, and the sound of his voice and the touch of his hand seemed to soothe her.

Mari, too, was relieved by his reaction. How many alphas would have shrugged off such a rebuke? It was true that Karin Jarlsdottir had let slide Mari's thinly veiled taunts—but, then, Karin was a woman, and females were far more sensible about such things.

"It is not our wish," Dawntreader continued without rancor or offense, "that your quest be delayed. If you could spare but a few moments, however, we would show you where it was that Arne stayed when he dwelt among us, and a few of those who knew him best would speak words in his honor, of his strength and brave deeds. Allow us to honor him, to bring a close to this grief."

"The matter was sealed with the fall of the Lawgiver's hammer," Brand said flatly. "The blood price is paid. Nothing remains to close."

Mari winced. She felt the double edge of the dagger Brand wielded. He slashed not only to Dawntreader's heart, but to his own soul as well. The cool waters of the spring might well have been a desert, the light of torches swallowed by impenetrable darkness.

"If you must hasten on your way," said Dawntreader, respectfully, sorrowfully, "then may Sister Luna watch over you, and Mother Gaia embrace you."

"And may their blessings flow over you like water," Kelonoke responded.

As they turned away from the spring and the willow, Mari

drew close to her tribemate. "I think that went well, don't you?"

Kelonoke drew in a deep breath and sighed as she reached into a pocket of her jacket.

The Fenrir six did not wait for the Furies before shifting into the Umbra.

"Come on," said Mari. "We'd better hurry, especially since you're the one who's supposed to know how to get where we're going."

Kelonoke shook her head, letting her frustration show now that she and Mari weren't under the scrutiny of the Get. "I get the feeling they'd rather charge blind into Serbia," Wildhair said.

"You think?" Mari asked sarcastically, then she took a deep breath. "Okay. Relax. Concentrate."

Hand in hand, the two women stepped across the Gauntlet, again leaving behind the mundane world for the spiritual. The branches of the giant willow loomed over them still, and the spring shone bright and clear, reflecting the light of Sister Luna. All else was less distinct, a shadow of its former self: the greenery, the meadow itself. Dawntreader and Oksana were not evident at all, though no one had left the glade. The transition to the Penumbra was a journey of awareness, not of distance.

The Red Star, hidden from the mundane world, was waiting here in the otherwise starless night sky. Mari looked away from it, but she couldn't dispatch the foreboding that filled her. She fought off the specters of visions and dreams.

The Fenrir were waiting as well. The way Brand stood, arms crossed, indignant, made Mari want to smack him. Dawntreader wasn't the enemy. Garou couldn't square off against Garou, not if they hoped to stand a chance against the forces aligned against them. But if Brand couldn't see that, no amount of talking or beating was going to pound it into his thick Fenrir head. Instead of confronting him, Mari turned away, pointedly ignoring him. She watched as Kelonoke flicked open a small, round metal object that she'd taken from her pocket just before they had stepped across.

"A compass?" Mari asked. It was the old clunky type, maybe World War II surplus, that old.

Kelonoke nodded. "More than a compass." And as she held it flat in her palm, a brilliant light illuminated the Penumbral meadow.

"A moon path," Jorn Gnaws-Steel said.

The light did, in fact, coalesce and form a lustrous path, smaller, narrower than the moon bridge they had just crossed, and more solid also. When Jorn stepped onto it, he did not sink into the ephemeral light; he stood squarely upon it. This characteristic, Mari knew—like love, like rage—was a two-edged sword. The path might be more substantial than a moon bridge, but it was also easier to step off.

"Let me see that," she said to Kelonoke, indicating the compass. Kelonoke handed it to her, and the pinprick tingles that ran up Mari's arm confirmed what she had suspected. She concentrated on the flat, cylindrical contraption of brass and glass, and on the indistinct swirl of motion that roamed, like an otter at play, around the compass and her hand. "A Lune," Mari said. "You've bound a Lune to this thing."

"What better spirit guide for a moon path?" Kelonoke asked.

"Why don't we just take a moon bridge to the caern?" Fangs First asked, perplexed.

"Even if a bridge exists from the Sept of the Dawn to the Sept of Bygone Visions," Brand said flatly, "the Furies would not open it to us."

Fangs First scratched his reddish beard. "Then why are we going to so much trouble to pull their bacon out of the fire?"

Mari tossed up her hands in frustration. "Didn't you listen to anything that was said during the concolation, or were you too busy drooling and clamoring for an execution? Do you think whatever happens in the Balkans, whatever Wyrm threat is there, is the concern only of the Garou who live next door? Why do you think I'm here, then?"

"That is a good question," Mars-Rising growled. He and a couple of the others stepped menacingly toward Mari—

Brand held out a hand to the side, and the Fenrir stopped in their tracks. "We have far to go," he said. Whether he agreed with Mari or merely wished to press on, she had no way to know.

Kelonoke took the lead with her compass fetish and its Lune, revealing the way for the Furies and the IceWind Pack to follow. As with the moon bridge, they soon left the familiar Penumbra behind. The moon path did not climb; it simply led...away. Away from the mundane world and its shadow, away into the swirling mists of the Near Umbra. Even walking behind Kelonoke, because the path was often too narrow for two abreast, Mari could feel the bustling energy of the Lune.

"Her name is Esh'm," Kelonoke said, as if privy to Mari's thoughts.

Mari cringed. For spirits, names were powerful, and to reveal them without permission was a perilous undertaking.

"She is a friend to our tribe," Kelonoke said, sensing Mari's discomfort and the cause. "She doesn't mind." Her words were pitched only for Mari, not for the Get who followed behind.

The longer the Garou walked and the farther they traveled through the Near Umbra, the less they seemed to actually walk, yet the more quickly they advanced. The path did not exactly move, escalator-like, beneath their feet, but the sojourners increasingly took on an aspect of weightlessness, movement becoming as much, or more, a function of will as of body. Each Garou placed one foot in front of the other out of habit, but their progress corresponded very little to their physical exertion. The mists, a wall of living cloud, closed in around them, then retreated seemingly at random, adding to the dislocation, the disorienting effects of the environs. None of these sensations were new to Mari; she was no cub to be put off by the Umbra, but she had seen enough and gathered enough wisdom to maintain a healthy respect for its mysteries—respect, and no small amount of wariness.

Kelonoke, too, seemed at ease traveling along the moon path. Her duties as diplomat for the Grecian Furies had taken her far afield across the earth and beyond. At irregular intervals as they progressed, Mari cast unobtrusive glances back at the

Fenrir. None among them seemed intimidated by the constantly shifting fogscape, though the younger of them—Fangs First and Jorn, most noticeably—kept trying to make their feet and legs work as they did in the realm of the mundane. As a result, they were expending ten times as much energy as the rest of the Garou, and to no effect. One did not change the Umbra, but rather adapted to it.

They'll figure it out sooner or later, Mari decided. Probably the older Get were having a laugh at the cubs' expense. It seemed harmless enough.

"Funny," Kelonoke whispered at one point as they traveled, "how, as the End Times draw closer, more and more of the tribes are looking to women for leadership."

"What do you mean?" Mari asked.

"Well, look at Karin Jarlsdottir. There have been female sept leaders for the Get before, but not many, and she's so young. She has a bright future. And there's Tamara Tvarivich of the Silver Fangs in Russia. With women leading important septs, there's that much more chance that we can cooperate. They're more likely to be sensible, reasonable. In a way, gender transcends tribal lines…if only they'd see that."

"You seemed to get along with Konietzko well enough," Mari said, "and he's not a woman."

Kelonoke slowed noticeably for a moment, her concentration lagging, then she resumed her normal pace. "I'm not one of the firebrands who thinks that males have absolutely no place in the world, Mari. The margrave has proven himself an able war leader. His sept also lies at the edge of the Balkans. Common interest can make for strange—"

"Bedfellows?"

"Allies, I was going to say," Kelonoke said reproachfully.

"Never thought I'd hear you say that about a Shadow Lord," Mari said, shaking her head.

"I never thought you'd play second fiddle to a Silver Fang," Kelonoke shot back with a smile that was not at all kind.

Mari felt color rising in her cheeks. In a fight, she never would have let someone goad her into saying or doing anything, but a verbal argument wasn't the same thing at all. Still, she didn't want to be squabbling in front of Brand and the other Get. That was probably the quickest way to confirm all of their chauvinistic suspicions. So she bit her tongue and let Kelonoke's dig pass. Sure, Jonas Albrecht wasn't perfect, but as far as she could tell he was the best the Fangs had to offer, and in recovering the legendary Silver Crown he'd finally shown some spine. Since then, he, Evan Heals-the-Past, and Mari had done some real good. If Kelonoke couldn't see that... Mari swallowed her pride for a moment and realized that was exactly what Kelonoke was saying about Konietzko. He was a Shadow Lord, but with the right influence maybe even he could be a credit to the Garou.

I hope she knows what she's doing, Mari thought. With a Silver Fang at least one knew what one was getting: a self-righteous warrior with a Jesus complex. Keep him from getting overly depressed or impressed with himself, and he might accomplish something. Somehow Mari didn't think it was so straightforward with a Shadow Lord. I hope she knows what she's doing, she thought again.

Having nothing else to say to Kelonoke for the moment, Mari peered for maybe the hundredth time in the last hour toward that place in the farthest Umbra where she could sense more than see the Red Star pulsing ominously. A sign of the End Times, the elders called it. Despite her respect for the spirit world, Mari wasn't one for all the prophecy and hocus pocus; she was more interested in the here and the now and what she could do to make it more bearable. Too often, the prophecies led to defeatism. If some cryptic couplet that came to somebody in a dream was going to cause the Garou to give up hope, then she had no use for it. Her inclination, however, didn't always square with her own dreams and visions. She couldn't help remembering them, searching for meaning in them. That was one reason she was here, after all. She couldn't escape the image of Luna's blood-red face, the screaming, the dark wings blotting out even the malignancy of the Red Star. She couldn't help but try to do something. If the End Times were so close, there was no more room for business as usual, for live and let live.

Feeling beaten down by the presence of the star, Mari

wondered if maybe New York, with its thick veil of obscuring spirit webs, wasn't preferable to the open Umbra.

"What's that?" called Fimbulwinter from behind the Furies.

Mari turned and looked to where he pointed and saw what she should have seen sooner if she hadn't let herself become distracted. Far ahead—exactly how far was difficult to assess because distances were so deceiving here—the moon path the Garou followed intersected with another. That, however, was not what had struck the note of concern in Fimbulwinter's voice. Having noticed the alternate path, Mari now saw that with each passing moment it was growing shorter, its farthest reaches consumed by a roiling mass of gray-black mist, an Umbral storm the likes of which Mari had never seen before. It appeared quickly, as if cresting a nonexistent horizon.

"Do you feel that?" Jorn Gnaws-Steel asked no one in particular, and indeed the moon path under their feet was beginning to vibrate.

"I don't like the looks of it," Fimbulwinter said.

The mists around the Garou were thinning, fleeing, it seemed, before the onslaught of the increasing turbulence. The storm, in just a few seconds, had spread its arms wide, like a thunderhead determined to surround them by miles on every side. Pockets of dynamic energy burst like thunder all around. Flashes of light shot in and out among the thicker fog banks in the distance.

"Let's go!" Kelonoke urged them over the rising noise of the storm. "If we hurry past where the paths intersect..."

"It's no good," Mari said. "It's too big, moving too fast." It had fallen on them so quickly, she realized it would have made little difference if she'd seen it earlier. The storm raged on three sides of them now, and it swept past the intersection of the paths, blotting out their light. "It's not following the paths," Mari saw. "It's swallowing them."

Before their eyes, the churning mass of angry vapor tore apart the moon paths as it advanced, scattering and then feeding upon the shredded fragments of moonbeam. On every side, smaller whirlwinds of violently whipping mist were spawned and then subsumed by the larger fury.

"Then back the way we came!" Brand yelled, barely able to be heard over the storm.

"It's too fast!" Mari yelled back. "Everybody hold tight!"

The moon path was pitching beneath them now. Mari instinctively shifted to Crinos and prepared to set her own rage against that of the storm. She tried to grip the path with her clawed feet, but such was not the way of light given direction. Though she strained every massive muscle of her woman-wolf body, it was her inner strength which would hold her—or not— to the path. The other Garou, also changed, were discovering much the same thing as the storm bore down upon them.

"Here! You're a Theurge!" said Kelonoke, handing Mari the compass. "Esh'm is frantic! You can control her better!"

Accepting the fetish, Mari could instantly feel the terror of the bound spirit—and feeling that terror she understood why. Mari looked again at the flashes of light darting maniacally in and out of and through the thunderhead. They weren't some type of Umbral lightning as she had assumed, a byproduct of the raging storm. Each streak of gold and flashing crimson amidst the darkness was a distinct spirit caught up in the fury of the storm. Perhaps they were even fueling it. But the immense power that would require…

Esh'm's panic began to infect Mari. She tried to soothe the Lune, urging it, lending her own strength of will, helping it to maintain the moon path that it revealed to them, without which they would be lost. But the black, swirling masses were rolling down on them now with the force of a hundred waterfalls. Kelonoke yelled something, but Mari couldn't hear over the din. She saw now that the other spirits were Lunes also—furious and vengeful, feeding and feeding on the rage of the storm. Mari couldn't block Esh'm's fear of these creatures that might well destroy a Lune obsequious enough to aid outsiders, those not of the spirit world.

Fangs First was the first to fall from the path—not down, but away. He scrabbled helplessly at the light but could not hold himself to it. Aeric Bleeds-Only-Ice instantly launched himself after Fangs First, and only Brand's quick reaction to grab his packmate's ankle kept Aeric from being lost as well, as Fangs

First drifted farther from the shuddering path.

Mari might have been able to help him, she might have been able to step far enough from the path to reach him and then make her way back, but she had her hands full trying to bolster the nerve of Esh'm. The spirit was wavering in the face of her angry brethren and the storm—and the worst was not yet upon them. Though it was rapidly approaching. Mari cupped the compass in her hands and tried to focus her strength, to reinforce the panicked Lune's resolve, and perhaps her efforts helped for a short while.

A concussive blast shook the path, and Mars-Rising drifted away. He lashed out at one of the Lunes that whipped within his reach, but the ribbon of light snaked through his grasp, evading his wrath. As if in retaliation, a whirlwind of mist spun into existence, pulling at Mars-Rising, dragging him farther away from the path, sucking him into the depths of the storm.

The Lunes swarmed all about now. Through Esh'm, Mari could more keenly feel their anger, their hatred. The storm was deafening. The buffeting winds and the shaking of the path were more than the Garou could handle, while the darting spirits lashed the Get to a near frenzy. Brand defended himself with one hand and gripped Aeric's ankle with the other. Jorn and Fimbulwinter stood back to back against the Lunes, but the undulating moon path sent them crashing one against the other, and the vengeful spirits slipped through their legs, past their sides, always just out of reach. Mars-Rising was concealed by black, roiling clouds, Fangs First a speck in the distance. Kelonoke's will was overcome and she fell away from the path.

There's not even a full moon! Mari thought in desperation. This shouldn't be happening!

But it was happening. All around her. Beneath and above. And as she looked on in horror, Esh'm could take the panic no longer; the storm snuffed the light of the spirit creature, and the moon path dissipated beneath their feet. The Garou, in the midst of the raging storm, floated lost in the Umbra.

Chapter 5

The sharp aroma of the sour apple tea brought tears to Karin Jarlsdottir's eyes. She wiped her face with her sleeve without realizing she did so. The bite of the tea on her tongue and throat was as stark and bitter as the steam in her face. The hall of Spearsreach was unnaturally quiet, empty except for her, as the Sept of the Anvil-Klaiven recovered from the collective exhaustion that had gripped it after the recent concolation. The Fenrir would soon bounce back, Karin knew, and wage their war against the Wyrm as ardently as ever. None were so hardy as they. Exerting to the point of collapse was how they grew strong, in body and in spirit. Already, much was returning to normal. Outside, cubs and young warriors were again testing one another's mettle in rites of combat and skill. Soren, grumbling all the while, was busy restocking the Icehouse cellar, which was practically bare. One other thing was the same as before: The mantle of Grand Elder, Alpha of the Sept of the Anvil-Klaiven, rested heavily upon Karin Jarlsdottir. No. It was not the same. Heavier.

Her thoughts were hopelessly scattered. As a result, in the hollow of the hall, she felt beset by problems from all sides. Unfocused this way, she grew overwhelmed. She knew this, but knowing and doing something about it were two quite different beasts.

She thought of Lord Arkady of the Silver Fangs, against whom she had rendered judgment in absentia. So many voices condemning him, and only a lone Fianna willing to speak in his defense. But if he had not gone over, why else would Black Spiral Dancers appear to speak on his behalf? Captured, perhaps? The great Fang warrior and leader of the Firebird Sept? Doubtful.

So many questions, yet as far as the Get were concerned, the time for questions had passed. Arkady stood condemned. Perhaps he might yet clear his name. Karin hoped so. Look at King Albrecht in America, after all: He overcame exile, by his own grandfather, and not only proved himself but claimed the throne of his birthright as well.

Others, also, the Jarlsdottir had sentenced, if not as explicitly. Warriors of her sept and of Threeships's were off to Hungary and the Sept of the Night Sky. Would they ever return from Margrave Konietzko's war?

Our war, Karin reminded herself. Or else she would never have agreed to send them. But the Garou were accustomed to thinking in such a provincial, territorial manner. Many of her tribe had railed against her when she had ascended to leadership of the sept. Though she was blood of their blood and born at the Sept of the Anvil, they had claimed she had lived too many of her tender years across the sea in the States. She was not suitable, she was not able, she was not fit. Sometimes she felt she had proved them all wrong. But sometimes, like now, she wondered if they didn't have cause to denounce her. Could someone else do better? Were her decisions in the constant struggle against Wyrm and Weaver the right ones?

She had agreed that two packs should investigate the growing threat in the Balkans. Three packs, she corrected herself, though only two had departed thus far. Antonine Teardrop, that eccentric Stargazer, had insisted on a third. Cries Havoc would be one member, that was all she knew. Teardrop would presumably see to the rest.

But what of the other packs, each named for Gaia's perfect breath given form in this imperfect world, Roving Wind and IceWind? Karin thought again of Brand, her septmate. Had she truly done the right thing in consenting to his demand? She had to believe that she had. If he'd stayed here, his grief would have consumed him, and the sept would have lost its Warder either way. At least this way there was a chance for him....

"Jarlsdottir!" came the call from beyond the walls of Spearsreach. Mountainsides, the newly appointed Warder, poked his head through the doorway. In his haste and urgency, he almost didn't see Karin, alone in the great hall. He continued past the door before realizing his mistake and returning. "Jarlsdottir, a Garou approaches by moon bridge."

Karin's doubts receded before the need of the moment. "What does Wavecrest say?"

"The Gatekeeper says the traveler is from Night Sky."

Karin's tea, like her doubts, was forgotten as she rushed to the Hill of Lamentations with Mountainsides dogging her heels. They approached Wavecrest as his hands completed a large circle above his head, fingers touching together. He raised a howl into the night, and his note seemed to take form on the wind, gaining substance and light. With a brilliant flash, Luna's beam took arcing shape and touched the hillside. A moment later, a Garou stepped from the Umbra and stood beside them.

A Garou, the traveler. The exactitude of Mountainside's words had not struck Karin until now, not until Mephi Faster-Than-Death appeared from the moon bridge. He and no other.

"You must stop them," he said, the words tumbling from his lips. "The IceWind Pack, and the American woman. Warn them. Don't let them go."

Karin's heart turned to ice in her chest. "What did you find?" she asked, gripping Mephi by the shoulders. "Where are the others?" She tried to hold him up.

He was bloodied and exhausted, trembling from the effort to stay on his feet, but fatigue, or the weight of the news he bore, drove him to his knees. "There are no others. Not any more."

"But the Roving Wind...?" Karin started to ask.

"Dead. There is no more Roving Wind," he said, his steely glare lost in the indeterminate distance, his mind replaying images the others could not see. "We found the caern at Owl's Rest. We recovered the pathstone and I delivered it to Konietzko."

Karin tried to absorb it all. Mephi was telling them what had occurred, but not explaining anything. "But what...what happened? How...? What happened to the others?"

Mephi looked up at her, his eyes focused again in the here and now. "Banes and Black Spiral Dancers and Wyrm spirits like I've never seen before," he said. "That's what happened. An army of Garou would have been hard pressed. The Tisza River is corrupted. Its spirit was destroying...some sort of chain, a mystic strand...I'm not sure what. And Banes were spawning from the broken pieces." His gaze began to slip away again, away to that place beyond sight.

Karin shook him. He was spouting too much too fast. He was going to have to explain in more detail after he rested. But not everything could wait that long. "The other pack..." she began.

"Just don't let them go," Mephi snapped.

"But they've already gone," Mountainsides said. "Brand is already gone."

Hearing that, Mephi slumped forward, and Karin's hope fell with his slouching shoulders. "Then they are doomed," he said.

His words, lent conviction by the recent loss of his companions, echoed in Karin's ears. Doomed. They are doomed. And though they stood upon the open, windswept face of the Hill of Lamentations, she felt the night, like all of her hidden doubts, closing in upon her.

Chapter 6

Mari's first impulse, as always, was to fight. But what? There was no longer a moon path to fight her way back to: Either it was destroyed or, without Esh'm's cooperation, it was closed to the Garou, or a little of both. Didn't really matter. The Lunes were a more attractive target, but the Get had tried that route and demonstrated that the spirits had the home-field advantage here in the Umbra. Mari was more likely to walk naked through a construction site in the Bronx and not get whistled at than she was to lay her hands on one of those Lunes. Should she fight the storm for having the nerve to mess up her little expedition? Spitting in the wind.

Still, as she was pulled and tossed this way and that by the churning mist, her rage flared at any piece of Umbral flotsam, no matter how incorporeal. She snapped her jaws shut on a tiny whirlwind and got a visceral thrill, a rush of adrenaline. Never mind that the next, larger whirlwind drew her into its current and sucked her deeper into the storm. She lashed out at—and missed—any Lune that came close, wishing desperately that she could slash the ribbon-like streams of light into confetti. She tried to stalk the infuriating spirits, willing herself in a certain direction through the featureless environs. The storm proved too strong, every time. But her rising anger, even a burgeoning hatred of the capricious beings, kept her going. Feeling waves of resentment emanating from them, she drank in the sentiments and returned them tenfold. But to no avail.

She began to wish that she would bump into one of the Get: This had to be their fault somehow. The whole tribe had had it in for the Black Furies since time immemorial. They fancied themselves such great warriors. She could show them a thing or two or three. How rewarding it would be to slash one and have his guts spill out—a damn sight better than floating here at the mercy of the storm, helpless, constantly assaulted by the spirits and the Umbral elements.

And what about Kelonoke? This trip was her idea in the first place! She could at least have brought a fetish that worked! One with a spirit that didn't cut and run at the first sign of trouble. Esh'm must be spirit language for wuss, she thought. She glared at the compass in her hand, cupped her Crinos palms around it and squeezed until the brass buckled and the glass cracked. "Stupid little...!"

She wanted to destroy something, someone; she wanted revenge for her misfortune, for the undeserved troubles that had befallen her. Albrecht was right: She should have stayed in the U.S. Damn him for being right! It was the kind of thing he'd be graceless about and not let her forget. She could have punched him right in the smug face. And damn Evan, too, for rubbing off on her. Mari had her work cut out for her in New York. She was the one who'd saved his butt when he was still shaking after his First Change and, if it weren't for him and his corny, We-Are-the-World vision of the Garou nation, she wouldn't be here right now.

Wherever here was. No matter what she tried, the storm did with her what it would: spinning her wildly until she had to close her eyes to keep from vomiting, plunging her over mile-long steamfalls into roiling masses of vaporous energy. Eventually time, like distance and direction before it, began to lose meaning. Mari raged at futility, at impotence, for as long as she could. Twice she thought she saw the familiar outline of dark wings in the distance, but if so, they drew away before she could be sure. At some point, she shifted back to Homid form, her senses and emotions dulled by the constant assault. The storm raged on. The buffeting vapors washed around her, through her. And then...

Nothing. It was over. The departure of chaos intruded only slowly within Mari's defensive cocoon. She emerged from the place deep within herself to which she had retreated. The noise of the storm had grown slight. The furious black thunderhead was receding. Even from a distance, it appeared miles wide, miles tall. The Lunes slashed their way through the vapors like lightning attacking a storm front.

Watching it all draw farther away, Mari noticed another piece of detritus, driftwood cast out by the tempest: Kelonoke. Mari struggled to concentrate. She was so drained, spent by the anger that had surged through her for...hours, days? Finally, she willed herself forward, too tired this time to bother with moving her feet. Slowly, she closed the distance to Kelonoke. Even now, Mari felt resentment flaring within her—wasn't this all Wildhair's fault?—but exhaustion won out.

"Are you all right?" Mari called.

Kelonoke stared at her, stunned, uncomprehending. Only gradually did recognition creep into her eyes. "Mari."

"The others?" Mari asked.

Kelonoke didn't seem to understand the question. "The others," she repeated vaguely, confused.

"Brand? The IceWind Pack?"

Kelonoke wasn't much help. She was staring at Mari, at Mari's hand. Mari looked down and remembered the battered compass, Esh'm. The noise of the storm was almost gone now. The more normal swirling mists—they seemed so gentle by contrast—closed in again, shifting constantly, playing tricks with sight and sound. Mari wasn't sure if she could see for miles, or merely feet. A far-flung vista, as often as not, turned out to be illusory, actually a mass of whirling vapor within reach, or just beyond, or half as far as it seemed....

"We'll never find them without help," Mari said, glancing again at the compass. She closed her eyes and felt for the tingle of energy, the spirit tickle, that had inhabited the fetish before. Esh'm, she called. The Lune was still there, she had to be; the mystic bindings were still in place. But what if the damage Mari had done the compass had weakened them enough for Esh'm to flee? Mari opened her eyes and gazed into the shattered face of glass. Three Maris stared back at her, concerned, angry, tired. Esh'm, we need you. Mari waited. Nothing. Esh'm, are you there? Frustrated, she shook the compass like a pocket watch that needed winding. Quickly she remembered herself, fought down the rage. The spirit had been panicked by the anger of the other Lunes and the fury of the storm. More anger wasn't going to help.

Esh'm, please… Mari could command the spirit, if it was in fact still present. The Lunes in the storm had been too numerous, and what good would ordering them about have done? They couldn't, she thought, have been the cause of the storm, just riders—maybe even victims like the Garou. Besides, Mari's own rage had been kindled too fiercely for her to have negotiated with the denizens of the spirit world. Now, she was calmer; she could reach her own spiritual nature, that which resided within each Garou. Esh'm.

A flicker of light shone within the compass, beneath the spider-web cracks of the glass. Mari breathed a sigh of relief: The spirit hadn't fled. Now another decision loomed. Mari required much of Esh'm, and willing cooperation was often far more effective than coerced.

"Kelonoke," Mari said. "The fetish belongs to you."

"Do what you must," Wildhair said.

Mari nodded. All things considered, the sacrifice was small enough. Esh'm, she said to the spirit, help us find the others and reach our destination, and freedom is yours.

The flicker within the compass grew brighter, though Mari could still sense the hesitancy of the spirit to emerge. Apparently the storm was not something to which Esh'm was accustomed either. But with more coaxing and assurances, the Lune snaked out from the compass and led the way for the Furies. They found Jorn Gnaws-Steel first, floating and mumbling incoherently. Slowly, like Kelonoke had, he came to his senses. Mars-Rising was next, alone in the mists, and then Brand, the alpha still clutching Aeric's ankle. As Mari drew close to the pair, she glimpsed a dark shape slipping away, quickly obscured by the wispy grayness. Like anything she saw in the Umbra, it could have been a trick of light and shadow at deceitful play among the mist, but that did little to explain the sense of dread that took hold of her. The shape was gone almost as soon as she saw it— thought she saw it; she couldn't be sure—and she was left with nothing more than the impression of black wings, and perhaps a lengthy tail switching back and forth as it slithered away.

Still, the work was not done. Mari struggled to urge Esh'm onward; the profound fatigue that afflicted her was evident in the spirit, as well as the other Garou. Physically they were unhurt, but to a person their eyes and slack faces showed how wrung out each was emotionally.

They continued through the shifting maze of vapor, finding Fimbulwinter next. He was slightly more coherent than the others. And finally Fangs First.

"And the first shall be last," Mari said. Thank you, Esh'm, she told the spirit. Now we just need you to get us where Kelonoke was leading us before, and your service is done.

The Lune was growing more active, less hesitant and fearful, slipping in and about the compass, twining up Mari's arm. When a moon path again appeared before the Garou, a glimmer of strength and volition seemed to rekindle within them.

"Have you ever encountered a storm like that before?" Fimbulwinter asked Mari.

She shook her head; she didn't want to talk about it, as if spoken words might call the storm back down upon them.

"We look forward," said Brand, "not back. Have you forgotten our quest? We have not come this far to tarry and discuss the weather. Danger and glory await us. Lead onward."

Mari looked curiously at the alpha and his peculiar outburst of vigor. She didn't think she'd heard him speak so many words unsolicited since they'd begun their journey, and certainly not with such a sense of encouragement. The determination was the same, but the morbidity had vanished; gone was the grim fatalism.

"You heard the man," she said. "Let's hit the road."

Chapter 7

"Can't remember when I've been this happy to put my feet back on solid ground," said Fangs First.

The last of the darkness before dawn clung to the copse of trees among which the travelers found themselves. Mari knew of what the young Get spoke—her own legs were rubbery and took a few minutes to become reacquainted with solid earth—but she couldn't disagree with him more. Stepping back across, piercing the Gauntlet and re-entering the mundane world, always left her feeling slightly wistful. Even after a hard journey, after a disaster like they had just experienced, part of her called out to what she left behind in the shadows. Humans always did more than enough to nurture her rage, but Garou were more than simply creatures of rage. Mari was born under the crescent moon, the spirit moon, and too infrequently did she pay attention to the mystical side of her nature: That was the greatest danger of life in the city, where the Penumbra was a maze of blights, and quiet contemplation was all too rare a luxury.

Mari thought of the last seconds before they had crossed back over. She had awarded Esh'm her freedom, as per their bargain, releasing the Lune from the mystic bonds that held her to the compass fetish. Esh'm had flitted about joyfully—as excited as the Lunes in the storm had been angry—before zipping away into the Umbra. The spirit world was not without its dangers and hardships, nonetheless Mari understood Esh'm's exuberance far more than Fangs First's relief at again assuming the mortal coil.

"Kelonoke," said a woman's voice from the darkness. The speaker, a middle-aged woman, attractive despite her weathered skin, approached the group. She grasped Kelonoke on the arm warmly; her eyes took in the rest less enthusiastically. "And you've brought...guests."

Brand stepped forward from his pack. "Greetings and respect from the IceWind Pack of the Sept of the Anvil-Klaiven. We are honored to be received by the sisters of Bygone Visions."

The woman's partial smile froze on her face. With raised eyebrows, she looked to Kelonoke.

"This is not the caern," Kelonoke said calmly to Brand.

Sensing that his display of formality and graciousness had been misguided, if not altogether wasted, his face drew grim. "What is this place, then?" he asked with forced patience.

"We are on Crete," Kelonoke explained. "You and the others will wait here, while Mari and I confer with the elders at the caern. There is a villa, just over there, where you will be made comfortable and—"

"Wait here," Brand growled. "While you women—"

"Surely you did not think," the new woman said sternly, "that males would be permitted at the caern? Especially males of the Fenrir."

"Why do we try to help these women?" Mars-Rising exclaimed. "We open our caern to them, come as friends to handle what they obviously cannot, and in return we are insulted!"

"Has any sister of the Furies ever attacked your caern?" the woman demanded.

"Please, Aegina..." said Kelonoke, attempting to calm tempers.

"They know better than to try!" Fangs First proclaimed defiantly. "Brand Garmson has long safeguarded the Sept of the Anvil-Klaiven. Even minions of the Wyrm know to keep their distance. Much less a gaggle of witless—"

"Women?" Aegina cut him off, the color rising in her cheeks. "Not so many years have passed since women of your tribe betrayed the trust and hospitality we were foolish enough to extend to them. We learn from our mistakes, while you, it would seem, do not even remember them. I shouldn't be surprised. You are men. Your minds are filled with lust and envy—no room for thought, so you have no recourse but to think with your—"

"Aegina," Kelonoke stepped in. "I am sure that Brand Garmson, long an honored Warder of his own caern, will respect the traditions of ours."

The younger Get all looked to Brand. Mari, too, watched as he consciously mastered his rage. This was not the grief-ridden, sonless father she had seen at the sept in Norway. He now possessed a new vitality, a volatility, that further insulated him from persuasion—not a new characteristic, Mari realized, looking at the other Get and seeing how they watched their alpha. This was the Brand to whom they were accustomed, not the hardened, brooding mourner whom she had met. She didn't understand the change that had come over him; she couldn't account for it.

"One day can't hurt anything," Mari added to the debate. "We wouldn't be heading back into the Umbra before nightfall anyway."

Brand flashed a challenging glare at Mari, then at Kelonoke and Aegina. Finally, he raised a hand toward his pack, who were appealing to his pride. "We leave at nightfall, then," he said grudgingly. "But let it be known that I am offended to be shunted off on Kinfolk."

"Aegina and the women at the villa are no mere Kinfolk," Kelonoke said placatingly, then added, "and I urge you to respect the limits of our hospitality."

The parting was tense, as Mari and Kelonoke drew away from the others. The two Furies did not pause at the villa, but continued past to the docks and the sea.

Chapter 8

The waters of the Aegean shimmered, bright and clear, beneath the rising sun. Kelonoke manned the oars of the small rowboat but, after a few perfunctory strokes to draw the two Furies away from the fishing docks, she had not needed to exert herself. Yet the boat maintained a brisk pace, skimming across the gentle swells as Crete fell away to stern. Water spirits: Mari felt their presence, their closeness, as they ushered the rowboat onward. Had unwelcome guests been aboard, the going would not have been so smooth, the seas so calm, the winds so favorable. At first, other vessels were visible, mostly trawlers, but they kept their distance; none seemed to notice the Furies' dinghy and, to a ship, each took a divergent course. Another consequence of spirit attentions, Mari suspected. As thin as the Gauntlet was here, with each passing mile she could feel it crumbling further, like sheer paper scorched by a relentless sun.

Palpable as the spirit-signs were to Mari, a human never would have noticed anything out of the ordinary, nor would many Garou not born of the crescent moon. Kelonoke, as was one of the few Garou actually born at the Sept of Bygone Visions, must have been aware. She was returning home. The caern and its surroundings were intimately familiar to her, but if she found any joy in her homecoming, Mari could not detect it. Kelonoke let the oars, now practically dry from the vigorous sea wind, rest against the gunwales as she stared to the east. Perhaps it was her squinting against the morning sun that made her appear distraught.

"Don't let the Get get to you," Mari said. Her voice sounded small amidst the distances of the sea and the squawking of nearby gulls drafting upon the wind.

"Hm? Oh." Kelonoke turned from the horizon to face her companion. "They don't bother me. They're just a lot of work. Valiant warriors. You just have to make allowances for their shortcomings."

"Ain't that the truth." Among themselves, the Furies sometimes referred to the Fenrir as the Can't-Get, for all the things they can't get through their thick heads. When the women's quiet laughter died away, Mari was certain of Kelonoke's distress but still in the dark as to the cause. "What, then?" she asked. "What's eating you, if it's not putting up with Brand and his bunch?"

"Nothing's bothering me," Kelonoke said unconvincingly; but then, after several seconds, felt the need to expand upon what wasn't bothering her. "It's just that...I guess the more I'm away from the caern, the less a part of it I feel." She paused again, and frowned, dissatisfied with what she'd said. "No, that's not right. I still feel a part. I still feel at home here. Iona, Kyra, even Teiresias and the others: We have a shared past, we have history in common. But we differ so greatly in our views of where the future must take us." Mari waited as her friend sorted out her thoughts. "It's such an insular world here," Kelonoke said. "In going beyond to represent our interests, I see more, experience more of the other tribes. Not everyone thinks that's a good thing."

"Yeah," said Mari. "Somebody once accused me of playing second fiddle to Albrecht."

Kelonoke tensed at the rebuke. She looked hurt for a moment, until she realized that Mari's dig was devoid of resentment or malice. Kelonoke smiled, but the pensive air did not leave her. "You've got a rough road ahead of you, Mari."

"It's the only kind of road I know," Mari said.

They sat in silence the remainder of the way as the water spirits took them to the island caern of Miria—Ecube to the outside world, though in truth the outside world paid no attention to this particular rock jutting from the Aegean. That was how the Furies—and their spirit guardians—liked it. By the time the boat eased into the confines of the small natural harbor, Mari could taste in the air, like the salt on the moist wind, the presence of spirits. The Sept of Bygone Visions had long stood as a marker, both symbolically and realistically, of Black Fury strength in this part of the world. Challenges from humans, from other Garou, had risen time and time again, but always they were met. Always the wisdom of the Circles had proven sufficient.

On the rocky beach that reached out from the cliffs of the island proper, a woman watched intently the approach of the rowboat. She was barefoot, despite the rough terrain. Her khaki shorts and white tank top were speckled from the surf spray. Mari, ever the martial artist, immediately noticed that the woman stood with most of her weight on her left leg. Also clear was the displeasure that furrowed her brow.

"She's hurt," Mari said to Kelonoke. "And pissed."

Kelonoke nodded. "The leg is an old injury. The rest is probably my fault."

The rowboat did not scrape ashore but came to rest gently upon the rocks as the surf, having risen slightly, now conveniently withdrew. Mari and Kelonoke were not forced to wade ashore.

"Kyra," Kelonoke called, "our guest is Mari Cabrah. She has come all the way from New York to honor us."

Kyra's eyes were as blue as the Mediterranean sky, though a storm brewed deep within them. In spite of her leg, more obviously crippled from close view but showing few signs of muscle atrophy, she was a strong woman, broad-shouldered and stolid, taller and older than the new arrivals. Her red hair was dark, almost black, except on her legs where in the sunshine it produced a fiery sheen. With ritual politeness, Kyra acknowledged Mari, but then turned to Kelonoke.

"How could you bring them here?" Kyra asked in low angry tones.

"They're not here," Kelonoke pointed out. "They're at the villa."

"Just as bad."

Mari felt the tension between the two women as distinctly as she felt the electric spirit presence on the island. "News travels fast," she said, trying to break the ice a bit. She doubted the

Kinfolk on Crete and the Garou here at the caern had telephone or radio communications. What spirits, she wondered, had raced ahead of the water spirits with the news of the Get visitors?

Kyra glared at Mari, but choked off a sharp, impulsive response. "I would not expect you to understand," she said instead. "This isn't the blighted city you're used to. There's still a reason to protect this place."

"There are plenty of people in 'the blighted city' who need protecting," Mari said.

"Humans," Kyra spat the word.

"If we hide away and leave them to themselves," Kelonoke said, "Weaver and Wyrm grow stronger. Should we let that happen, Kyra?"

"Without humans to feed on, Weaver and Wyrm would starve," Kyra said.

"The humans aren't going to fade away," Kelonoke pointed out. "If they kill each other off, they're going to take us—and Gaia—with them."

Kyra scoffed. "There is no reason that could justify bringing Get here."

"I did not bring—"

Kyra waved off Kelonoke's protest. "Iona is waiting for you. You can answer to her." Before hobbling away, Kyra turned once more to Mari. "Welcome, Mari Cabrah." Her words were almost apologetic, but her anger maintained the sharp edge. "Our tribe would be better off if more of the younger generation made a pilgrimage here."

As Kelonoke led Mari along the shore in the opposite direction, Wildhair didn't attempt to conceal her exasperation. "If all kinds of Furies made pilgrimages here, she'd complain about the number of visitors and the threat to the caern's security."

"She's the Warder, then," Mari said.

Kelonoke nodded. "And a good friend...despite everything."

They followed the coastline eastward, into the morning sun which by now had risen high into the sky. The harbor gave way to natural terraces, while always the cliffs rose steeply to the left. Vines and shrubs grew robustly wherever the soil was thick enough on the rocky island. Brushing her hair back from her face, Mari was struck by the contrast between the warm, moist breeze here and the biting arctic chill at the Sept of the Anvil-Klaiven. But caerns needed to be protected wherever the Garou found them. She supposed they were lucky that the Get seemed to prefer the harsher climes. Mari stripped down to her T-shirt, peeling off her long-sleeve shirt and carrying it along with her coat, which she'd removed on the boat.

Within a mile or so, Mari began to hear a dull rumble that grew louder with each step she and Kelonoke took. As they rounded a particularly narrow stretch of shore, where only a snaking path existed between cliff and sea, the rumbling continued to increase in volume. By the time the waterfall came into view, the roar was nearly deafening. The path continued closer, turning sharply toward the cliff and then winding its way up the craggy rockface very close to the cascading water. The climb wasn't easy. Mari stuffed her coat and extra shirt into her pack. At many points she was on all fours, scrabbling up after Kelonoke. The rocks were slick in places from drainage and spray. Careful to concentrate on every hand and foothold, Mari still managed to savor the splattering water. Between the sun and wind on the boat ride, and the hot sweaty climb, she'd worked up a ravaging thirst; but she couldn't get more than a few drops of spray at a time, just enough to tease her, to hint at how deliciously cold a mouthful would be.

The sun was almost directly overhead, perhaps slightly past noon, when Kelonoke and Mari pulled themselves over the last few steep yards of the trail and stood upon the lush green plateau atop the island. The vegetation reminded Mari of a tropical landscape as much as a Mediterranean vista. The Furies of the sept had had many years to import and nurture whatever exotic plants they desired, and the time had not been wasted. Pausing before plunging into the thick undergrowth, Mari stretched. She actually felt better after the tough climb. At home she was accustomed to multiple daily workouts and practice sessions: conditioning, forms, sparring, not to mention teaching the self-defense classes. Other than her brief altercation with Mars-Rising, she'd had precious little opportunity for physical activity since the beginning of the concolation.

"This way," Kelonoke said. She brushed aside a collection of heavy vines to reveal that the path did indeed continue toward the interior of the island.

The roar of the waterfall faded back to a distant rumble surprisingly quickly, though the sound of running water was never far. The two Furies followed the stream that fed the falls until it opened into a broad, clear pool. Beside the pool, framed by massive trees that appeared to be as old as the island itself, stood a woman nearly as old. Her skin was the leathery tanned-olive of an islander, and her black hair was streaked with white. Despite her age, she held herself tall and erect, her body a series of tightly woven muscles where not covered by the elegant white shift that graced her Homid form. The spear she held to her side was not for support, nor for show.

"Welcome, Mari Cabrah," she said, "to the Sept of Bygone Visions. I am Iona Kinslayer." Her eyes were as dark as Kyra's had been blue.

Mari bowed deferentially as she tried to remember the stories of this Fury icon and how she'd earned her name: something about a purge in her sept and Nazi infiltrators back during World War II—but Mari had never paid close attention to the tales of faraway places and times that seemed to have no bearing on her own day-to-day existence.

"I understand that your stay is to be brief," Iona said, without the slightest smile or change of expression. "Considering your choice of traveling companions, perhaps that is for the best."

"If there is fault to be found," Kelonoke said, interceding, "it is with me, not Mari. But I contend that all I have done is in the best interest of tribe and sept."

"Ah," said Iona, with raised eyebrows. "But which tribe, and which sept?" She waved away Kelonoke's fervent protestation. "Do not worry, child. We will discuss this further, I assure you. At length. Now, however, you must allow me to attend to our guest."

Mari was fidgeting throughout the exchange between the two sept members. She felt like a kid again, getting reamed out by a friend's parents for staying out too late or wandering into a part of the city that was better off avoided. "Hey, I didn't mean to cause trouble for you folks," she said. "Kelonoke told me about how bad things are. You know, Serbia, Kosovo, even though everybody thinks all the fighting is over now. And Konietzko was all bent out of shape about the spread of Wyrm-taint. So I volunteered to help investigate. Kelonoke thought it'd be a good idea if we came here first. But, you know—no disrespect or anything—if it's a problem, maybe I should just be on my way now."

Iona listened impassively, her black-eyed gaze boring into Mari. A long, tense silence spread out between them after the younger Fury had spoken.... And then Iona smiled. The corners of her thin lips turned up ever so slightly, sending a play of rune-work wrinkles dancing across her face. Still, though, her eyes were fixed, probing, and the tension was not undone as much as it might have been. "You do not care to be ordered about by an old woman, do you?"

Mari tried to gauge the words. How much should she say to this venerable sept leader? How much was too much—or had she already crossed that line? "I never met a Garou who like being bossed around," she said. "And like I said, this is your sept. If my being here is offensive—"

"Your being here is hardly the issue," Iona said. She paused, and finally shifted her sharp gaze back to Kelonoke. "Or is it, Sister Wildhair?"

Mari felt that she'd missed something. She looked back and forth between the other two women, whose interlocking stares seemed to bind them in a sort of contest of wills. "What do you mean?" Mari asked.

Iona did not shift her gaze from Kelonoke. "Why venture so far from your home, sister?" she asked evenly, not in an accusing manner as the Fenrir had asked the same question.

"I just told you," Mari said. "If it's that bad over here, I want to help if I can." She was tempted to mention her dream, her visions—the blood-glow of Luna, the screams, the dark wings— but those were too personal somehow.

"Many have ventured into Yugoslavia before you," said Iona. "Many have not returned. Those who have, they have been...broken. You are willing to face the same risks. Why?"

"I teach women how to keep from being victims," Mari said. "That's what I do. Kelonoke said something on the way here: She said that gender transcends tribal lines. Well, I think it crosses the line between Garou and human, too. Some humans shouldn't have to live in fear just because they're women. I've heard about the wars in Bosnia and Kosovo: the rape camps, sexual slavery, torture. It makes me sick to think about it. It makes me want to gut the nearest man at hand. Kelonoke came asking for help. She's my sister. All those women are my sisters."

"I wanted you to come here, and then take word back to the States," Kelonoke said to Mari, but without looking away from Iona. "It's not a one-woman job, Mari."

"So you are willing to take this risk for the sake of all those women," Iona continued. "And for Kelonoke. Perhaps in the name of all Furies. Are you willing, also, to take this risk for the sake of the Shadow Lords?"

It wasn't a question Mari had been expecting, nor one that she understood completely.

"Answer, girl," Iona prompted her.

"The danger is larger than the Furies," Kelonoke broke in. "It's larger than the Shadow Lords, Iona. If each tribe tries to face each threat alone, then each tribe will fall alone."

"Some of the Sisterhood," Iona said, and obviously meaning Kelonoke among the some, "have consulted very closely with Margrave Konietzko despite the fact that the Shadow Lords have long sought to capture this caern. He is not like those others, the sisters say. Perhaps. And perhaps the Get that sit at our doorstep are not like those of their tribe who directly attacked us—and many of those Fenrir were women. Their gender did not transcend tribal loyalty. And now some would conspire with—"

"I have conspired with no one," Kelonoke said hotly.

"Tell me, Sister Mari," Iona said, "why do you think Kelonoke has sought the aid of other tribes? Why of the Get? Because they are more capable warriors than are we?"

"Of course not," Mari said.

"Of course not," Iona echoed quietly. "But too many sisters

have died, broken against the walls of the Hellhole to our north. Perhaps it is easier to send Garou of other tribes to their deaths, rather than our own sisters?"

"Not true!" said Kelonoke.

"Not true, then," Iona conceded calmly, "but just as necessary?"

Kelonoke had no answer for her elder but turned instead to Mari. "I never thought you would volunteer for this," Wildhair said. "We needed you to rally support in the States. What we need is an army, a massive assault—"

"Ah, but won't a martyr serve to rally support?" Iona asked. "Just as a pack of Fenrir martyrs will rally support among the Get? And the other packs that are being sent into deathtraps? Is this not the cruel thinking of a Shadow Lord?"

In spite of the hot afternoon sun, Mari felt cold suddenly.

"There is a chance of success," Kelonoke insisted. "And we must find out what it is we are fighting. We would not have anyone undertake these tasks if they were hopeless."

"But in failure," Iona pressed, "there is also accomplishment: the other tribes rushing to meet the threat."

"If the Garou on the expeditions die," Kelonoke said somberly, "they will not die in vain. Would that every warrior's death carried such meaning."

For the first time in what seemed like hours, Iona turned her black, steely gaze from Kelonoke and turned to face Mari again. "So you understand why your accompanying the others pains dear Kelonoke. Will you tell your Get friends, or let them throw their lives away unknowing?" The old woman paused. "Will you throw your own life away?"

Had Iona challenged Mari's courage or ability, Mari would not have hesitated to answer, to reaffirm her willingness to walk into danger. But to suggest that Kelonoke had betrayed her… Kelonoke stared now at the crystal pool, at the near-blinding sunlight that glittered on the surface of the water. The signs had been there all along, Mari realized: Wildhair's dismay and anger at Mari having volunteered. And now, unrefuted by Kelonoke, the reason was clear. Yet the underlying facts remained the same.

"Look," Mari said, growing angry at having her motives constantly called into question, "something is going on there, in the Balkans. Nobody is denying that—not you, not Kelonoke, not Konietzko. Now, maybe it's exactly what the TV and newspapers say, and the humans have run amok and are killing and torturing each other. Gaia knows they're capable of horrible atrocities left to their own. And even if that's all that going on—'if that's all'; listen to that, like none of them matter because they're not Garou—even if that's what's happening, it's bad enough. Somebody needs to put her foot down. I know war happens, and people are killed and raped and tortured, but this is ethnic cleansing, one step away from genocide. Most of the people being hurt are unarmed innocents, women!" Mari tried to imagine the horror of it; she tried to imagine the suffering she had seen multiplied hundredfold, and in doing so she practically quivered with fury. "Maybe I can't change everything," she said, balling her hands into fists, "but maybe I can save an Albanian woman, or a Serbian woman. Maybe I can't even save them. Maybe all I can do is hand some paramilitary predator his balls on a bloody platter and make sure he doesn't hurt anybody else."

Mari took a deep breath, trying to regain control of her emotions before she stepped over the line and irrevocably insulted the Grand Elder. But even trying to forget for a moment—because to acknowledge them consciously was to provoke her rage—Mari could not escape the images of her dreams.

"Worse yet," she said, "there's a Red Star up there that means our time is running out. We don't have the luxury anymore of picking our battles. We have to take on the Wyrm where and when we can. And you know the whole region is rotten with Wyrm-taint. How else do you explain all of those packs not coming back?"

Mari paused. For a moment, she thought she was done; she knew that if she kept going, she would go too far—but her passion got the best of her. "So to answer your question, I guess I am willing to risk throwing my life away, if that's what it takes. Because I'm proud of the Furies that have gone before

me, and I know their cause—my cause—is worthwhile. As for
the Get, I don't think they have any illusions about this being
a cakewalk. But that doesn't scare them. At least they aren't so
worried about Shadow Lords or who the hell else that they can't
face the real threat."

Mari's temper having run its course, a profound silence—
despite the sounds of running water and wind in the trees—fell
over the glade. The three women did not speak for some while.
If Kelonoke was relieved by Mari's words, she did not let on;
instead, she seemed to struggle with both defiance and guilt,
neither quite gaining the upper hand. Iona, if not pleased with
Mari's frankness, did not appear overtly antagonized.

When again the Grand Elder spoke, she took a small wooden
bowl resting atop a flat rock, dipped the bowl into the pool, and
handed the vessel to Mari. "Your mind and heart are one," Iona
said. "You have come seeking the wisdom of our caern. I will
not stand in your way."

Hesitantly, Mari took the bowl and raised it to her lips.

Chapter 9

Kyra Firefoot felt no need to disturb Iona, who was busy with the American sister. The spirit wards were sufficiently strong to turn back this pitiful assault on the caern. Actually assault was too generous a term for what was happening: a lone Garou attempting unilaterally to establish a moon bridge to Miria. What hope of success could this person hold? Still, the interloper seemed to be of the Fenrir, so the effort could be a diversion. Kyra would contact Aegina at the villa and instruct her to take appropriate safeguards against the Get there. Only if a more formidable threat became apparent would Kyra alert Iona.

Standing over the mosaic tile that was Hecate's Gate, the point of contact for all moon bridges leading to and from the caern, Kyra listened to the lesser spirit guardians that swarmed about her—not to voices, but to their moods and movements, the natural rhythms of their existence that intersected with the spiritual being of the Garou. She melted into her natural wolf-form to attune herself to the guardians more easily. The Fenrir trespasser, Kyra knew, would turn back or suffer horrible consequences. Kyra hoped the Get proved persistent.

Caught between worlds, Karin Jarlsdottir tried to keep pressing forward, but the Umbra would not release her, and those in the mundane world would not accept her. Her left foot was planted at the ragged edge of the moon bridge Wavecrest had opened from the Sept of the Anvil-Klaiven. It was not a proper moon bridge—it had no end. Or rather, it ended before it got where Karin wanted to go. Rites existed to open a bridge into a hostile caern, but that was not what Karin desired. If she tried anything that gave the impression of an attack, the Furies would turn her insides into her outsides before so much as listening to a word. No, she simply wanted to get someone's attention, so she could pass along the warning that Mephi Faster-Than-Death had brought back.

But so far, the Gatekeeper or Warder of the Sept of Bygone Visions was content to block access and seemed disinclined to make contact with the uninvited guest. Karin's right foot was poised to step forward, but was blocked, held motionless in the cloudy Umbra.

At last a sound, perhaps a response from the caern or some spirit guardian: a woman's voice, gentle but insistent, tickled Karin's brain. "Turn back," she said. "This way is closed to you. You are not welcome here. Turn back."

"I must reach Mari Cabrah!" Karin called. "I must give her a warning. She must know what the other pack found."

"Turn back. This way is closed to you."

"Listen to me!" Karin persisted, not knowing if the woman could actually hear her. "I must warn your sister! This is for her benefit, and that of my septmates!" Forewarning of the strange Banes Mephi had described, and of the mystic bonds destroyed by the corrupted river spirit—these things might be the difference between life and death for Mari and Brand.

But the voice was unyielding. "You are not welcome here. Turn back."

Nonetheless, Karin pressed forward with all her might. She resisted her growing rage and the urge to shift to Crinos—too threatening to the Furies; they would never let her through, and the added physical strength would make little difference here in the land of spirit. As Karin pushed, the invisible resistance before her gave way. Suddenly she was falling—no longer at the edge of the moon bridge but tumbling through space. Then she heard the screaming of demons, and they beset her from all sides.

Chapter 10

The world was passing by overhead. From beneath, the surface of the pool was as solid as ice—more solid. Mari pounded her fists against it, but the water in which she was submerged blunted the force of her blows. She dug her claws into the impenetrable plane that separated her from the world above of air and breath and light. Her lungs burning, she opened her rage-beast jaws and smashed them against the barrier. Frustration, anger, fear—these all mingled in her breast and formed a primal howl that gurgled from her throat in a stream of bubbles, only to burst against the transparent undersurface of the pool.

A crack formed. Choking down her fear, Mari released her rage against the barrier. She clawed and pounded and bit and kicked. The crack stretched longer. At last the surface ruptured. Mari erupted into the world of air. Gasping and sucking in breath, she managed a roar of triumph.

But now a current formed in the pool, an undertow that took hold and threatened to pull her back beneath the surface. Mari flailed at the water, at the intangible danger that would not release her. She kept afloat, but the current was pulling her along, drawing her from the pool and down the impossibly wide stream. She swam for shore, but the water was dragging her along too quickly. No vines, no branches, nothing close enough to grab. Mari paused in her struggle for a moment as she heard the dull roar of the waterfall—and then she redoubled her efforts. She fought against the current with all her might, all her rage, but her thrashing made little more than a ripple, and that ripple was cast over the edge along with her.

Freefall. She might as well have been one of the infinite

droplets of water seemingly suspended in air, yet ever plummeting, caught by the inexorable pull of gravity. Somewhere in the distance, obscured by the glaring sun, lay the horizon, where sea and sky became one. For a brief moment she knew peace; she was the roar of the waterfall; the downward arc was her sunrise and sunset. Then her body crashed against the rocks and was broken.

For quite some time, the numbness partially obscured the constant churning, as more and more water crashed down upon her and she was again and again dashed against the rocks. Her blood was diluted, lost amidst the hundreds of gallons of pounding water; her voice shattered; her bones ground to dust. Eventually, she slipped free of the cyclic churning and floated, limp, out into the tidal pool. She had escaped through no doing of her own. The pain had little enough meaning now. Transcendence. Someone earlier had spoken of transcendence, yet only now, with her body battered beyond recognition and use, had she truly transcended anything.

Slowly, sensation, returning. Pebbles rubbing against her belly as she bobbed in the shallows. Hands taking hold under her arms, dragging her from the water. A wooden bowl raised to her lips. Choking on the water again. Now swallowing, drinking.

"Rest easy," said the woman tending Mari. "Nothing can harm you here. Themis will be back shortly."

Themis, weaver of dreams, mistress of visions.

Mari's body was already healing: fragments of bone fusing together, torn skin reknitting until it was whole. The healing was more gradual—and more painful—than the harming had been. Mari tried to focus on the pleasant warmth of the sun, the coolness of the water. Nothing can harm you here. The roar of the falls hung over the tidal pool, and Mari knew relief that she was no longer caught in the ceaseless churning. Her eyes began to pick out distinct shapes now, and she saw clearly the woman who was aiding her—saw her and recognized her. Diana Howl-Strong.

But what was it that someone had said about Diana? Mari's thoughts were slow to form, sluggish like a lizard sunning itself on a warm rock. Diana and her whole pack. Gone. Disappeared. Lost to whatever lurked in Serbia.

A new sound distracted Mari from wondering what Diana was doing here, what either of them were doing here. Mari cocked her head—it was all the motion she was yet capable of—and picked through the roar of the falls. The dull thunder was not the crash of water against the rocks, but instead a woven tapestry of screams and moans, dirges of the dead and dying as they plummeted to their dooms.

"Nothing can harm you here," Diana said again.

Mari looked up at the other woman, the other Garou. Diana bore scars and bruises that had not yet healed. She gazed blankly away from the falls, as if she could not hear the screams. Yet tears streamed down her face.

"Nothing can harm you here," she whispered, a mantra against desperation.

Mari tried to rise to her feet, but her legs were not yet whole. So she pulled herself back toward the water, back toward the falls. Amidst the spray, she could see now a body crashing to the rocks, and another. And the screams grew together like vines blotting out the sun, until there was no roaring of water whatsoever—only screams. Of men, women, children. Smashed and rent. Their death wails lingering and blending together.

"Stay here," Diana pleaded.

But Mari could not block out the cries of anguish; she could not pretend she did not hear them. She pulled herself farther from the stony shore, farther into the water.

"You cannot help them," Diana said.

Still, knowing it was true, Mari dragged herself along.

Beyond the shallows, the buoyancy of the water compensated for her crippled legs, and even they were beginning to reform, as the torturous mending of flesh and bone attested. But what then, what when she was again whole? She couldn't catch each body as it hurtled toward the rocks. She couldn't climb to the top of the falls and stop them; she'd merely be flung over again herself. What, then?

"You cannot help them," cried Diana. "But you will not stay."

"I can't stay," Mari said, feeling her own tears wet against her face. "I have to try."

Diana turned her face to the sun and howled a mournful cry, as if Mari with her words had plunged a silver dagger into her breast. And as the wail died away, drawn into the amorphous cry of the falls and the fallen, so too was Diana undone. Her skin tore open, and her bones snapped. In the face of Mari's determination, Diana suffered defeat a second time. A moment later she was no more, and a grisly collection of bones and stringy flesh floated in the water around Mari, who could not avoid them. A ragged scalp brushed against her shoulder. Scattered teeth touched her and held fast, as if they were trying to bite in some random pattern. The water was red with blood. As Mari choked on bile and vomit, the churning waters pulled her in again. But at least the death wails of the innocent were lost again to the roaring of the falls.

Chapter 11

The sky gradually came into focus. The blue was still luscious, but deeper, darker than what Mari had seen before. Much of the light was gone, and the horizon had gone to pinks and reds in the west. Gentle motion. Rising and falling. Scent of sea salt. Slight Mediterranean breeze with just a hint of late-afternoon chill. Slowly, Mari recognized the small rowboat. Kelonoke sat at the oars which rested, idle, on the gunwales.

"Rest while you can," Kelonoke said. "Iona said that you should be fine, but just rest."

Mari didn't try to speak. She felt weak, even though she was seated. Weak and thirsty. A well-used water skin rested on the bench beside her. She raised it to her lips, then paused, remembering the bowl of water Iona had offered her: the ice-cold liquid fire that had plunged her into a world of visions, pain and futility. The pain and futility were already there, she told herself. That's part of what the vision was about. Part, but not all.

"Just normal water," Kelonoke said, seeing Mari's reluctance to drink from the skin.

Mari hadn't realized the depth of her thirst until the first drops touched her tongue. She drank deeply, savoring each swallow. When she put down the skin, her knee bumped against her pack, which lay in the bottom of the dinghy. Someone had strapped an extra parcel on the pack.

"Maps," Kelonoke explained. "Greece, Macedonia, Kosovo and Serbia. You should be able to find spirit guides through the Umbra. That will be faster. But we've marked less inhabited areas in case you need to hoof it."

"And the other packs?" Mari asked. "The ones that didn't come back?"

"We've marked what we know of their routes."

"Diana's pack?" Mari asked, as bits and pieces of the vision replayed themselves in her mind.

"Marked," Kelonoke said.

They rode in silence for some while as the water spirits took the boat south. Miria was out of sight altogether, and the sun was rapidly following its example. Mari didn't know what to think about the questions Iona had raised about this expedition. It was true that Kelonoke had not been pleased that she had volunteered, and that the Garou needed to find out exactly what was going on in this place. Was it a suicide mission? In failure there is also accomplishment, Iona had said. But Mari couldn't think about that. She might use the bigger picture to justify her actions, but it was each and every scream cascading over the waterfall, crashing into the rocks, that drove her—that, and the chill of dark wings blotting out Luna's light.

Absently, Mari rubbed her arm, and her hand touched a bracelet she had not worn before. A glint of silver caught her eye. Fastened loosely about her wrist by a clasp of Lunar metal were two sizeable teeth—eyeteeth, canines, fangs from a Crinos Garou. Mari stared at the bracelet; she felt the cold burn of the silver, though the amount was little enough not to cause real harm. Her thoughts drifted back to the tidal pool of her vision, to Diana—or Diana's ghost. Themis will be back shortly, she had said. But perhaps Themis had been with them all the while; perhaps the mistress of visions had imparted to Mari a gift of wisdom.

Lost among her own thoughts, Mari did not notice their approach to the much larger island, Crete, until the boat tapped against the dock near the villa.

"Be well, sisterfriend," Kelonoke intoned, as if she were marching off to certain death.

"Be well, sisterfriend," Mari replied, and then she gathered her belongings and gifts, and climbed onto the dock.

Finding the Get was simple enough. By the time Mari reached the villa, she was inundated by the kind of snarling and growling that generally accompanied carnage. Her heart skipped a beat. She followed the sound and rushed past the main building. Behind it, spread across a hillside, were rows upon rows of olive trees—wiry, gnarled trees that clung tenaciously to the rocky soil—and amidst the orchard were the berserking Fenrir. The six were spread in a rough circle, the back of each protected by his packmates, and as Mari, breathless, raced to the edge of the orchard, they seemed ferociously determined to keep at bay... the olive trees?

Fangs First darted and slashed at one of the nearby trunks. Jorn Gnaws-Steel pounced on a branch that had the audacity to sway in the breeze, savagely snapping it in his jaws. Mars-Rising seized a tree, uprooting it with one mighty yank, and brandished it over his head like a fallen foe, while clots of dirt peppered his companions.

Mari stood mystified, practically entranced by the bizarre scene of Garou, with unbridled savagery, cavorting in the light of Luna rising and laying waste to an olive orchard. Slack-jawed, she noticed Aegina standing not far away in the shadows, the woman's arm draped around the shoulder of a young girl no older than thirteen or fourteen. Aegina's eyes shone with grim satisfaction, while the girl's were anxious and wide, missing no detail of the display before her.

"Aegina...?" Mari said, moving closer to woman and girl.

"Barbarians," Aegina said, not taking her eyes from the Get, as they sliced and pummeled more olive trees. "There is no civilization to the north. It has always been so. Mark my words." She lifted the chin of the girl, making sure her message took root.

"What happened?" Mari asked, completely confused. "What's happening?"

"They are good for nothing but slaughter," Aegina said, "so I turned them loose where they can do little harm...except to this year's harvest." She noticed Mari's continuing puzzlement. "To them, the trees are Wyrm minions: Banes, Black Spiral Dancers, and worse. I hope you have come to take the barbarians away. They are the worst sort: male and Fenrir," she added, again for the girl's benefit.

"Okay..." said Mari, beginning to understand, though she wasn't sure of the power Aegina had brought to bear on the Get— some illusion or other trick of the mind, but powerful enough to affect the entire IceWind Pack. "Did they hurt anyone?"

"Fortunately for them, they did not," Aegina said. She hugged the girl closer. "They frightened the girl, and she was only taking water to them, so that their stay might be more comfortable. But they are...less than even the humans."

Mari could see the obvious fear in the girl's eyes, and she supposed it would grow into hatred, as it had with Aegina. "No wonder she's scared of them," Mari said sharply. "You've probably raised her on stories of the Fenrir carrying off babies and virgins. And they're not less than human. They are full Garou—which you are not."

Maybe it was Mari's imagination that the wind suddenly blew colder, but Aegina was not accustomed to, or pleased by, such a rebuke from an outsider of the caern, Fury or no. "I have been kinder to them than they deserved," Aegina said in icy tones. "The Warder told me to make sure they did not—"

"I don't care what Kyra said," Mari cut her off. "And you know what? I don't care what you have to say. Now, release them. We're leaving."

The girl now seemed as frightened by Mari as by the Get. Probably she'd never heard anyone speak so to Aegina. But Mari suspected as much fault lay with these servants of the Furies as with the Fenrir. She wasn't out to make enemies, but she couldn't stand this sort of superior attitude in other tribes; it was worse coming from Furies, and especially humans, even the Kinfolk witches of the Argassi Strega.

"Release them," she said again.

With stiff jaw and raised chin, Aegina turned her back on the orchard. "Come, child," she said to the girl, and they began to walk back to the villa.

At the same time, the snarling battle cries of the Get wavered. Jorn Gnaws-Steel was surprised to realize that he was gnawing wood. Fimbulwinter tried to stop midair as he stomped the life from a sapling. Like turnkey toys winding down at the same time, the Fenrir slowed and then ceased their assault on the orchard.

Brand was the first to slip back to man-form. "What witchery is this?"

"Those women!" Jorn bellowed, his confusion shifting to embarrassment and then indignation. "Those Furies!"

Mari stalked through the center of them. The shock of realization had been enough to snap them from their frenzy, but now she had to put up with their rationalization and self-justification. "Let's just go," she grumbled.

"You were part of this!" Mars-Rising accused her.

"Whatever you say." Mari kept walking. She covered twenty yards, and the Get still stood muttering curses. "Hey, Brand," she called. "You want to bring your OliveOil Pack and get out of here, or what?"

The Get heaped more curses upon her—but after a moment they followed.

Nightmares of horrid black fancy assaulted Karin relentlessly. Here she labored unsuccessfully beneath the Sisyphean weight of the Anvil of Thor; there stood her father, the Old Jarl, shaking his head in disappointment at her impotence—her hubris, to imagine that she could lead the people and take his place. She saw the great hall of Spearsreach transformed to a brothel, and she its most voracious whore, as one after another after another Fenrir warrior mounted her, and all before the eyes of countless metis cubs that crawled about the floors searching for food amongst the filth. She saw the Icehouse forge, fiery and hot, but a metal-skinned abomination wielded the blacksmith's hammer and churned out Baneswords, which it piled higher than the Hill of Lamentations, itself the scene of a garish orgy of prancing Black Spiral Dancers.

Against all these desecrations, Karin could summon no rage—only a woman's tears. Every utterance and slight against her since the day of her birth was proven true, her every doubt made whole and real.

For a moment, the demons drew away and the nightmares receded. She felt the ragged edge of the unfulfilled moon bridge beneath her knees as she quivered. The dark clouds of the Umbra closed about her to take the place of the demons and scenes of outrage.

"This way is closed to you. You are not welcome here. Turn back," spoke a woman's voice, gentle yet insistent.

Karin vaguely recognized the voice, knew that she had heard it before and disregarded its warning. She could sense, too, that nothing she did would change the guardian's mind; no warning would reach the Sept of Bygone Visions. Even so, she could not allow herself to turn back. She would not. Again, she tried to press forward; again, she failed utterly. But she would not give up. Barely could she remember why she needed to proceed, where she was trying to go.

As if sensing Karin's uncertainty, as well as her undaunted determination, the voice spoke to her again: The one you seek has already departed, the woman said. There is no need for your suffering. Turn back.

Karin heard truth in the words. The one you seek... But there was more than one, she remembered more clearly now. Mari, and Brand, and the rest of his pack. ...already departed. Karin cared little about her suffering; it was the price of leadership, and gladly would she have endured it if there were the slightest hope. But recognizing truth in the woman's voice, the last of hope dwindled. There is no need....

"There was need, damn you," Karin said, climbing to her feet, angry despite her lack of surprise. She turned back along the bridge. How long Wavecrest had held the passage for her, she did not know. But the time had come for her to return to the Sept of the Anvil-Klaiven. For good or ill, the IceWind Pack would meet its ordained fate, and the weight of their destiny rested no longer solely on Karin's head, but on those of the Furies as well.

Chapter 12

Mari stepped, alone, through the Gauntlet and awaited the Fenrir. They joined her a few minutes later, coming to the other side as one. Now the only outsider among the group, Mari tried to disregard the isolation, the distinct loneliness. Her own pack with Albrecht and Evan was looser than most, but time among these Get made her keenly aware of the bond with her own friends, who were many miles away. Perhaps the sensation was more poignant in the Umbra, where the Garou's spiritual nature held sway. Evan would understand. Albrecht, he would never admit it—and neither would Mari, not to him. You just can't stand to lose sight of my face, he would say, or something equally as inane. And Mari would be forced to kick his ass.

"You Furies' hospitality leaves something to be desired," said Brand, disgruntled, approaching her with his tree-like arms folded across his chest.

Mari shrugged. "Yeah, well…Motel 6 it ain't, but we're out of there now."

"And better off having left one of your sisters behind," Jorn chimed in. "Little Miss Kelonoke Wild-Hair-Up-Her-Ass."

"Whatever you say, Jorn Gnaws-Olive-Trees," said Mari dryly, eliciting chuckles even from Mars-Rising and Brand. "You know," she added, moving closer to Jorn and building up a head of steam, "you can say what you want about Kelonoke, but she's taking a lot of heat for bringing you guys here. She's the only one I heard defending you. So don't bitch about her to me. And don't try to tell me that you Get don't have just as many close-minded, bigoted elders as we do, 'cause I've met some of them."

The Fenrir were taken aback by Mari's frank criticism of her own tribe, so much so that they failed to grow angry at her equally harsh assessment of their own. If anything, they regarded her with grudging approval and perhaps a bit more respect. Brand was almost smiling. Mari decided she liked the old gloomy him better.

"Your stay was worthwhile?" the alpha asked.

"Yeah. I got some maps, routes marked from the other packs. That kind of thing." Mari glanced at the bracelet on her arm, the Garou teeth. She didn't know what to say about it; she didn't know what to think about the vision of which it was such a tangible reminder. She tried not to think about Diana Howl-Strong's tattered body spreading across the pool.

"Good," Brand said. "We will go as soon as you are ready."

Mari watched him swagger back to his pack. Strange. He was so much more animated now, so much…freer, not weighed down. The change had come over him after the storm, she recalled. What had happened to him? It didn't make sense. She studied the other Fenrir. They seemed relieved at their alpha's transformation, at the way he shared their mirth—all except Aeric Bleeds-Only-Ice, who kept a wary eye on Brand. Of the lot, he was the only one who noticed Mari's observation of them, and his hostility toward her seemed tempered by other concerns.

Not wanting to hold up the show, Mari turned to the maps Kelonoke had provided. From Crete to the northern border of Macedonia looked to be about six hundred miles. If Mari summoned a spirit, one moon path should be able to cover much of that distance. From that point, she and the Get would need to decide how to proceed. The Umbra might well prove too dangerous. In the mundane world, the threats might be submerged enough to allow passage and reconnaissance. Was that what the other packs—all the packs that hadn't returned—had assumed? she wondered.

She folded away the maps and sat cross-legged on the ground to prepare herself for the Rite of Summoning she must perform. These Penumbral surroundings lent themselves nicely to a quieting of the mind, she found. There was much of the

Wyld here. She could just make out the orchard—its trees largely undamaged in this realm—and several grove spirits flitting in and out among the branches. Great, she thought. I'll probably summon some olive Gaffling, and it'll be able to take us as far as the next tree.

The landscape in the spirit world was actually more lush than the mundane. Whatever shortcomings the Furies and the Argassi had in their dealings with other tribes, they had been ideal stewards of this place. What would they think of New York? she wondered, feeling a twinge of guilt at her harsh words to Aegina. But there was more to the fight against the Wyrm than tending one's own little patch of Gaia, she reminded herself. There had to be. That was what this whole expedition was about. She glanced up at the Red Star, the only light save Luna in the Umbral sky, and took it as proof that the Garou must fight a larger battle than those to which they had grown accustomed.

Letting those thoughts slip away, Mari found the quiet place within herself—the place where mystery rather than rage was master, where the invisible winds of the spirit world could flow through her until they and she were one. Her breaths grew slow and deep; the beating of her heart stretched out to embrace infinity. From deep within, she felt her lips moving, her tongue forming the spirit speech as it had been handed down to her by elders of the tribe, and to them by their elders before. Though her eyes were closed, she was aware of the Get nearby. Whatever they thought of her personally, they respected the ways of ritual, and following Brand's example, each knelt and recited quietly his own prayers of thanks and petition to the spirits.

Mari's soft chanting had not gone on very long when she sensed a familiar presence, an electric flow of motion, a tingle so light as to be barely noticeable but as distinctive as a signature. She opened her eyes and saw that she was not mistaken. "Esh'm," Mari said, surprised. She raised her hands from her lap, and the golden band of light wound about her like the smile of an old friend. Often spirits had long memories only for grievances, but the Lune obviously remembered that she had given it freedom from the compass fetish, and now the creature was pleased to come to her.

"We must travel far," Mari whispered to her, still tapping that quiet place within herself and partaking of the gifts of her moon, so that the Lune would understand her meaning. "Will you show us the way, Esh'm?" Through its writhings and pulsations and means ineffable, the spirit indicated that it would. Pleased, Mari checked her gear one more time, and then, when the moon path revealed itself to the Garou, they began the final leg of their journey. Perhaps it was Mari's imagination that the Get followed her slightly less grudgingly. Regardless, there was no time for gloating, as her thoughts turned to what lay ahead.

Esh'm didn't seem to care if Mari stayed close or not. In fact the Lune, no longer bound to a fetish, ranged far and wide from the moon path that it so obligingly revealed for the Garou's use. The spirit alternated between ringing the path in tight corkscrew spirals and then shooting off into the Umbral mists to reappear minutes later. Mari sensed contentment, even playfulness, from the Lune. And why not, at home in its element? Not needed at the fore, Mari let the others outpace her as the group progressed. She reminded herself that she had nothing to prove to the Fenrir; she was here to work, not compete, with them, and a bit of deference in such an inconsequential matter might pay dividends down the road. Brand, all vigor and determination, if not so grim as before, gravitated naturally to the head of his pack. Though not a part of the banter among the Get, Mari could appreciate the camaraderie that such ribbing gave voice to. Jorn and Fimbulwinter were often the culprits, with Mars-Rising taking part at times. Fangs First, most junior in the pack, often as not was the target of their jests, though Brand himself stepped in with a jibe on occasion when the youngster seemed particularly overmatched.

Keeping half an eye on Esh'm, Mari soaked in the dynamics of the Fenrir, and was surprised to find herself thinking that they weren't completely unlikable when left to themselves. She was sure, however, that the instant she joined the mix more actively, the defenses would go back up, and the tribal us-versus-them mentality would take over. So she kept to herself. She had found on previous occasions that this sort of contemplative, almost meditative, attitude lent itself very well to travel in the Umbra, as if the spiritual world not only welcomed but elicited quiet, soulful thoughts that were so often crowded out of the hectic mundane world. Her feet, out of habit, continued to move over the gleaming moon path as she advanced, more or less weightless, through the Umbra. The path twisted and turned, intersecting other paths at infrequent and irregular intervals, but Esh'm seemed sure of their route.

Eventually, as the other Get strove to keep pace with Brand, Mari found herself part of the rearguard along with Aeric Bleeds-Only-Ice. He had not joined in the banter of his packmates, nor did he seem inclined to surge forward to keep up with the others. Mari noticed again Aeric's guarded glances toward the Fenrir alpha.

"Brand really seems to have caught his second wind," she said casually.

Aeric regarded her with skepticism, as if weighing how much was wise to say to someone from beyond the pack. Apparently he decided that Mari already knew what he was about to say, and so he was betraying no confidence. "Something is...not right," he said, watching her closely for any reaction.

His words chilled Mari. She had assumed that whatever had changed with Brand was just him regaining some of his manner from before—before the death of his son. "He's been through a lot," she said cautiously.

Despite his hesitance, Aeric was relieved to speak to someone about what was troubling him. "At the villa," he explained in doomsday tones, "he spoke of Arne."

"That must have been difficult for him," Mari said in agreement.

But Aeric was shaking his head. She didn't understand his point. "He spoke as if Arne were still alive," he said.

Mari looked ahead on the path to where Brand kept the lead. The alpha was driven, still determined that his pack should acquit itself well, yet the pallor of fatalism was lifted from him. He drove himself and the others hard, but not out of the desperation that had seemed to animate him before. Aeric's words gave shape to what she had noticed before.

"I say none of this with malice," Aeric added self-consciously. "It is true that I challenged him during the concolation, and I do not resent his defeating me. But the manner..." Aeric paused, tried to gather his thoughts.

Mari had heard about the challenge, though she hadn't witnessed it. Some of the more militant Garou—must have been Red Talons, to out-bloodlust a Get—had goaded Aeric into the challenge. As such was often the case, the details, except for the fact that Aeric had been soundly beaten, had varied wildly from account to account.

"I don't know what the others saw," Aeric said, "but a great shade arose from within Brand. A shade as cold and bottomless as the grave, and as bitter as unshed tears."

"I've felt it," Mari whispered, again chilled. It was the doom that had hung over Brand, the desperate longing—and it was what now was absent. She didn't feel much better having her vague unease clarified by someone who knew Brand well enough to offer insight. *I'd rather have been flat wrong,* she thought.

Aeric, too, seemed to garner little comfort from sharing his worries. "The others have seen it too," he said. "But they won't say anything." Aeric's shame made it clear that he, too, had been unwilling to say anything until now. "They want everything to be like it was before. They want Brand to be like he was before."

"Maybe he is," Mari said, not believing it, but able to tell that it was what Aeric wanted to be true. It was what she wanted to be true. But in the pit of her stomach she felt otherwise.

"And while we were lost," Aeric said, even more hesitantly, "in the storm, there was something, some...creature."

Mari's throat tightened. She remembered dark wings, the lashing tail slipping away into the mists.

"I didn't see it clearly," Aeric said. "I didn't see anything clearly. Perhaps I was mistaken...confused by the storm...."

Mari placed a hand on his arm, silently communicating that she believed him, that she shared his concerns. The storm. That was when the change in Brand had come about. Something had happened in the storm—or rather, if Aeric was correct, something in the storm had gotten to Brand. But what? And was it a bad something? The alpha's suffering, his consuming grief, was so obviously lifted from him. She should be relieved instead of concerned. But she was concerned, as was Aeric. Gradually they drifted apart, as if by confiding their worries they were also somehow conspiring against Brand. Aeric kept to the rear while Mari, still thinking about what he'd said and what she herself had seen of the alpha, made up ground on the others.

The gap narrowed quickly when the leading Fenrir stopped. Mari and then Aeric drew even with them. The Get were perplexed by Esh'm, who had ceased her ranging and her advance altogether. Instead, she gyrated spastically, back and forth in front of the Garou.

"What is this?" Brand asked, when Mari was at his side.

To Mari, with her Theurge sensibilities, the Lune's distress was clear enough, but the reason was not. "What's wrong, Esh'm?" she tried to soothe the spirit.

"What is it?" Brand wanted to know.

The other Get began to chime in, but Mari shushed them. "Esh'm?" she tried to reach the spirit, but the Lune's rising panic, now apparent to all, was too intense to penetrate. A moment later, however, Mari understood the reason. "Look," she said, her throat suddenly dry.

They all turned—and saw in the distance a mass of violently churning mists and jagged streaks of light, so similar to what had overwhelmed them before. Except...

"It's bigger than the last one," Fimbulwinter said in anxious awe.

"I didn't think that was possible," Fangs First muttered under his breath.

It was bigger, Mari could tell. Taller, wider, darker, angrier— and moving quickly. "Esh'm," she called out, forcing herself to remain calm. She had no desire to tangle again with...with whatever that storm was. They might simply have been lucky to be spat out before, lucky to have survived at all. It didn't feel lucky at the time, but worse could be in store. Mari quickly centered herself, allowing her spirit to attune to the mystical gnosis, the spirit sense, that was her moonsign's birthright. *Esh'm*, she thought, piercing the Lune's agitation with undeniable will. *You must lead us back the other way before it's too late. Along one of the other paths. Hurry and we can escape it.*

The spirit's desperation translated into almost immediate reaction. The Lune shot past the Garou—who were quickly in pursuit—back along the path they had traveled. The Get, who would have fearlessly charged an army of Black Spiral Dancers, were eager to avoid the storm. Behind them, the roiling clouds swept forward with the roar and mindless fury of an avalanche, a tidal wave. Mari hoped they had detected it early enough this time. That was all she could do: hope and flee—and wonder if she saw the silhouette of wings amidst the clouds.

Without hesitating in the least, Esh'm zipped onto the first intersecting moon path. Mari devoted all her energy to keeping up, fighting the strong urge to constantly look back over her shoulder. Some of the Get were not so single-minded.

"It's catching up!" Fangs First warned, with a note of alarm in his voice.

"Just keep going!" Mari yelled at him. Her legs felt like they were moving in slow motion, as if in a dream, but she knew the distance was falling away behind her more rapidly than her actual steps could have accounted for in the mundane world. Still, the storm was growing louder, the thunder of its rage and the crackle of maddened Lunes drawing closer, closer….

The moon path they traversed zigged and zagged crazily. Looking ahead—always ahead—Mari saw that it dove and climbed at impossibly steep angles, but the path always seemed level under their feet. The Garou crossed two more paths before Esh'm turned again, and again. The Umbral winds tugged at Mari, tried to drag her back into the tempest that, from the sound and feel of it, must surely be on top of them by now.

But ahead a shape began to take form. It was merely the gentle slope of a hillside, growing more real each second as the mists thinned and the moon path underfoot brought the Garou back to the shadow world of the Penumbra.

Save yourself! Mari urged Esh'm. *We can make it now! And thank you!*

The spirit understood, and shot away, no longer needing to stay close to the path. Mari hoped the Lune, on her own, would be able to outrun the storm somehow. A few feet away, hungry whirlpools began to whip into existence, reminding Mari in no uncertain terms that she still had her own skin to worry about. She pressed forward, hurtling across the final yards, finally feeling her feet touch the spiritual reflection of the mundane world. She paused for an instant to see the Fenrir join her just as the fury of the storm broke upon them. The earth beneath their feet provided the grounding they needed to keep from being swept back into the Umbra—barely—and a second later, the Garou stepped across.

The quiet of the serene hillside was deafening. Mari's ears rang, absent the bluster and violence of the storm. The rocky soil beneath her feet felt disconcertingly substantial; gravity latched onto her with what seemed increased enthusiasm, making her arms, her legs, heavy. The Get felt the sudden change as well. Jorn let himself crumple to the ground. A deep-felt, nearly collective sigh escaped the Garou. The relief was short-lived.

"Fangs First," said Fimbulwinter. "Where is he?"

The realization struck all the other Garou at the same instant, choking off all oxygen to that peaceful hillside. Mari and Brand looked to one another, and without a word, their decision was made.

"Wait here," Brand instructed his pack. He stepped closer to Mari and, one beside the other, they stepped back across.

It was as if the brief respite on the hillside had been a fleeting fantasy, never actually real. In the Penumbra, the storm still raged. Again, Mari felt that if she weren't standing on the ground, if she were deeper in the Umbra, on a moon path, she would have been swept away. Was that what had become of Fangs First?

Brand stepped through almost simultaneously with her. Instinctively, they latched arms against the buffeting gusts, the swirling fog. A whirlwind, several whirlwinds, drew close and threatened to drag the two away into the heart of the storm.

"It's no use!" Mari yelled. She barely heard her own words. Brand had no idea what she'd said until she yelled again directly in his ear. They were going to be lucky, she knew, to get back out of this themselves, much less find Fangs First. And without Esh'm, if they were swept away they'd likely never find each other again, nor make it back to the pack.

"There!" Brand shouted, pointing into the roiling mists and trying to pull away from Mari.

She looked where he pointed and saw Fangs First—for an instant. Then she saw more clearly; she recognized the deceitful play of the ribbons of light, the trap that the storm-crazed Lunes were setting—and among them, barely discernible amidst the raging storm, a shadow black as night.

"Not him!" Mari shouted. "The spirits! Not him!"

But Brand jerked away from her. "Arne!" he yelled, his voice hopeful, desperate.

"Arne is dead!" Mari tried to tell him, but the howling winds drowned out her voice. "It's the spirits!" She grabbed at Brand, but he slapped her hands away. Suddenly, inexplicably, her rage leapt from deep within her to take control. Her body shifted in response, growing taller, massive. Claws and muscle were ready—aching—to slice open the Fenrir, he whose tribe had threatened and warred on her people for so long. Brand saw and shifted to match her Crinos. They faced off as the winds tore at them equally, each primed for violence. Mari's heart pumped vengeance through her body. All was forgotten save striking down the enemy of her people.

Then a driving gust took hold of Brand, pulled him away from the solid ground. Mari roared as her prey was stolen from her—then realized what that meant. The sudden, irrational hatred buckled and then gave way. Mari was left with the sight of her ally being sucked into the storm. She lunged for Brand, grabbing, not attacking. But the Fenrir's eyes still flashed violence. He slashed at her and tore a ragged gash across her shoulder. Mari roared again, this time in pain and anger. But she held on.

"Arne!" Brand bellowed, his face contorted with heartache, but there was no shape among the mischievous Lunes now— no Fangs First, no Arne. The alpha looked back to Mari, and from deep within him, a spark of recognition grew: Mari was not fighting him, she was trying to help. Reluctantly he turned his efforts to resisting the wind. He broke free of the mists that had enveloped him and the Lunes that flashed with rage and licked at him like angry tongues of flame. Deeper in the storm, ominous shadows retreated beyond view.

"Not him!" Mari shouted in his ear when Brand was again beside her. "No use!"

Brand looked again to where he thought he'd seen... someone. But the image was gone. Finally, he nodded. The loss that had been so plain on his face receded, as if a fading memory. Empty handed, the two Garou slipped again from the storm and returned to the pack.

Chapter 13

The trek north through the hills of Macedonia was a somber journey, and understandably so. Mars-Rising and Jorn Gnaws-Steel volunteered—all but demanded—to step back across the Gauntlet and continue the search for Fangs First. Brand's repeated refusals did little to deter them until the alpha grew visibly angry. At a certain point, they all realized that continued argument would constitute a direct challenge, but only then did the two younger Get back down. Mari didn't enter the debate, not even when the furious Get tried to draw her in.

"What in blazes did we bring her for?" Mars-Rising snarled. "Spirits and the Umbra, that's supposed to be her responsibility."

Mari held her tongue. This was a pack matter, and she knew better than to interfere except as a last resort. She busied herself dressing the gash on her shoulder. Besides, Brand had experienced the power of that storm. He knew.

"We did all we could hope to do," the alpha said. "The storm was too strong, too big, and time is too short. If he survives—like we all did before—he might make it out on his own."

He might make it…. Brand seemed to be talking about Fangs First; the alpha didn't seem to remember having seen—having thought he'd seen—his son Arne. But Mari remembered. The throbbing laceration on her shoulder was reminder enough. She remembered, too, her own willingness, even eagerness, to gut Brand, to stab her claws into his flesh and rip him open. The bloodlust had been so strong, as had Brand's desperation— the desperation that now again seemed suppressed, forgotten. As Mari tended her shoulder, Brand looked away from her; he did seem to remember attacking her, at least—he seemed embarrassed by the fact, and intent upon moving forward instead of looking back.

What were Fangs First's chances? It was possible he might survive, but Mari wasn't laying odds. She didn't understand enough of what was happening with these Umbral tempests, but the first storm they had encountered had been just a squall compared to the second.

While the other Get argued, Aeric Bleeds-Only-Ice and Fimbulwinter did some quick scouting. Consulting Mari's maps, they decided that the stream in the valley below must be a tributary of the Vardar River. This meant that they were still thirty miles shy of the Yugoslavian border, and then another twenty or so from the city of Vrajne, in Serbia, just east of the so-called buffer zone along the Serbia-Kosovo border. The buffer zone was patrolled by international peacekeepers, but there was trouble south of the border as well, where Albanian rebels were attacking Macedonian villages. Judging by Kelonoke's notations, several of the Fury packs that did not return had ventured into the buffer zone area. One of those packs was Diana Howl-Strong's.

"Is something wrong?" Fimbulwinter asked Mari as they looked over the maps.

She wasn't sure what he meant until he gestured to her left arm. Looking down, she realized how vigorously she'd been scratching it—scratching at the silver and Garou-tooth bracelet that somehow had grown very tight around her forearm, where before it had rustled loosely. "Nothing's wrong," she said, though Fimbulwinter eyed her skeptically.

Before embarking, the Garou dropped to all fours and, shifting to wolf-form, raised to Luna a howling dirge for their missing comrade.

Only a few hours of darkness remained, but they made good time keeping to the rough and largely empty hills. They steered clear of the few small towns they saw, and of the remains of refugee camps that had been brimming with human squalor during the worst of the war in Kosovo. Even from the ridges above, Mari could smell the lingering stench of suffering and death. She imagined that the Penumbra here—if it weren't being scoured by raging storms—would be a seething mass of Wyrm-spirits feeding, now that the humans had left, on one another. In time, without sustenance, they might cannibalize themselves to the point that they died out, or they might persist and bedevil whatever human or animal inhabitants eventually migrated into the area. For that reason, the abandoned camps were worth keeping an eye on, though the threat they posed was relatively minor compared with what must lie ahead.

The closer the Garou drew to the Yugoslav border, the more humans they saw, military types mostly: Macedonian troops, one of whom took a few pot shots at what to him must have seemed a passing pack of wolves or wild dogs in the distance; a few tanks on flatbed trucks being rushed north; and then, beyond the crossover, American KFOR troops, better equipped, more disciplined. By the time Mari and the pack swam the southern branch of the Morava River, the sky was light in the east.

When they climbed again into the hills and came upon the trail of a mountain goat, the chase was short and its outcome never in question. Hungry as she was, Mari had only a few bites. The absence of Fangs First cast a pall over the meal. The Get, without exception, were tense and foul of temper, so Mari used the opportunity to withdraw, shift back to her natural woman-form, and consult the maps again. This time, though, as soon as she assumed Homid shape, the pain in her left arm was unmistakable. The bracelet, the gift of her vision, was tighter still, digging into her forearm. Mari tugged at it, but to no effect. She started to rip it off, then reconsidered. What the hell had Diana—or Diana's ghost?—been trying to tell her in the vision: to stay at the caern? That seemed to be in keeping with Iona's wishes, and it might even have soothed Kelonoke's conscience, but more than one person in Mari's life had called her stubborn. Somebody had to come, though, so was it really stubborn or her to persist? She decided not to raise that question with the Get. At any rate, in her experience, visions were never precise, never clear, and the bracelet was bound to serve a purpose, so she decided to keep it and try to ignore the discomfort.

"Mari," said Brand, done eating and striding, two-legged,

to where she sat nestled among the rocks. "There is a village just over the ridge. We will take shelter here, out of sight, and continue at dark."

"A village?" Mari said, looking at her maps. "It's not marked here."

"Very small," said Brand. "There would be no reason." He looked down over her shoulder. "Or maybe no Fury pack came back from here."

Mari glared at him, wondering if he was going out of his way to be callous, insulting, or if that was simply his stupid Get way. She searched his face for any lingering shame at having attacked her before, but found mostly disdain. His dismissive attitude kindled Mari's ire—not as fiercely as his hostility in the second storm had, but enough. With her hands balled into fists, she felt the constriction of the bracelet more keenly; her arm began to throb. "Show me," she said.

He led her up the slope to the ridge top. The other Get except for Fimbulwinter were already there, sprawled on the ground keeping out of sight, all Homid, looking down into the vale and the town, with its plentiful burnt-out buildings.

"There," said Brand. "I've sent Fimbulwinter for a closer look."

"We'll be better off if the villagers don't see us," Mari said.

Brand scoffed. "We are the Fenrir."

"Yeah," Mari said. "That's what worries me."

"They will not see him," Brand, not amused, assured her.

Mari fought down the urge to punch him, to lay her forearm across his windpipe, or to smash her elbow into the bridge of his nose. For a few seconds, she pictured herself back amidst the Umbral storm, the painful gash in her shoulder reminding her that she owed Brand one. But then motion from below drew her attention: Fimbulwinter. Even having spotted him, she had trouble tracking his progress. His Lupus coat of mottled grays blended in well with the rocks and dried grass on the hillside as he lost himself amongst the scenery. Not bad, Mari admitted to herself, though not aloud to the other Get.

Fimbulwinter, she saw after a minute, was making his way back up the hill to their hiding place. He circled around behind the ridge and approached his friends from the opposite direction of the village. Over the last few yards, his legs and arms grew longer, and his back straightened. In just a few steps, he appeared as human as did the rest of them.

"Looks to be deserted," he said. "And shot up. Lots of bullet holes in the buildings."

Mari's arm throbbed more intensely beneath the bracelet. "We need a closer look at that village," she said, not sure whether the Garou teeth digging into her flesh were urging her forward or warning her away—but resolute that they must investigate, once she saw that Brand obviously disagreed.

"We wanted to strike farther into Serbia," he growled, "not waste time in a pointless little—"

"You said yourself that we were going to rest through the day," Mari pointed out. She could have told him about the bracelet, could have explained that the pain it inflicted meant that there was something important about the village; they couldn't just skirt it and keep going. But Brand's sudden haughtiness fed Mari's own consternation, and so she lashed out at the ample Get pride. "We wouldn't be covering any ground anyway. You guys all tired, even after your rest at the villa?" Mars-Rising stepped forward to take exception, but Mari didn't give him a chance. "I'm going down for a closer look. If you guys are scared..."

"Bite your tongue, woman," Brand snapped. "I should have known better than to agree to bring along a woman—a Fury, no less. Aside from my son, you are the most stubborn—"

"Your son is dead, Brand." Mari wielded the words like a knife. In the back of her mind were all the lofty words she had spoken about Garou uniting against the common threat, yet in the face of Brand's tirade, his manner, she was unable to contain the vitriol that welled up within herself. Something had happened to Brand in the storms: He was imagining Arne back to life. After what the alpha was saying about the Furies, Mari wasn't willing to allow him that luxury.

His expression was all she needed to know that her blow had struck to the heart. Shock, indignation...and then dawning realization. She had spoken the truth and Brand, confronted with that fact, had nowhere to hide. The shroud of grief that, for a short while, had been lifted, now lowered over him again like a suffocating pillow. Mari saw the twin specters of hatred and death in his eyes. She glanced at Aeric Bleeds-Only-Ice, and he also regarded her with hatred: she who had betrayed his confidence to strike a petty but grievous wound against his packmate.

"We will go down into that village," Brand said, somehow more defiant in acceding to Mari's wishes than if he had refused her until Luna rose in the east.

As the Garou collected their gear, seething rage and thinly veiled contempt washed over Mari from all directions. She wondered what the Get would do to any humans they found, if the village was not in fact deserted; she wondered what she would do.

Chapter 14

The wooden and stone structures were relatively modern, most seeming to have been built in the last forty years or so; but the destruction, the bloodshed, were as old as the hard-packed earth. The burnt shells of buildings could have been put to the torch by invading Turks, by Christians seeking to cleanse the land of infidels, by Moslems seeking revenge, by numerous Serb warlords, by Nazis, by Tito's communists. Mari wasn't prepared for the history, the deep-seated suffering, which seeped from Gaia like a widow's tears.

The Garou spread out and entered the village, each having assumed his or her most lethal visage of bulging muscles, claws, and teeth. Whoever had attacked the town might still be lingering. Besides that, though, the coiled fury of the rage-beast felt right in this place. Brand, every second slipping more deeply into his newly found grief, was spoiling for a fight. So were the other Get, and Mari wouldn't have been too unhappy to provide them with one. She'd had enough of their condescension and misplaced sense of superiority; keeping a lid on her own animosity toward them—based on wrongs personal and historical—was all she could manage. The hills themselves seemed to urge her to vengeance. Thankfully, the bracelet constricting her arm kept her grounded; the pulsing ache reminded her of the immediate task: to bring back some clue for Kelonoke and Konietzko and the others who were so bent out of shape, and maybe even to find out what had happened to the previous packs to explore this region. Too much was at stake. If not for the bracelet, she might have given in to the red haze, to the mindless rage.

Even so, Mari ignored the Get, kept her distance. She

slipped down a side-street that none of them seemed interested in investigating—and she found the first bodies.

Her hunter's nose caught sign of the blood before she saw them, so when she pulled the bullet-pocked table away from the outside wall of the house, she wasn't surprised. There were three: an old man and woman, and a middle-aged woman, all shot, one bullet apiece, through the back of the head. Looking down at them, Mari knew nothing about them: not their names— were the old couple married? could the younger woman be their daughter? a neighbor?—or which ethnic or religious group they belonged to that had drawn someone's wrath. All Mari knew was that they were dead. Shot down in the street. She drew her claws down the stone wall that stood in place of a headstone.

The day was dawning sunny and brisk. Clouds and rain and biting cold would have better suited the morbid streets. She wondered, as she continued through town, if the Umbral storm still raged. Had its churning anger contributed to this slaughter somehow? Or was the storm perhaps a result of what was taking place all across this land? She wondered if Diana Howl-Strong and her pack had come upon similar scenes, here or elsewhere, or if they had encountered the storms.

Not every street was home to murdered villagers, but enough were. Too many were. Mari began to dread turning each corner, or passing close to the larger piles of rubbish— whether from looting or vandalism, most buildings' contents had been thrown into the streets—that concealed bodies also. She wasn't squeamish, but with sight and smell of each dead human, her control of her rage slipped that much more. Many of the bodies bore the telltale execution-style wounds, like the first three, but many of the people had been shot down attempting to flee. Some lay sprawled in the road, perhaps where they had fallen; others looked to have been heaved out of the way, against walls or into gutters, like so many sacks of grain. Not all of the women were stripped, but some were, completely naked or left lying among the rags of their tattered dresses. Mari didn't allow herself to contemplate what they certainly had endured before their deaths; to do so would have sent her rampaging through the countryside in search of whatever male was unlucky enough to cross her path, whether he be human or Garou.

Gaia knew Mari had seen murder and cruelty and rape and abuse in New York, but at least there such crimes were the exception. How could she hope to mourn for or avenge the wronged when victims were everywhere? Though this was but one small village, the scale of the human suffering was overwhelming. None of the stories, nothing that she had seen before, had prepared Mari for this.

An unexpected sound brought her up short as she inspected one fire-ravaged shack: an embittered, sorrowful howl from elsewhere in the village, playing mournfully over the rooftops. Fimbulwinter. Mari recognized his voice and knew that she wasn't alone, that the streets she walked were not the only ones cradling shattered bodies. In his howl, she heard echoes of her own anger at the waste, frustration that the deeds were done, completed, and the purveyors of torture likely escaped; she heard in the howl helplessness in knowing similar acts were still occurring across the war-torn region. She was surprised that Fimbulwinter would care, that a man, a Get, would share her grief.

Watching rats scrabble through the material and human devastation, Mari's thoughts turned to Brand and his loss. Surely he had howled his pain to Luna, cathartic release similar to that which Fimbulwinter sought now, which Mari joined by raising her own voice on that obscenely bright morning. But nothing Brand had attempted had cleansed his spirit, nothing had eased the pain of his loss. Nothing except forgetting, Mari thought. He would never be able to erase the death of his son, much less forget it. But he did. He was different after we were caught in the storm. Whatever that was in the Umbra, it made him forget. The black wings of Mari's vision; the black wings of the storm.

"For a couple of days, he had peace," she muttered to herself. "And then I rubbed his face in it all over again." Would he have been better off, she wondered, if a few hours ago she'd let him traipse after what he thought was Arne? Brand had been so reluctant to come back, and particularly hostile toward Mari since—and she toward him.

Slowly, as Fimbulwinter's dirge faded from the morning, Mari began to see the surrounding destruction in a different light. The ruined homes, the burned churches, the limbs of old women and children, dirty and stiff—they were not the full story. She recognized her own prejudices and uncharitable impulses, so many given outlet, and with little enough provocation. In the Umbra, she'd been ready to hand Brand his head; her reaction, even before he'd clawed her, had come out of nowhere. Or maybe not. The black winged creatures—could they have done more than make Brand forget his pain? And just a short while ago, though Brand had been insulting, Mari had, without hesitation, hurt him in the most vicious way she could. The spirits again?

Or is that me looking for an excuse? she wondered.

The human carnage was awful enough, and Gaia knew, too, that humans were all too capable of this sort of thing—but something else was at work. If the atrocities of war were the full explanation, then Garou packs would not have ventured into this place never to be heard from again, and Kelonoke would not have grown desperate to the point of falling into Margrave Konietzko's camp.

Raging spirits, she must be desperate! Mari thought. And what's worse is that Iona isn't worried about what's happening here half as much as she is the fact that Kelonoke is talking to the Shadow Lords.

The first human sound Mari heard in the village was not so different from Fimbulwinter's mournful cry: not a lupine howl, but a woman's anguished moan. Mari raced to the noise, hurried to the side of the building from which it had emanated. She listened for sign of conflict, hopeful that she had caught a soldier or terrorist red-handed. Her heart pounded like jaws snapping shut, over and over again. But after the moan, only a woman's soft sobbing escaped the small house. Disappointed, Mari shifted to her more human face and form and cautiously stepped over the door, which had been torn from its hinges.

The woman did not turn to face her guest. Mari scanned the room for any immediate threat; she cautiously opened a door to check in the other room of the small dwelling, and, finding nothing, turned back to the woman, who was leaning over a box and sobbing. Spasms of uncontrollable grief wracked her body. A trap door was open in the center of the floor. So that's why she's alive, Mari thought. She hid down there while the killing was going on, and was lucky enough not to be found.

But the woman didn't appear lucky. Her sobs, rising to near hysteria and then quickly ebbing, suggested she'd rather be dead. Mari moved closer. She didn't know what she could say or do that wouldn't alarm the poor woman. I don't even know what language she speaks, Mari realized. Looking more closely at the box beneath the woman's shawl and tangles of long hair, Mari could tell how crudely it was fashioned, as if the boards, rough and uneven, were torn from fences and cobbled together with whatever tools were at hand. Mari could guess, too, from the size of the box, why this woman wept so inconsolably.

Had the man who burst through the doorway that instant not been bellowing at the top of his lungs, Mari might not have heard him in time. As it was, she spotted his face contorted in rage, and the hatchet in his upraised hand, and trained reaction took over. She didn't cower, but rushed forward to meet him before he could get the full force of a swing behind the hatchet. Forearm block of the weapon arm. Grab the wrist with her free hand. Blocking elbow smashed into his chin. As her attacker's shout was abruptly cut short, Mari pivoted and twisted his weapon arm around her body. He fell forward—the only alternative to having his arm snapped in two—and landed hard on his face. Mari knelt with him as he fell, pressed his arm across her knee.

"I'll break it, you bastard!" she warned him.

Whether he understood her or not, the hatchet fell from his hand to the floor. Mari barely managed to keep herself from snapping his arm anyway. Not only would it have more satisfactorily put him out of commission, but she wanted to break something—someone. Instead, she kicked the hatchet through the trap door, out of reach.

Mari glanced up at the woman, who had stopped sobbing and was watching the deadly dance with a look of sick horror. Mari pressed enough on the arm to make sure she had the man's attention. "She's been hurt enough," she said. "You're not going to do anything else to her! You got that?"

The man jabbered at her, words she couldn't understand, but he was obviously panicked. And then suddenly he burst out in English: "I'm not going to hurt her! You don't hurt her! Or I'll kill you! I'll kill—!"

Mari cut off his threats with another twist of his arm. "Pipe down, buddy." She looked up at the woman, who still watched in terror, fresh tears running down her face. "I'm not going to hurt her," Mari said. "I'm keeping you from killing her."

The man laughed, a sick, ironic sound. "She is my wife," he said. "I would not hurt her."

Mari looked to the woman. "He's your...you're his wife? He's your husband?" But the woman only stared in response, not understanding, or paralyzed by trauma. "You speak English," Mari said to the man.

"Yes. I studied in the U.S. Go Yankees."

Mari released his arm and stood, still watching him closely. She wasn't of a mind to trust somebody who had just attacked her with a hatchet. "I hate the Yankees," she said.

The man climbed painfully to his feet, favoring his arm all the while. He wasn't old, probably late twenties. Mari saw now that the woman was roughly the same age, maybe a few years younger, though grime and grief added years to her face. The man went quickly to his wife, wrapped his arms around her. She returned the embrace, but as if out of habit. Her eyes stared blankly over his shoulder. He spoke quiet, comforting words to her.

"This is your home?" Mari asked.

"Yes," said the man with undisguised bitterness. "What is left of it. This is our home. I am Milosh."

"Does she speak English?" Mari asked him. Milosh shook his head, no. "What's her name?"

"Katerina," he said. His gaze drifted toward the box behind his wife, and his eyes began to brim with tears. "Our daughter was named Katerina also, for her mother."

Katerina started to turn back to the box, the coffin, but Milosh held her firmly. She struggled and screeched an anguished wail until he let her go to her daughter. She pressed her face against the boards again and sobbed, her hair cascading over her like a veil.

"Did the Serbs do this?" Mari asked, wanting—needing—to know who to blame.

Milosh drew himself up tall and fairly snarled at her: "We are Serbs." His words stunned Mari. "This was mostly a Serb village. You Americans think we are monsters, you bomb us, you try to kill us. You do not know us. You have not suffered as we have suffered." He spat on the floor and surveyed the wreckage of his home. "You think the KLA are all 'freedom fighters.'" Milosh scoffed. "The NLA are even worse. National Liberation Army." He spat again. "They will kill whomever they can until there is an Albanian Kosovo with equal parts carved out of Serbia and Macedonia."

"Hey, hold it," Mari said, to cut off the building steam of his tirade. "I'm sorry. I didn't mean anything by it. But this village— it's mostly Serb. Was it mostly Serb before the war, before the ethnic cleansing? How many Albanians were run out of town, or worse?"

Milosh's face reddened. "The Albanians did this to my daughter!" he screamed, pointing at the coffin. Katerina, giving no indication that she knew the argument was going on directly behind her, slid down the side of the coffin and dropped to her knees. Milosh turned and knelt beside her, placed his arm around her to keep her from slumping to the floor. "They did this to my wife," he said more weakly, the energy of his rage spent. "My beautiful wife, my daughter…" He laid a hand on the side of the coffin and wept into his wife's tangled hair. She stared, unseeing, at Mari.

In the pit of Mari's stomach, anger and guilt wrestled and rolled into a hard, tight ball. Of course not all of the Serbs were monsters, no more than all of the ethnic Albanians were blameless. Milosh and Katerina and their little girl were not combatants. None of the bodies Mari had seen in the streets seemed to be those of soldiers. But in how many other villages, she wondered, were the bodies those of Albanians, whose survivors railed against the inhuman Serbs?

I can't fix this, Mari told herself. I can't make this right. I can't bring back Milosh's daughter. I can't track down everyone—maybe anyone—who's responsible. She knew this was true, and she hated it. She knew, too, that there was nothing to be gained by arguing with Milosh; she would only fan the flames of his grief and hatred. He was too close to it all—part of it. And Mari was not. She was a visitor. She could taste the hatred that tinged the breeze, but it was not part of her—not this particular hatred.

Howling again, from outside. Different this time, not mournful, a warning. Mari's ears perked up. "Armed men coming into town from the east."

If Milosh was worried by the wolf calls, he gave no indication. Perhaps he had survived too much horror already to truly fear anything beyond humanity ever again. "From that direction," he said, "probably Serb police, or maybe paramilitaries. The NLA come more from the west, and usually at night." He started rousing Katerina from her stupor.

"What are you going to do?" Mari asked.

Milosh gestured toward the trap door. "Hide. The paramilitaries are no better than the NLA sometimes, Serb or not." He didn't appear embarrassed to make that admission despite his earlier rant. Survival was the primary concern.

Mari slipped out of the house and left them. In the distance, she heard scattered gunfire. As she slipped through the streets, she gave herself over to the rage, flexing her claws, and salivating at the thought of vengeance.

Chapter 15

By the time Mari found the Get, any doubts she might have harbored about what she was going to do to the gun-toting humans had taken a back seat to her inexorable rage. A few hours in the wreckage of the village had left no room for doubt. Gone were all reservations, all thoughts that the men entering the village might be NATO troops trying to enforce the peace; gone was any care that the teeth and silver biting ever more deeply into her arm might be warning her away. Danger was at hand. Whatever had happened to Diana and the others, there would be a reckoning.

Approaching Mars-Rising, Mari could read in the glint of his eyes, for the first time, her own sentiments: Humans with guns did this to these people; these newcomers are humans with guns. Enough said.

Jorn Gnaws-Steel joined them a few moments later. His claws and snout dripped blood. "Serb paramilitaries," he growled. "Three squads, five or six men each." And then, with his gruesome, gap-toothed grin, he added: "One squad a few less than that."

"Where are the other Get?" Mari asked.

"Circling around," said Mars-Rising. He pointed out where. "A squad in those ruins across the square. Brand will signal."

That was good enough for Mari. She sharpened her claws on what was left of a door frame and waited with the two Fenrir, Garou with whom she'd been at odds for much of the past days, yet who now seemed brother warriors in the face of bloodletting.

"What in all blazes…?" Mars-Rising muttered as he peered around a corner.

Mari joined him, and was just as baffled. Making his way across the square was Fimbulwinter. But Brand had not yet given a signal, and what was more, Fimbulwinter was in his vulnerable Homid form despite impending battle, to untrained eyes no different than a human.

"What's the hell is wrong with him?" Jorn asked.

Watching a moment longer, Mari saw what he meant. In addition to exposing himself to harm, Fimbulwinter was moving awkwardly. Every few steps he staggered, his knees appeared about to buckle. He looked to be assailed by some type of spasm or seizure, again and again. Mari thought he might collapse, but he kept going, his eyes glazed over with a vacant stare. Beyond him, from the other side of the square, a reflected glint of the morning's bright sunshine caught Mari's eye. First she saw the barrel of the assault rifle, and then the camouflaged gunner aiming through a broken window.

"He's going to get himself killed," she growled of Fimbulwinter, and started around the corner—but Mars-Rising grabbed her arm, stopped her.

"No signal yet," he said.

Mari bared her teeth and started to argue, but at that instant gunfire commenced. Even Mars-Rising considered that signal enough. He charged along with Mari, Jorn just a step behind.

The gunman Mari had seen was not alone. He and several others found Fimbulwinter a likely target and unleashed their fire. The cause of the Garou's spasms this time was readily apparent, as bullets tore into his body. Mari and the others ran headlong toward the ruined building, snarling bloody murder with each step. By the time they reached Fimbulwinter, he had fallen to his knees. He wore a pained and perplexed expression as he toppled forward onto the dirt. Mari paused at his body, taking bullets herself. The pain drove her forward, though Mars-Rising shot past and through the closest window. Within seconds, growls and screams echoed through the square.

The paramilitaries were prepared to shoot civilians or perhaps armed separatists. Nothing in their sporadic training had ever begun to ready them for what they faced now. As the Garou closed the final yards to the ruined building, those soldiers who weren't completely paralyzed by their fear chose flight over fight. One frantic young man ran, still holding the trigger of his AK-47, and in the course of emptying his clip shot down one of his comrades. Mari, her earlier wounds already healed, dragged down the careless soldier and shoved her claws through his abdomen. The other two men met similar fates at the hands, and teeth, of Jorn and Mars-Rising. It was over almost before it began, but not quickly enough to save Fimbulwinter.

"What in blazing hells was he doing?" Mars-Rising growled at everyone and no one, while he took out his anger and frustration on one of the Serb bodies. "What in blazing hells?"

Her own rage for the moment sated, Mari grew aware of a sharp pain—not a bullet wound, nor even the gash Brand had given her, but the silver bracelet grown incredibly tight, the two Garou teeth, as if biting, digging deep into her forearm. She saw and smelled her own blood trickling down the back of her hand. It wasn't the shift between forms that had caused the problem; earlier in the morning she'd moved through Crinos, Homid, Lupus, and the constriction hadn't been so severe.

Something is happening, she thought, if I can just manage to see it. What are the spirits trying to show me? She stared out at Fimbulwinter's body and tried to let the pain from the bracelet flow through her, to see what it was trying to reveal.

"What in blazing hells?" Mars-Rising was saying over and over again, though he wasn't likely to get any answers from the dead Serb he continued to mangle.

Then suddenly Brand was among them all, furious, frothing and hardly able to speak through his bared fangs. "Who attacked…? No signal!"

"What in blazing hells?" Mars-Rising said.

Jorn ran into the square to retrieve Fimbulwinter's body and attracted a few gunshots. That other squad of paramilitaries couldn't know how surely they had just sealed their own doom.

To Mari, the whole world seemed to be moving very slowly now: Jorn shrugging off gunshot wounds as he brought Fimbulwinter back to the pack; Mars-Rising, splattered with gore, seeking answers from a dead man; Brand realizing this, his most recent loss, and his eyes clouding over, growing sore with unspeakable grief; Aeric Bleeds-Only-Ice joining them in the ruined building, his glare telling Mari that all of their pain was her fault. Mari took it all in as if separated from the scene, as if watching herself. She sensed motion from just beyond her field of vision—no, just beyond what she or any of them could see—the rustle of black wings brushing past. The Garou fangs bit deep, gnawing into flesh and bone, drawing deadly silver into her blood. The moment rewound, played forward again.

"What in blazing...?"

"No signal!"

Fimbulwinter walked through the door—no, Jorn carried him. Fimbulwinter's dead eyes stared at them. Had he but shifted forms, the bullets would have been like mosquito bites to him. But he didn't know, Mari realized. Somehow, he hadn't known. His eyes had been blank, now were forever blank. Mari looked at Brand: at his eyes which had lost sight of that which could not be lost, at his unassuageable grief which the storm had swept away, which Mari had so cruelly inflicted on him again. She couldn't imagine the heartbreak of losing a son a second time.

The Get were in motion now, hellbent on vengeance, but Mari could only watch. Fangs digging through her arm held her in place. Silver coursing through her blood trapped her between the worlds. And suddenly what had been beyond sight was visible. The spirit winds pulled at Mari. She hovered, straddling the Gauntlet, and saw the congregating Banes, wings spread like black, shimmering vultures gliding on the storm, their whiplash tails switching hungrily back and forth; she saw the way they lusted after the Fenrir and fed upon their rage; she saw the whip-scar wounds across Fimbulwinter's body.

As Mari slipped fully into the Umbra, the Banes flocked to her like sharks grateful to the fisherman for chumming the water. Between their black wings was nothing but a cavernous, slavering maw. They embraced her with their spiked tails, and the rage of a thousand deaths shot through her, wracking her body with convulsions. The great storm still churned full force, fed by the Banes, fed by Mari's essence, her rage, which the Wyrm minions siphoned off so they could more readily sift through less threatening portions of her inner life.

The Get must have heard her cries somehow, for they were charging back now. Mari could see them; she saw flickers of the mundane world, and a red haze of rage surrounding the Fenrir. They stepped across into the tempest and laid into the Banes. But the winged monstrosities commanded the gusts and the whirlwinds, and the Get, despite their efforts to stay close, were soon scattered. All about them, maddened Lunes darted, harassing, distracting, enraging the Garou, while the tails of the Banes, thick with barbs, struck true.

As one strangled scream stretched out across a full lifetime, Mari was bound and lashed, her spirit probed, each second of torture lingering beyond endurance. Like her rage, her will and her identity were being stripped away. With each instant, she grew farther from herself. Increasingly numb of spirit, she watched helplessly as the Get struggled.

Brand struck again and again in a frenzy of rage, heedless of the danger to himself—no, not heedless, but welcoming it, inviting the oblivion that would remove from him his pain. He had felt before the sting of these slavering Banes, and fought blindly, guided by the knowledge that he would achieve either victory or release. Brand sliced the belly of one of the creatures, spilled its steaming entrails into the scattering winds, only to have two more of the spirits swoop down upon him, and then two more, their tails striking and holding, forming a cocoon around the thrashing Get.

Mars-Rising wielded his klaive with deadly power and bloody grace. He fought toward Mari, cleaving his way through the ranks of swarming Banes. "You'll not perish on my watch!" he yelled at her defiantly. He remained defiant to the end—even after a trio of Banes lashed their tails around his klaive-arm, and another snapped its black jaws around his bicep, severing arm from shoulder.

Aeric and Jorn stood back to back—until the fury of the storm separated them, and the enraged Lunes bound their arms and legs, and the ravenous Banes descended upon them with warbling banshee wails of carnivorous lust.

The last Mari remembered of any of the Fenrir was the

expression of pained rapture on Brand's face—agonizing loss, blessed oblivion—as the Banes dragged him into the storm. No charge was ever more valiant, nor more surely doomed to failure, than the one in which the IceWind Pack ceased to be. And all throughout the storm-churned mists, diminutive spirits whirled—spirits that flowed from the corpses of the Banes like blood, flitting away into the Umbra.

Then Mari was too far from herself to know the other Garou, to recognize them or feel for them, one way or the other. She was empty, except for a remote, dwindling reservoir of rage. Alone amidst the tempest, she lashed out, one last futile attempt at defiance, fueled by a strength that was not completely her own. Drawing on the will of those of her tribemates who had gone before, she refused to go quietly, to submit, until her last breath was crushed from her body, until the last spark of her mind was extinguished. In her striving, she didn't manage to harm the Banes—no more than the Fenrir could have hoped to overcome the endless legions—but her desperate thrust of will touched...something. The mind of the Banes, or if not the mind, the force that gave them direction. She could harm it no more than she could harm the Banes, but like a suicide facing the rock-hard water rushing to greet her, she knew it. And with her final scintilla of rage, she latched on to that knowledge. She made it part of her—in a way, all of her, because there was so little else left.

By the time they finished with her, she was beyond caring, beyond feeling, beyond rage. Uncoiled from within the leeching tails, the Umbral winds took her, dragging her into the heart of the roiling tempest.

Chapter 16

"Jarlsdottir," said Mountainsides, his furrowed wrinkles so deep that his brows nearly concealed his eyes altogether. "It would be best for you to come with me."

Karin looked up from her seat in Spearsreach, where she was adjudicating between two cubs, chronic rabble rousers, a dispute regarding a Kinfolk's pilfered—and eaten—menagerie. She could not mistake the Warder's grim countenance, and joined him immediately. He led her to the Hill of Lamentations, where a woman sat shivering, wearing only jeans and a ripped T-shirt against the wind.

"Bring her a blanket," Karin ordered, cross that Mountainsides had not done this on his own. Karin kneeled at Mari Cabrah's side. "You have come back to us," the Jarlsdottir said, uncomfortably reminded of another lone Garou returned without a pack. Where Mephi Faster-Than-Death had spoke warnings, however, Mari stared, her eyes as blank as her tongue was silent. "Where is Brand?" Karin asked softly. "Where is the IceWind Pack?" But the Jarlsdottir could see that she would have no answer. Not today, perhaps not ever. The fact that the Fury had returned at all was a miracle in itself. She didn't seem in any shape to have gotten anywhere on her own, yet here she was.

Mari did not respond, did not so much as look at the Fenrir. In another moment, Mountainsides returned with a blanket. Karin laid it over Mari's shoulders, careful of one ragged wound that looked as if it could be from the claw of a Garou. Mari jerked away regardless, favoring not her shoulder but her hand. She did look up at Karin now, with the eyes of a child struck without cause. Karin flinched herself, though she had meant no harm.

Gently, she inspected Mari's left hand and arm. Burned deeply into the flesh, more like a rune than a brand, was a silver pattern that could have been the woven strands of a bracelet, and two large fang shapes. Mari pulled her hand away, firmly, determinedly, until Karin released it. Then Mari opened her mouth, and with breath as cold as the wind rushing from the sea and that rattled deep in her chest, she spoke: "Jo'cllath'mattric."

Karin leaned closer. The Fury was in shock; violent trembling overtook her. "Save your strength," Karin told her.

But the gibberish was like bile that, having risen, must be expelled or choke her. "Jo'cllath'mattric," Mari muttered weakly. "Jo'cllath'mattric." And then she lay back in Karin's arms, consciousness having passed.

Curious about other Crossroad Press books?
Stop by our site:
https://www.crossroadpress.com
We offer quality writing
in digital, audio, and print formats.

www.ingramcontent.com/pod-product-compliance
Lightning Source LLC
Chambersburg PA
CBHW031126210626
46816CB00015B/709